INVISIBLE GIRL

ALSO BY PADGETT GERLER

Getting the Important Things Right

Lessons I Learned from Nick Nack

The Gifts of Pelican Isle

What Does Love Sound Like?

INVISIBLE GIRL

Carol,

So hope you enjoy!

Thanks for your support!

Love,

Muffin

10.24.19

PADGETT GERLER

ISBN-13:978-1-64516-082-3

DISCLAIMER

This book is a work of fiction. Names, characters, places, and incidents are either products of the author's imagination or are used fictitiously. Any resemblance to actual events, locales, or persons, living or dead, is entirely coincidental.

DEDICATED TO

Mandi

ACKNOWLEDGMENTS

A very special thank you to all the invisible girls whose experiences helped me write this book. Please know that you are not alone, that we all feel invisible or want to be invisible at some point. But rest assured we see you, we appreciate you, and we respect you.

Loving thanks to the late Anne Barnhill, fellow author and delight to all who knew her. Anne, you taught us how to write with joy, laugh with abandon, and live life with grace, dignity, and wit. You could light up a room with your smile alone. Thank you for sharing your glow with us.

Heartfelt thanks to you, Amanda Nordin and Suzanne Boswell, my first readers, for taking my characters seriously and treated them with love and respect. Amanda and Suzanne, I am so very grateful for your honesty and candor, and I thank you for your guidance, your advice, and your never-ending encouragement.

My sincerest gratitude, Harry James Krebs, my friend and author extraordinaire, for sharing your courtroom and forensics expertise with me. Without your guidance, the trial scenes would have made no sense at all. I owe you one, Harry. The next time you're stuck on a tear-jerking scene, buzz me. I'm your girl.

My thanks to you, Deborah Bradseth at Tugboat Design, for your beautiful cover design for *Invisible Girl*. I am in awe of your amazing talent and your ability to capture my vision. Thanks, too, to you, Anand Vadnere, for your haunting cover photography. Your photo of my invisible girl is breathtaking.

Thank you, Ed, for showing the same interest and enthusiasm for book #5 that you showed for book #1. Without you by my side, there would be no books at all. You are my muse, my guide, my best friend, and the very best giver of *atta girls* and yellow sticky notes of validation.

INVISIBLE
GIRL

One

I don't know the exact day I became completely invisible, but if I was forced to name a date that the process commenced, I'd say that would be October 17, 2015. That's the day my grandmother called, screaming all crazy-like, and changed my world forever and ever. Amen.

Now, up until that point I'd been pretty much transparent, people just sort of looking right through me, but I didn't feel completely invisible. It took my grandmother's meltdown to put me on the road to my Power of Invisibility.

That morning Mama yelled down the stairs, "Briley, the phone is ringing."

That's me, Briley. I was loosely named after my mother, Bronwyn, and her dead brother, Riley. Mama saw my Uncle Riley die, so she thought it'd be a great idea to keep that memory alive by naming her one and only child after him. And herself, of course.

So Mama was screaming that the phone was ringing. Well, I knew the phone was ringing. I was sitting right beside it. But it didn't make one bit of sense for me to answer it. I knew it wasn't for me. Never was. The phone rang only for my perpetually popular mama, Bronwyn Talmidge Beckwith.

So I just yelled, "Yes, ma'am," and kept on eating my Cheerios and reading my book.

Mama came clattering down the stairs in her fancy pink satin bedroom slippers—the ones with the clickety heels and the fuzzy pompoms on the toes—and stomped into the kitchen and said, "Briley, I said the phone is ringing."

Once again, I said, "Yes, ma'am," without looking up from my Cheerios and my book.

Even without seeing her, I knew she was rolling her eyes at me. A daughter just senses these things about her mama.

Yanking the phone out of its stand, my mama nearly sang, "Good morning, this is Bronwyn speaking."

That woman could turn on a dime.

"Mother? Is that you, Mother?"

Here in Bynum, Georgia, we call our mothers Mama. But that wasn't good enough for my Granny Evadelle. She insisted her daughter call her Mother. She said Mama was so trivial and beneath her. So there my mama was, bellowing *Mother* into the phone.

"What are you crying about? Calm down, Mother!" I can't understand a word you're saying when you're screeching at me like that."

My ears perked up, and I lost interest in my Cheerios and my book. Nothing could divert my attention like my grandmother crying and screeching on a Saturday morning, 'cause my grandmother didn't take to crying and screeching casually. My Granny Evadelle was what one might call stoic. She didn't show her hand, whether she be overjoyed or devastated. She was always the same, lips pursed and nostrils flared. It's like she was forever smelling something rather unpleasant. About the only thing that would bring even the slightest hint of a smile to Granny Evadelle's lips was the mention of her precious daughter, my mama, Bronwyn Gail Talmidge Beckwith. But she wasn't smiling at her precious daughter; she was bellowing at her like the Wild Woman of Borneo. Now, I have no idea who the Wild Woman of Borneo is, but when someone was acting all crazy, Granny Evadelle would say she was acting like the Wild Woman of Borneo.

"Okay, Mother, tell me what's wrong." After listening to why her mama was crying but refusing to tell me why when I poked at her and gave her my questiony face, she said, "What station, Mother?"

And while my Granny Evadelle shouted through the phone—even I could hear her shouting—Mama flicked on the TV, the little one on the kitchen counter, the one she watched while she was cooking, and scrolled to station WSAV over in Savannah. The screen sprang to life, and I found myself staring at a bunch of police cars, all of them with their yellow and red lights spinning, and a bunch of people crowding around, craning their necks. And there was a strip of yellow crime tape wrapped all around the outside of a house. I got closer to the screen and squinted my eyes through my smudged glasses and realized that it wasn't just any old house I was looking at.

"Mama, Mama," I screamed and pointed, "that's Dr. Joe Bobby's house! I'd recognize that house anywhere!"

Mama just stood there and stared at the picture of Dr. Joe Bobby Tisdale's house on the television screen, like she had been slapped silly. Then, without saying a word, she just hung up the phone while Granny Evadelle was still screeching.

I could sort of understand Mama's unnatural reaction to seeing Dr. Joe Bobby's house on the TV news, all wrapped up in crime tape like that. That's because Mama and Dr. Joe Bobby go way back. Fact is, they go back all the way to the beginning. Actually, if we were getting real technical, and Mama says I usually am, she and Dr. Joe Bobby go back even before the beginning.

That's 'cause my Granny Evadelle and Miss Eulalee, Dr. Joe Bobby's mama, were the dearest of friends, having met at Miss Delta's School for the Refinement of Young Cultured Southern Women at the age of four. They also happened to be members in extraordinary standing of the DAR and the Dames of the WNA, which, of course, stands for War of Northern Aggression (miscalled by those of great ignorance and ill breeding—Granny Evadelle's words, not mine—as The Civil War).

So since their mamas had been best friends for so long, naturally Dr. Joe Bobby and Mama automatically became best friends at birth. They grew up right here in Bynum, Georgia, across the street from each other. They teethed on identical Waterford crystal cut glass knife rests, took summer naps side-by-side, swinging in a Pawleys Island rope hammock on Granny Evadelle's veranda, and were baptized on the same sultry July Sunday morning right down there on Main Street at the Holier-than-thou Episcopal Church, which is right between and head and shoulders above the First Presbyterian and the First-and-only-one-that-matters Southern Baptist Church. Mama and Dr. Joe Bobby started school at Miss Minnie's Preschool for the Privileged Progeny of Bynum and spent every year in the same classroom from Bynum Elementary school all the way up through Bynum Central High School. They went to sleep-away camp together over at Lake Waccaneechee, where they sang Ricky Ticky Nicky

Hicky Doo Roo Roo around a campfire and practiced kissing. And when they graduated from Bynum Central High School, they went to college together over at Georgia Tech.

Mama turned up the volume on the television, I assumed so she could find out why her best friend from before birth's house was all wrapped up in crime tape. Andrew Morgan, a field reporter from over at WSAV, was talking directly into the camera. He held a microphone up to his mouth with one hand, and with the other he pressed a hearing-aid-looking thing in his ear, like he was trying to get some message from Command Central, which, I guess, is exactly what he was doing.

Turning and motioning at Dr. Joe Bobby's house, Andrew said, "We have just arrived at the home of prominent and well-respected Bynum OB-GYN, Dr. Joe Bobby Tisdale, and his wife, Libby Beth." Pausing for his next fresh-off-the-press installment, he shook his head up and down in understanding and said, "When the Tisdales' maid, Bertha Ransom, arrived at the home this morning at around seven o'clock, Mrs. Tisdale did not respond to Bertha's yoo-hoos. So the domestic ventured into the home in search of her employer. It was there, in the Tisdales' bedroom, that Ms. Ransom found a very grizzly sight." Andrew paused and squinted as he took in the next feed of his report through his ear piece. A shocked look crossed his face as he continued, "That's where Ms. Ransom found Mrs. Tisdale, face-down on her and Dr. Tisdale's bed, a fatal wound to her temple, a gun in her hand. Though it appears to have been a suicide, the police are not speculating or making any statement at this time, pending the autopsy report and complete forensic analysis."

Andrew squinted as he, once again, pressed his finger to his ear. After his next info feed, he shook his head and continued, "It is our understanding that Dr. Tisdale is at this time out of town with friends, on their annual hunting trip up in Jacksonboro, South Carolina. We do not know if he has been contacted in the wake of this devastating tragedy."

When he didn't have anything else to say, Andrew just scrunched his face all up and squeezed his lips tight together, all the while shaking his head in stunned disbelief. I think all news reporters take a class in making those serious, I-just-can't-believe-this-has-happened faces, 'cause they all seem to know how to do it. And the face scrunching and lip pinching just sort of fill in the spaces between the times that they have something to say.

There were cars from the Bynum Sheriff's Department sitting in the Tisdales' driveway and parked along the front of the house. There was also an ambulance sitting in the driveway, which I assumed had something to do with Miss Libby Beth.

By the way, I have always felt that Libby Beth is a redundant name. It would appear that it consists of two nicknames for Elizabeth. So the woman's real name would be Elizabeth Elizabeth. Come to find out, though, Libby Beth is Dr. Joe Bobby's wife's real given name. Or *was* her real given name.

Anyway, while I was sitting there staring at Dr. Joe Bobby's house all wrapped up in yellow crime tape, the front door opened and out came two deputies, followed by two men wearing rubber gloves and carrying plastic bags.

Andrew Morgan squinted again and pressed his finger against his ear. Then he said, "Leaving the home of Dr. and Mrs. Joe Bobby Tisdale are several gentlemen carrying large plastic bags. They seem to be removing evidence from the house."

Following those two men were two other guys rolling a gurney with a big, old lumpy black bag on top of it.

Just as I was assuming that Libby Beth was in that bag, Andrew whispered real reverently into his microphone, "It appears the investigators are, at this time, removing the body of Mrs. Libby Beth Tisdale from the home she shared with her husband, Dr. Joe Bobby Tisdale."

Then the investigators put that lumpy black bag in the back of a big old van, closed the doors, hopped in, and drove away, leaving Andrew with an empty house wrapped in yellow crime tape and nothing more to say. So he motioned with his microphone to the short, squat, gray-haired lady standing off to one side. "We have with us Dr. and Mrs. Tisdale's next door neighbor, Clara…" Andrew hesitated and looked down at his notes.

"That's Miss Clara," I said to the television screen before Mama turned around and shushed me.

But before Andrew could locate Miss Clara's last name, she yanked the microphone out of his hand and said, "McGill, the name's McGill, Clara McGill. That's M-C-G-I-double-L, for the record. Now, I been living next door to Dr. Joe Bobby and Libby Beth just forever. Never has anything like this happened. We live on a peaceful, quiet street in a peaceful, quiet town. This just don't make no sense, no sense a'tall," Miss Clara said and shoved the microphone back at the reporter. Then she turned and shuffled back over to her house next door on the heels of her worn, dirty bedroom slippers.

Miss Clara is sort of an eccentric, always seeing UFOs and hearing voices. So it's kind of hard to sort out truth from fiction where she is concerned. But what she was saying was truth: she did, most certainly, live on a peaceful, quiet street in a peaceful, quiet town.

"That was Clara McGill, next-door neighbor of Dr. and Mrs. Joe Bobby Tisdale. Miss McGill says that this tragedy is uncharacteristic for this peaceful, quiet town, where folks have never experienced anything like this."

And he said this like none of us had just heard Miss Clara say the very same thing.

Mama just stood and stared expressionless at the screen, seemingly suffering from shock over the news that her best friend's wife was dead, from an apparent—but the police weren't saying for sure—suicide. As the news feed switched from Andrew back to the anchor desk in Savannah, Daddy came in the back door, sweating and panting from his morning run.

He took one look at Mama's ashen face and said, "What's going on, Bronwyn?"

Mama just stared and pointed at the screen.

"We will be suspending all regular programming this morning so that we can cover this tragedy over in Bynum," said usually perky Holly Hendrickson, the blonde-and-beautiful morning anchor at WSAV. Turning the corners of her lips down in appropriate grief, Holly said, "We are all here at WSAV saddened by this news, and we send our sincerest condolences to the family of Mrs. Libby Beth Tisdale. We will work tirelessly to bring all the details to you as we receive them." With that she put her face in her hands, and professional, helmet-haired Rob Mixon gave her a pat on the shoulder, cleared his throat of the grief lodged there, and bravely took over.

"What?" Daddy said to the screen, and, turning to Mama, asked, "What happened, Bronwyn?"

Mama just shook her head, tears puddling in her sad eyes, and said, "Libby Beth. Libby Beth is dead. Looks like suicide. Poor Joe Bobby, up there in South Carolina hunting and not even knowing about this."

That was so like my mama, feeling sorry for her best friend, Dr. Joe Bobby, at a time like this. Then she busted out crying and ran from the room. Daddy followed her, leaving me there all by myself with just the TV, my Cheerios, and my book, two of which no longer interested me.

Then I heard a knock at the door. Since Mama was up in her and Daddy's bedroom wailing away and Daddy was up there trying to console her, I figured I was the only one left to see who was calling on a Saturday morning.

I opened the door to find Miss Delphine Dudley, our next-door neighbor, standing on the porch. Being relatively new—or newly returned—to the neighborhood, it was the very first time she'd paid us a visit.

Miss Delphine had grown up in the house next door, but she had hightailed it out of Bynum in the direction of New York City at the ripe old age of seventeen, long before I was born. She'd worked in Broadway theatre doing odd jobs for a good many years—I'd heard about thirty-five or so—before returning to Bynum, Georgia, only when she was absolutely positive that her mama and daddy were good and dead.

Her daddy had died ten years back, when I was just four years old. There are only two things that I remember about Mr. Dudley: he had a few wispy white hairs that he combed from the left side of his head over the top to hide his baldness, but the hairs never stayed put; instead, they just stood straight up in the air, like a flag, sort of advertising Mr. Dudley's baldness.

The other thing I remember is that he'd give me a Luden's menthol cough drop every time he saw me, like he was giving me a piece of candy. I'd put it in my mouth to be polite and not hurt his feelings, and then I'd spit it right out in my hand as soon as I was sure he wasn't looking.

They'd buried Miss Delphine's mama just seven weeks before. We were all sure she was good and dead because we saw her laid out in her casket, all painted up and waxy looking on visitation night at Cletus Clemmons Funeral Home. So Miss Delphine moved back into her mama and daddy's home since she was Mr. and Mrs. Dudley's only young'un and the sole heir to their estate, an estate consisting of one paid-for house, a 1976 orange Chrysler LeBaron, and a whole bunch of money stashed in odd places that nobody knew about till their lawyer started poking around in the Dudleys' business.

"Hey, Miss Delphine," I said, surprised to see her standing on our porch.

"You're Briley, right?" she asked, pointing a well-manicured green fingernail at me.

"Yes, ma'am, I am. We met at your mama's funeral."

"Why, yes, I remember now. But that whole day is a bit of a blur," she said, shrugging her shoulders at me.

"Sure, I understand, Miss Delphine."

"Well, I heard about Joe Bobby's wife, and I remembered that Bronwyn and Joe Bobby were real good friends when they were little kids."

"Yes, ma'am, they've been best friends since way back when."

"Well, I just wanted to come over and see how y'all were doing, see if there's anything I can do to help."

The woman had been away from the South for over thirty-five years, but she still knew how to say *y'all.* I liked that in a person. As Grandma Evadelle would say, she hadn't gotten above her raising.

"Well, I guess I'm okay, Miss Delphine. Mama's all shook up, though. Just don't know what to make of it."

"Well, it's a sad situation. Sorry to say I hadn't been back in Bynum long enough to have met Libby Beth. But how dreadful to be so despondent to take one's own life," Miss Delphine said, shaking her head.

"Yeah, it's a sadness all right and a real mystery. Miss Libby Beth always seemed like a real cheerful sort to me. We just never know what goes on inside other folks' houses or other folks' heads, no matter how good we think we know 'em. Isn't that right, Miss Delphine?"

"That's right, Briley."

"Well, Miss Delphine, would you like for me to go get my mama for you?"

"No, that won't be necessary, Briley. You just let your folks know that I stopped by. If y'all need anything at all, just holler. I'm right next door, all alone."

"Thank you, I'll tell them when Mama composes herself and

comes out of her bedroom."

"You do that," Miss Delphine said and trudged down our steps, across our grass, and through the hedgerow into her own yard.

I waited until I saw her climb the steps to her big, wide porch, cross the creaking boards, and wave at me before disappearing into her house. Then I went on back in the kitchen and took up my post in front of the television, listening to Andrew say the same thing over and over and over. But I figured something different was bound to happen at some point, and I just didn't want to miss it.

Mama finally pulled herself together somewhat around lunch time and came out of her bedroom, her eyes all puffy and her face splotched real red. She was wringing a wad of wet Kleenex in her hands, and her nose was all runny from crying.

"Mama, you okay?" I asked her, scared by the looks of my up-until-that-time perfectly made-up mother.

"No, Briley, I am not," she answered in a woeful sort of way, wringing her wad of Kleenex till her knuckles turned white.

"I'm sorry about Miss Libby Beth, Mama."

"I'm sure you are, Briley. We all are."

"Mama, that reminds me, Miss Delphine from next door came over to see how you were getting along."

"Well, that was right neighborly of her," was all Mama said as she slumped into the kitchen where WSAV was continuing to report on the Tragedy of Bynum, Georgia.

She stayed right by the television all day long, ready to spring into action the moment Dr. Joe Bobby needed her. Of course she figured he'd need her, seeing as how she was Dr. Joe Bobby's best friend and all. She would be ready with casseroles, mostly chicken and rice with mushroom soup, which were already prepared and waiting in the freezer for births, deaths, sicknesses, or any other occasion that called for frozen dishes. She'd also be ready with a warm heart and a shoulder for a best friend to cry on. But she waited and waited, her eyes flitting from the television screen to the phone, like they were playing ping pong. Seems Dr. Joe Bobby didn't need her, though, because the phone stayed silent all day long. Mama kept picking up the receiver to see if there was something wrong with the telephone, like the line was dead, but everything was working fine. Then she'd check her cell phone, thinking Dr. Joe Bobby would, perhaps, be calling her on her cell. But Dr. Joe Bobby wasn't calling, much to my mama's despair.

Then about seven o'clock Liz Ketchum, the evening anchor at WSAV got all excited-like and said, "It appears, ladies and gentlemen, as if Dr. Joe Bobby Tisdale has been notified and is returning to his home in Bynum as we report to you. Let's go back to our camera crew that has been waiting outside the Tisdale home since early this morning."

Andrew Morgan, looking disheveled and a little worse for wear after hanging out the entire day in Dr. Joe Bobby's front yard, said, "Yes, Liz, we are here in Bynum, Georgia, at the home of Dr. Joe Bobby Tisdale. An automobile has just pulled into the driveway, and I see two men emerging."

I saw Dr. Joe Bobby's silver Lexus SUV pull up and Dr. Joe Bobby get out of the passenger side, his head all hanging down.

Mama gasped when she saw him and croaked, "There he is. There's Joe Bobby right there," like Daddy and I didn't recognize him at all. "Oh my, he looks dreadful, poor thing."

"Well, Bronwyn, he did just drive back from Jacksonboro after learning that his wife is dead," Daddy told her.

"Shhhhhh…." Mama said and flapped her hand in Daddy's direction.

Bayless Bramble, one of Dr. Joe Bobby's hunting buddies, jumped out of the driver's side and rushed around the front of the car, shielding his eyes from the lights of the TV cameras. He caught up with Dr. Joe Bobby, put his arm around his shoulders, and ushered him into the house, closing the door behind them.

"Well, from what we know," Andrew Morgan said, looking at his notes on his iPhone, "Dr. Joe Bobby Tisdale was on a hunting trip with three other gentlemen up in Jacksonboro, South Carolina, when Mrs. Tisdale was found dead in their bed, a single gunshot wound to her temple. Dr. Tisdale was apparently contacted by the authorities while in South Carolina and has just returned to his home. He is accompanied by one gentleman, whose identity we have yet to ascertain."

"That's Bayless, Bayless Bramble, you moron," Mama yelled at the TV. "You should get all your facts together before you start reporting."

"Calm down, Bronwyn," Daddy said. "The reporters had no way of knowing that it was Bayless who was going to come home with

Joe Bobby."

Mama just crossed her arms over her chest and said, "Pffft."

"We are withholding further reports on the incident, pending an autopsy and complete forensic evidence," reporter Morgan said.

Every time there was a new bit of information, whoever was reporting would just tack all the old stuff on to it to make it look like they were making great progress.

"Didn't we just hear that a few minutes ago?" I said to Mama, after hearing the same thing for about the eleventeenth time.

"Shhh," Mama said, "they might just say something else, and I don't want to miss it."

Daddy put his arm around Mama and patted her, saying, "Calm down, Bronwyn, calm down."

"I will not calm down, Kyle," Mama said, shrugging out of Daddy's arm. "Joe Bobby needs me. Needs us. I think we ought to get on over there right this minute."

"Now, hold on, Bronwyn. We are not going to go over there and get tangled up in all those newspaper and TV reporters. Why, they probably wouldn't even let us get past all that yellow crime tape."

"But, Kyle…"

"No, Bronwyn. We're going to wait right here until Joe Bobby calls to tell us he needs us," Daddy said, stroking Mama's hair like she was a pet of some kind. "You know very well we'll be here for him, and he knows that too. He'll call. You know he will."

Two

Mama didn't move from her spot in the kitchen right in front of the television all weekend long. We didn't go to church, and she didn't even make me go to Sunday school. I'm sorry Miss Libby Beth had to die to get me out of going to Sunday school, but staying home suited me just fine. Truth is, I'm the only person in my Sunday school class down at the Holier-than-thou Episcopal Church. That's 'cause everybody else my age belongs to the First-and-only-one-that-matters Southern Baptist Church. But most every Sunday, except when something like Miss Libby Beth killing herself happens, I go into my Sunday school class and sit in front of Mr. Jeffries, who drones on and on about some Bible story I've heard before and heard told better.

After he teaches for a while, he'll say, "You understand, Briley?"

Understand? It's a Bible story, not calculus! I want to say. But I don't. Mr. Jeffries is teaching me out of the goodness of his heart, so the least I can do is pay attention and be respectful and appreciative.

So I just say, "Yes, sir, I understand."

But the day after they found Miss Libby Beth's body, Mama said she wanted to stay close to home, just in case the news reporters were to tell us something new about the Libby Beth case. Mama also wanted to stay right by the phone, so she could be ready when Dr. Joe Bobby called.

Even though I was glad I didn't have to go to Sunday school, I felt kind of guilty knowing that Mr. Jeffries had planned a Sunday school lesson just for me. I was hoping he wouldn't wait around too long for me to show up, and I thought maybe he could just save my lesson till the next Sunday. I started to call and tell him that I wouldn't object to a leftover Bible story if he didn't want to plan a new one, but I figured he was old enough to figure that out himself. What's more, I wouldn't know if it was a leftover Bible story, no matter what he chose to do.

And even though we missed Sunday school and church just so Mama could be by the phone when Dr. Joe Bobby called, Dr. Joe Bobby never called.

"I just don't understand why," she wailed, cut to the core by the indignity of Dr. Joe Bobby's slight.

"Bronwyn, you have to get a grip," Daddy said, taking her by the arms and talking to her real sternly.

"But I'm his best friend, Kyle," she wailed and pulled away from Daddy, plopping down in a kitchen chair and laying her head on the table. Her long, chestnut hair made a curtain all around her face, her arms hanging limp down by her sides.

I've often thought Mama would have made a really good actress.

Daddy is a very patient man, but eventually he got right put out with Mama and said, "Bronwyn, you're just being self-centered. This is not about you. Joe Bobby's wife is dead. Though I know Joe Bobby cares deeply for your friendship, you are not on his mind right now."

Mama picked her head up off the table, a big red spot taking shape on her forehead, and looked at Daddy with a pout, her eyes all bloodshot by now and her face splotchier than ever.

She said to him, "Now, Kyle, that was a mean-spirited thing to say." Then she put her head back down on the table and resumed her sobbing.

Daddy just shook his head and said, "Briley, why don't you fix us some bologna sandwiches and Fritos for lunch."

"Yes, sir, I'll do that," I told him and headed for the refrigerator to get the fresh package of bologna that Mama had just had Mr. Pete slice on Thursday down at his butcher shop. I got out the Wonder Bread, 'cause only white Wonder Bread will do when you're making a bologna sandwich. I pulled out six slices and slathered lots of Duke's mayonnaise on every slice. I gave us each two pieces of Mr. Pete's bologna, 'cause I figured a tragic day like we were experiencing called for extra bologna.

Daddy and I ate our bologna sandwiches, but Mama refused to

touch hers.

"But, Mama, I put extra Duke's on yours, just the way you like it."

"You're so thoughful, Briley," Mama said in a muffled, sobby voice, without even lifting her head off the table. "But I just couldn't choke down a thing right now. Thank you for asking, though."

She also refused to touch her Campbell's chicken noodle soup I fixed at suppertime, even though we had those little oyster crackers she loved to sprinkle all over the top.

"Bronwyn, you have to eat something," Daddy begged her.

Lifting her head with much effort, she said, "Thank you, Kyle, I appreciate your caring, truly I do, but I just couldn't eat a thing right now." Then she put her head back down on the kitchen table, that red spot on her forehead getting bigger and brighter.

Her drama made both Daddy and me just shake our heads. I rolled my eyes, but she was so caught up in her performance that she didn't even sense it.

I cleaned up the supper dishes and went to take my shower. Afterward I read for about an hour, then came down to tell my mama and daddy that I was going to bed. I found Daddy in the living room, reading the paper.

"Night, Daddy. See you in the morning."

"Sleep tight, Briley," Daddy said, as I leaned over to give him a good-night hug.

"Where's Mama?"

"Where do you think?" he said, shaking his paper real exasperated and cutting his eyes toward the kitchen.

I shuffled down the hall and found Mama sitting at the kitchen table, right where I'd left her hours before.

"Night, Mama."

"Night, Sugar."

Mama's forehead was glowing red in the light of the TV screen. I leaned over and kissed her on her cheek, and she reached up and patted my back, never taking her eyes off WSAV.

Still Dr. Joe Bobby didn't call.

Daddy tried to reason with Mama. "You don't know how a fellow is going to behave under such circumstances, Bronwyn. Now, you just leave him be. He'll let us know what he needs from us and when he needs it."

Mama huffed and fumed around the house, cut to the quick by Dr. Joe Bobby's betrayal of their abiding friendship. Yet none of us saw Mama's forever best friend until we showed up at Miss Libby Beth's funeral, down at the Holier-than-thou Episcopal Church.

I came downstairs in my blue jeans, ready to head out to the church. Mama took one look at me and screamed like crazy.

"Briley, have you taken leave of your senses? Blue jeans at a funeral? Why, the disrespect! It's bad enough that you refuse to put on heels, a battle, it appears, I shall never win. But you can most certainly do something about those jeans. Now, get on back upstairs and put on your Sunday school dress."

Well, I had at least put on a clean shirt. I thought that was respectful enough, but apparently not, by Bronwyn Talmidge Beckwith's standards. So I trudged back upstairs, shrugged out of my clothes, threw them in a pile on my bedroom floor, and yanked down my Sunday school dress from the closet rod. Actually, it's not just my Sunday school dress; it's my one-and-only-dress-since-I-hate-dresses-with-a-passion dress. It's a navy blue print sundress that I wear in summer just plain and every other time of year with a sweater over it. I stepped in, zipped it up the back as high as I could reach, tugged on my navy blue sweater, and headed for the door. Realizing I was wearing my tennis shoes, I kicked them off, slamming them against my bedroom wall, leaving a smudgy tread mark in the blue paint, and dragged my blue flats out of the closet with my toes. I hate my blue flats as much as I hate dresses. They hurt my feet something awful. I could only imagine how bad high heels would hurt. I planned never to find out. I slid my feet in and hobbled down the stairs to see how I ranked on Bronwyn's respect-o-meter.

"Better," was all Mama said, checking her teeth for lipstick smudges in the hall mirror.

Daddy looked real presentable in his everyday business suit, but Mama was dressed to kill in her black mourning dress and her black hat with the big old wide brim. Daddy said she looked like Zorro when she wore it, but he just said that to me, so as not to hurt my mama's feelings. But she was the only person in all of Bynum who still wore a hat. However, that was Bronwyn's idea of respectful.

When we arrived at the church, we found that lots of folks had already gotten there and were filling up the pews. Mama tried to get the usher to seat us down where the family was supposed to sit, but everybody in Bynum, including the ushers at Miss Libby Beth's funeral, knew we were of no relation whatsoever to Miss Libby Beth or Dr. Joe Bobby Tisdale, never mind how tight Dr. Joe Bobby and Mama were. Shortly after we took our seats, as close to the family as the usher would allow, the organist started playing a real mournful hymn. That hymn was the cue for Dr. Joe Bobby and his Real Family to begin processing down the center isle of the church. Clutching onto Joe Bobby's arms were his mama, Miss Eulalee, and Miss Eulalee's identical twin sister, Miss Eugenia, each of them dabbing at their eyes with monogrammed, linen hankies with lace edges. Parading behind the main three was a whole pack of cousins and cousins' spouses and cousins' children, only a few of them familiar to us.

"Why, those strangers are less family to Joe Bobby than I am," Mama whisper-screamed.

Several people turned around and glared at her, and Daddy just put his arm around her and pulled her to him, trying to quiet her down. She glared at him, yanked away, and stabbed him in the eye with the brim of her Zorro hat.

While speaker after speaker got up to praise the wonderfulness of beautiful, kind Libby Beth Tisdale, I looked at her closed casket sitting up there at the front of the church. It was a basic, shiny wooden box with brass hinges. It made me sad that a human being's whole life, from beginning to end, could be wrapped up and stuffed inside a wooden box. Something about it just didn't seem, you know, respectful. I don't know what the inside of Libby Beth's life box looked like because the funeral directors said no matter how hard they'd worked on Libby Beth, they just couldn't get her fixed up good enough to have an open casket. Guess when you give yourself a gunshot wound to the head, it's hard to fix that where it can be presentable. And respectful. And while I stared at Miss Libby Beth's casket, wondering just what the insides looked like, one after another person droned on and on about their remembrances of their deceased friend.

"Libby Beth was beautiful, inside and out."

Isn't that what everybody says about somebody who has died? Who's going to argue, even if it's a lie?

"Libby Beth loved her family and friends."

Still no surprises and an awfully generic statement.

"Libby Beth was one of a kind."

Well, shoot, everybody's one of a kind.

Didn't the citizens of Bynum, Georgia have any creativity, any originality? Apparently not.

"Libby Beth loved life."

Well, if the lady loved life so much, why the heck did she put a gun to her own head?

When the last droner stepped down from the pulpit and I had mentally unraveled every word they'd said, Father Caleb gave a brief homily and pronounced the funeral ended, thank goodness, and we all filed up the aisle.

When we got outside, we found Dr. Joe Bobby and his real blood-relative family standing in a straight line, ready to shake hands with everyone who had come and to thank them for being there.

Mama shook, shook, shook hands, being as cordial as she could be with people whom she deemed less than fit to be called Joe Bobby's family. When she got all the way down to Dr. Joe Bobby, she threw her arms around his neck, stabbed him in the eye with her hat, and wailed uncontrollably, "Joe Bobby, you didn't call. I was so worried."

Clutching Mama's wrists and prying them from around his neck, Dr. Joe Bobby smiled an uncomfortable smile and said, "I've been a little busy, Bronwyn. When things settle down, I'll give you and Kyle a call." And shoving her along, he reached for the next mourner, who so happened to be me, and said, "Hi there, Briley. So good of you to come."

"Course, Dr. Joe Bobby," I said, but I didn't really think it was a good thing I'd done. Mama had said, "Briley, put on your dress and go get in the car."

And I'd done it.

Three

The morning after Miss Libby Beth's funeral, I woke up and got dressed for school, an activity I always dreaded—the school part, not so much the getting up and getting dressed part. I went downstairs to the kitchen to get a Pop-Tart, where I found my mama already dressed in her blue scrubs, fixing herself a tall, insulated cup of coffee to carry along to work with her.

My mama was a nurse. She worked at the Urgent Care over on Gladiola Place. She loved her job, always liked taking care of people. And, if I do say so myself, she was a dang good nurse. She could give you a shot without you even knowing it. She'd wanted to be a nurse ever since Joe Bobby told her he wanted to be a doctor.

"You doing all right this morning, Mama?"

"I reckon, Briley, good as can be expected, given the circumstances," she said dramatically, screwing the top on her coffee and grabbing a Tupperware container of salad from the refrigerator, slamming the door with her knee. "Daddy has already left for work. He had an early-morning conference call." I'm guessing Daddy left early for work just to get away from all the Miss Libby Beth and Dr. Joe Bobby drama. "I'll be home about the usual time. Now, you have a good day at school today, and try not to think of all this sadness, you hear?"

I hadn't planned on thinking of all the sadness until my mama reminded me of it.

Then giving me a one-armed hug and kissing me on the side of my head, she said, "Bye, Honey," and headed for the door.

I watched my mama back her car out of the drive, and then I rummaged in the pantry till I found the Pop-Tarts. Blueberry was all we had. I'd have preferred strawberry with sprinkles, but I figured blueberry would do in a pinch. I dropped two in the toaster and poured myself a glass of milk. I had a half hour to kill before the bus showed up. Usually I'd turn on the TV for company, but I didn't want to run the risk of hearing more—or the same—about Miss Libby Beth's suicide. So I ate in silence, and while I was eating, something in the back of my head started rumbling around, troubling me really awful. Then that something popped up and told me that our lives would just never, ever be the same again.

I thought I knew why, but I didn't know just how.

When I finished my breakfast, I put my plate and glass in the dishwasher and went upstairs to brush my teeth and get my backpack. Loading all my school books, none of which I'd even cracked because I'd been sidetracked by the Libby Beth news, I trudged back down the stairs, school dread in my step. I reached into my backpack for my latest novel, opened it to where I'd left off, and buried my face in it as I headed out the door to the bus stop, right at the end of our driveway.

I always left home with my nose in a book. It was my shield of protection against a world where I felt I didn't belong: high school. It was a world where everybody else seemed to have a place; it was a world where everybody else seemed confident and self-assured; it was a world where everybody else seemed to look right and wear the right clothes and say the right, clever things.

So there I was, standing at the bus stop, eyes on my book, minding my own business, trying to hide my lack of belonging, when I heard, "Briley, yoo-hoo, Briley."

I looked over at the group of kids standing in a cluster on the other side of our driveway. There were about a dozen of them, shifting from foot to foot, talking in twos and threes. In the center of the pack was Kurt, captain of the football team, talking to the Bitsy-Buffy-Binkys, my names for the spirit squad girls. It was spirit day at school, and the Bitsy-Buffy-Binkys were wearing their spirit uniforms, short blue and white skirts and cropped, tight tops that showed off their belly buttons and their perky boobs. While Kurt charmed them with his hooded eyes and hair tossing, they smiled adoringly up at him, but I knew they were ignoring every word he was saying. Instead, they were practicing, in their heads, their favorite spirit routines. They bobbed their heads ever so slightly and shuffled their feet to the beat going on in their heads.

I could tell that Bitsy was going through the routine to Uptown Funk, everybody's favorite. When the spirit girls would perform it, we'd all cheer and want them to do that one again. I had seen it so many times that I knew the routine by heart. I'd tried it once in front of my full-length mirror in my bedroom. That's when I knew, for sure, that I wasn't cut out to be a spirit girl.

But if Kurt had been talking to me, I wouldn't have been thinking about spirit routines. Or anything else. Kurt has that kind of effect on girls. Well, some girls.

"Did you call me?" I asked no one in particular. No one looked my way, so I said a little louder, "Did somebody call me?"

Kurt and the Bitsy-Buffy-Binkys finally turned toward me, looks of surprise on their faces, as if a unicorn had spoken to them.

"No, I didn't call you," Kurt said. And, looking around, he said to his admirers, "Did y'all call Briley?" When no one answered, he just shrugged and gave me an awkward smile.

But there was really no reason they'd have called me. I'm not one of the popular kids. In fact, I'm not even one of the unpopular kids. I'm, like I said, a non-belonging kid. And I'd learned well how to play my part. I did my best just to blend into the background. I stayed to myself, kept my nose in a book, and tried not to make any sudden moves.

I hadn't always been the lone non-belonging kid, though. There used to be three more just like me: Whitney Burroughs, Kevin Whitcomb, and Randall Bullock. Whitney and I were good friends, even had sleepovers and everything. But her daddy got a job in New York, and her family had to move away. We both cried and clung to each other the day she left, vowing to be best friends till the end of time. At first we texted a lot, but then she got new friends in New York. And as the group of new friends grew, the texts dwindled. That's just the way life works, even if you plan it differently. That left just Kevin, Randall, and me. Kevin's parents thought he was too much of a recluse since all the three of us did was sit in his room and play video games, so they sent him to boarding school up in Virginia. He didn't text at all, which was fine since he'd never promised to.

With Whitney and Kevin gone, I realized that Randall was just plain weird. Among other weird things, he picked his nose. I told him that it was one thing to pick your nose in second grade, but once you got into high school, that crap just had to stop. I said it was either me or his nose picking.

He looked at me real bored-like, said, "Okay," and turned and walked down the hall. He already had his finger in his nose before he disappeared around the corner.

So there I was, all by myself. My lack of involvement in high school and inability—or lack of courage—to make new friends baffled my mother. My mama, Miss Bronwyn Gail Talmidge, had been the queen, president, and chairman of everything at Bynum Central High School back in the day. Guess it helped that she's pretty as all get out. She's tall, with that long, thick chestnut hair and great big blue eyes. She has full lips and big old straight white teeth, for which she never had to wear braces or Crest White Strips.

Me, I take after my daddy. We make a passable-looking grown man, but not so much a teenage girl. Being fourteen with thick glasses, braces, and lanky mouse-brown hair is just pure ammunition for ridicule. And it didn't help that I was scrawny with boobs the size of mosquito bites. Mama got me a training bra, but I refused to wear it. Why bother? What was I training for?

"Briley, Sugar, why don't you try out for majorette?" Mama said real casually one day while she was loading the dishwasher.

Majorette? Is Mama delusional? Has she ever looked at me? Doesn't she know I'm anything but majorette material? Maybe she's just living proof that love is blind. And she does love me. I'm pretty sure of that.

"You know, I used to be a majorette," she said off-handedly, still loading the dishwasher while I sat at the kitchen table eating Lucky Charms right out of the box.

Of course I know she used to be a majorette. Everybody in Bynum, Georgia, and surrounding areas knows my mama was a majorette. And not just any majorette. Miss Bronwyn Gail Talmidge was head majorette of Bynum Central High School, which happens to be the only high school in Bynum, so I don't understand why it isn't just named Bynum High School. But, anyway, not only was my mama head majorette of Bynum Central High School, class of '89, she was also the Georgia State Champion Twirler three years running. Why, she even earned a majorette scholarship to Georgia Tech. I was stunned to learn that there was actually a scholarship for such a thing. And there's evidence of her majoretteness everywhere: pictures on the coffee table of her flinging her flaming batons way up in the air; pictures on the mantle of her receiving ribbon after ribbon after ribbon for her twirling abilities; pictures of her on her bedside table of her being crowned Bynum Central High Homecoming Queen her senior year. I guess I failed to mention that in addition to being head majorette, Miss Bronwyn Talmidge was also homecoming queen. And in case we might forget all of Bronwyn's accomplishments, we could find identical pictures in Granny Evadelle's house, parading across her mantle and lining the shelves of her whatnot cabinet. Pictures of her little girl, Bronwyn, were the only whatnots Granny Evadelle ever wanted.

"I believe my old batons are still upstairs in the attic," Mama said, as if no one knew she went up there from time to time to twirl and prance to music she'd play on her old boom box.

When I didn't say a thing, Mama turned to me and said, "Briley, don't you think that would be a good idea? You could try out for majorette? Hmmm, sound good?"

I stretched my tee shirt tight over my teeny boobs, squinted my eyes through my thick glasses, smiled real big around my braces, and lisped, "Yeth, ma'am, I think thath's an ecthellent idea. I'll get right on it."

And her ability to believe that I could be anything she wanted me to be made her ignore my sarcasm and smile her sparkly smile. And keep on loading the dishwasher.

But I wasn't going to be a majorette or homecoming queen. Because I didn't belong—to anyone but my mama, my daddy, and my Granny Evadelle. And sometimes I had my doubts about my Granny Evadelle.

Then I heard that *yoo-hoo* again and looked up from my book. This time Kurt pointed toward the house next door and said, "I believe she's calling you."

When I looked to where he was pointing, I found Miss Delphine standing on her bare tiptoes, waving to me with one hand, holding her silky red kimono together with the other.

I pointed to myself with my *you-talkin'-to-me?* move.

She nodded her head vigorously up and down and motioned me

to her.

I closed my book, stuck it under my arm, and shuffled down her oyster shell driveway, curious about what Miss Delphine just might want with me. She'd already asked if I was all right. I assured her I was. What more was there to say? Halfway up the drive I turned to the kids still standing at the bus stop to gauge their reaction. They'd already lost interest and had returned to their huddle of teen chatter, the Bitsy-Buffy-Binkys still shuffling their feet ever so slightly, Kurt flinging his hair, attempting to charm his female audience.

"How are you doing this morning?" she asked me.

I cocked my head curiously and said, "Okay."

"Well, I know the events of the past weekend have been hard on your family."

"Yes, ma'am, you might say that."

"Want to watch TV with me and bake some apple bread?"

I pointed toward the bus stop and said, "But I gotta go to school."

"Do you really?" Jutting out her hip and cocking her head at me, she screwed up her face and asked, "Will just one day of hooky hurt?"

I'd never had a grown-up—or anybody, for that matter—suggest that I skip school.

"I like you, Briley. I liked you the minute I met you. I think we just clicked, don't you?" Then she smiled and squinted her eyes at me.

I hadn't detected any clicking when Miss Delphine showed up on our doorstep. But, then, I wasn't familiar with instantaneous clicking, so I didn't dispute her word. Instead I looked back at the cluster of kids at the bus stop. I saw the bus coming down the street and the students breaking their huddles to line up single-file. They'd long forgotten that I'd ever been there, that I'd broken rank to sidle up Miss Delphine's driveway. Who would know and who would care if I didn't show up for school that day? Or any day?

So I shrugged and said, "Guess one day can't hurt."

"Goody!" she yipped and jumped up and down on bare feet—feet that I hadn't noticed until then were so tiny—and clapped her hands. "I hate watching TV alone. And you can read out the apple bread recipe while I mix all the ingredients together. Okay?"

"Okay."

It really didn't sound like an exciting day, but anything sounded more exciting than a day at Bynum Central High School, where I would probably spend the day thinking about Miss Libby Beth and where I would never be a majorette or homecoming queen.

Four

So from Miss Delphine's front porch I watched my classmates file onto the bus and jostle for seating, the guys pushing and shoving, punching one other on the arm, like they didn't have a lick of sense. Our bus driver, a pudgy, pimply-faced guy with BO named Francis who had graduated from Bynum Central High a couple of years before, yelled at them to cut that crap—just like he did every morning—slammed the doors, and drove off, without even noticing that I was standing there on Miss Delphine's front porch, playing hooky for the first time in my entire academic life.

I just shrugged my shoulders, turned, and walked on into the house, Miss Delphine following me, clapping her hands and saying, "We're just gonna have so much fun."

I figured Miss Delphine must be real lonely, if she considered hanging out with a fourteen-year-old truant so much fun.

Miss Delphine's house smelled real good, like some sort of exotic perfume you couldn't get in Bynum. Or even over in Savannah. Maybe in Atlanta. But I figured Miss Delphine had gotten whatever that sweet-smelling stuff was up in New York City, where she'd been living all those years. When I got to know her better, I'd ask her what that sweet smell was 'cause I wanted my bedroom to smell just like that.

"How about a Yoo-hoo?" Miss Delphine asked.

I'd just eaten my breakfast and wasn't really hungry or thirsty, but I figured, why not? You can never be too full for a Yoo-hoo.

"Sure, I'd like me a Yoo-hoo. I really love Yoo-hoo, but my mama won't ever buy it for me. She says she can't figure out if Yoo-hoo is an insult to chocolate milk or if it's an insult to soda. Me, I don't really care what or who Yoo-hoo insults. To me it just tastes delicious."

Miss Delphine laughed and said, "There you go," popping the top and handing me the icy-cold bottle.

I liked Miss Delphine's laugh. And her smile was so kind and welcoming. Even at that early hour in the morning, she had her lips painted bright red, the color sort of creeping into the little lines fanning out around her mouth. But the creeping lipstick didn't affect her kind smile in the least. Her hair was mostly gray, with a few black hairs mixed in, and she wore it long and sort of untamed, like she'd slept on it and hadn't bothered to comb it when she got out of bed. It just kind of hung there, down around her shoulders, and from time to time she'd brush it away from her face with the back of her hand. It looked like a very dramatic gesture to me—as if she had learned it on Broadway, back when she was living in New York and working in the theatre.

Still smiling with her bright red lips, she held out a recipe card and said, "Now you call out all the ingredients while I mix them together for our apple bread. But first we must have some baking music. Can't bake without the perfect music."

She reached for the knob on the radio sitting on the kitchen counter. It was rather large and looked like it was made out of wood, with rounded corners and weathered with age. Miss Delphine turned the big knob back and forth, stations fading in and out, as the dial passed them by. When she hit upon the station she wanted, she yipped, "Found it!" and began to sway. She turned to me, closed her eyes, held up her arms as if they were floating on air, and inhaled deeply, sort of breathing in the music.

"Opera," she said, reverently, as if it were something to worship. Opening her eyes and halting her swaying, Miss Delphine said, "Briley, don't you just love opera?"

She didn't ask if I *liked* opera, but jumped right to *love,* as if that were the only feeling one could have for opera. Frankly, I hadn't heard much opera in my life and had never really dwelled on it when I heard it. Guess you could say that I just knew *of* opera.

Sensing my operatic ignorance, she said, "Or, perhaps, you haven't been exposed to the opera. Sad. Everyone should have the joy of knowing opera. But give it time. Opera is an acquired taste.

Soon it will ooze into your soul. Listen, Briley, it's magic."

Resuming her swaying, she floated around her kitchen, preparing to make apple bread.

She had already assembled bowls, measuring spoons, measuring cups, and a big stirring spoon; flour and sugar and eggs and cooking oil sat on the counter next to the bowl; there were little containers of cinnamon, vanilla, and nutmeg; salt and baking soda; and apples, lots of chopped apples, 'cause, as I found out, it takes lots of chopped apples to make Miss Delphine's apple bread.

She also had a great big bag of shelled pecans which she slid down the counter to me. Still floating to the rhythm of the opera coming from the old radio, Miss Delphine said, "Here, chomp on these while you're coordinating this effort."

Then she said, "You ready?" When I let her know that I was, she said, "Then start reading."

"All right," I said, taking a swig of Yoo-hoo and a deep breath, "put three cups of flour in that bowl and add a teaspoon of cinnamon, a teaspoon of salt, and a teaspoon of nutmeg."

"You're mighty good at this, Briley. Thanks for helping. I have a hard time reading, measuring, and swaying to the music at the same time."

So as I ate pecans and called out ingredients, Miss Delphine floated on her tiptoes, her bright red kimono with the Japanese fans and lanterns on it swirling around her, the full, flowing sleeves flapping as she stirred the batter. When she had, at last, added the apples and the nuts, she measured the batter into two loaf plans and stuck them in the oven.

"Well, Briley," she said, rinsing her hands and drying them on a dish towel, "we have about an hour and a half to kill. What do you want to do?"

I didn't quite know what you did when you skipped school. I'd never done it before. And, what's more, she was the one who had said we were going to have so much fun. I figured she'd have had the fun all figured out.

So I told her, "I'm not sure, Miss Delphine. I've never skipped school before. Normally I'd be doing algebra about now."

"I never was too good at algebra, so we won't be doing any algebra today, if it's all the same to you."

That suited me fine. Even though I was a good math student, I wouldn't miss an hour of doing Miss Matheny's word problems.

"How about we watch a movie?" she asked, clapping her hands together excitedly.

I was hoping for *Twilight* or *The Fault in Our Stars*, but Miss Delphine said, "I have a wonderful collection of French movies. You're just going to love them."

She ran to the bookshelves beside the fireplace, crouched down, and pulled out a movie. Shoving it in the DVD player, she scurried to join me on the pink flowered sofa and gathered her tiny feet under her kimono before the movie appeared on the TV screen.

A crackling, popping black and white movie sprang to life, its title *Clair de Lune*. Miss Delphine informed me that *clair de lune* meant *moonlight* in French. To this day I have no idea why the movie was named *Clair de Lune* since it had absolutely nothing to do with moonlight.

I don't think.

Since the movie was made in France, all the actors spoke French, and there were English words at the bottom of the screen to go with the French words they were saying. But I had a hard time reading the words and watching the actors at the same time.

So Miss Delphine explained to me that the movie was set in France, during the occupation of France by the German army during World War II. Gerta, whose real name was Monette, was pretending to be a German spy, when, in real life, she was a member of the French Resistance and was spying on the Germans to get information for the French. She pretended to be in love with Ludwig, a handsome young German officer, so she could sweet talk him into telling her his secrets. Trouble is Gerta/Monette really did fall in love with Ludwig, and that just complicated everything.

I finally got the gist of what was going on, but I had one big question: If Ludwig was German and all the other officers were German and Gerta/Monette was pretending to be German, then why was everyone speaking French?

Miss Delphine explained that since the movie was made in France, everybody spoke French for convenience sake.

Convenience for whom? I was watching it, and I wasn't French.

But then Miss Delphine's apple bread was done, and I'd just have to save my confusion for another day.

Now, Miss Delphine's apple bread was fun—or as fun as a day of food could be. When she pulled it out of the oven, all puffed up and golden brown, it smelled delicious. My mouth started watering, and I wanted to taste it so bad. I was hoping she was planning to give me a piece.

"Briley, we're going to have to let it cool before we cut it, but we can turn it out of the pan and dust it with powdered sugar now."

And, with that, she flipped the loaf pan over and slammed it down on the counter, making a cracking noise so loud that it startled me and made me jump. Then she slowly lifted the pan from the loaf, leaving it sitting there upside down with steam coming off of it. When she turned the second loaf upside down and slammed it on the counter, I was expecting it and didn't even flinch. It, too, was golden, perfect, and steaming. Then she turned both loaves right-side up, filled a sifter with powdered sugar, and sprinkled it all over the tops of those loaves. I'd never seen anything so pretty or anything that smelled so good. Miss Delphine's opera was still playing in the background. To this day, whenever I hear opera, I can smell Miss Delphine's apple bread.

"What you say we do pedicures while we wait for our bread to cool?"

"That sounds fine to me."

"Oh, goody, I hoped you'd say that," she chirped and skipped down the hall and disappeared into a room I wasn't familiar with. She returned shortly, carrying a big wicker basket of nail polish bottles. There must have been fifty of them, each one a different color.

"Take your pick," she said, "and I'll paint your toenails. Then you can paint mine. Deal?"

"Deal."

While I was sorting through the bottles of nail polish, Miss Delphine pulled a pack of Pall Mall filter cigarettes out of her kimono pocket, tilted it toward me, and said, "Smoke?"

"No, ma'am. Better not."

"But if you change your mind…" she said, pulling out a cigarette, pinching it between her lips, and tossing the pack onto the coffee table. Then she took a pink Bic lighter from her pocket, cupped the cigarette with her hands, and lit the end.

"I think I'll take this blue," I said, handing the bottle to her.

"Good choice," she said, turning the bottle over and inspecting its name. "Hey, it's called *Clair de Lune*! What do you think of that?

Sounds like an omen to me."

I wasn't sure about omens, but I certainly did think it was a coincidence, seeing as how we had just watched the *Clair de Lune* movie.

Miss Delphine painted my toenails, and she was right: the blue I picked was a good choice. Miss Delphine chose black.

"Sometimes I'm in a black mood. How about you, Briley? Are you ever in a black mood?"

I told her that I had never assigned colors to my moods but that I'd give it some thought. Then I asked her if she was in a black mood and that was why she had chosen black polish for her toenails.

"Why, no, Briley. Just my toenails are in a black mood today. I am actually personally in a very yellow mood. That's the best mood there is. Thank you for helping me achieve yellow mood."

I'd been at Miss Delphine's for only about four hours, and already I was accumulating a list of questions to ask her, like *What makes your house smell so good? Why do the people in the movie speak French if Americans are going to watch it? How do you know what color your mood is? And how do you know the color of your toenails' mood?*

By the time our toenails were dry and Miss Delphine had smoked another cigarette, our apple bread was cool enough to cut. I was mighty glad, too, 'cause it was past my regular lunch time, and I was getting mighty hungry.

"Let's have apple bread for lunch," she giggled, as if we were getting away with something.

I usually eat at least a bologna sandwich and maybe some chips or an orange for lunch, but a good old slab of sugary apple bread sounded like a fine lunch to me. Miss Delphine cut two big slices and put them on real pretty, delicate pink flowered dessert plates. Then she reached into her silverware chest, which was just like my Granny Evadelle's, and got us two fancy, decorative sterling silver dessert forks. She even got out two linen napkins, instead of old Scott paper napkins, like the ones we used at home. Miss Delphine fixed herself a cup of tea.

"Would you care for a cup of tea, Briley?"

"No, thank you, Miss Delphine. I'm not much of a hot tea drinker, but, if it's all the same to you, I'd drink another Yoo-hoo."

It was the best lunch I have ever eaten or ever plan to eat for the rest of my life. Miss Delphine's apple bread was so moist, and it was so sweet it made my tongue curl—in a good way. It had lots of pecans that made a crunch among all the soft moistness. You know, lots of folks don't like that word *moist*, but you just can't describe Miss Delphine's apple bread without using the word *moist*.

We were still sitting there eating our apple bread—we had a second slice—when I saw the school bus stop at the end of my driveway and my classmates tumble out. I didn't realize we'd eaten and talked so long.

Wiping my mouth with my delicate linen napkin, I said, "This has been fun, Miss Delphine, but I think I better be getting on home. Mama will be coming home from work pretty soon."

"Well, okay, Briley. I hate to see you go, but I'm glad you spent the day with me. Your presence just made it real yellow."

"Thank you, Miss Delphine."

And scurrying to the kitchen, she said, "Now, you take this loaf of apple bread with you. I'm sure your mama isn't going to have time for baking, what with her grief and her concern for Joe Bobby."

"Yes, ma'am, you're probably right," I said, as she wrapped the second loaf of bread in aluminum foil and handed it to me.

I grabbed my backpack and headed for the door.

"Well, do you love it?"

"Love what?"

"Opera!"

"Oh, that," I said, scrunching up my nose a bit. "Don't think it's quite my style, Miss Delphine."

"I understand, Briley. Opera is an acquired taste. But it'll grow on you."

Wasn't sure I believed her, but I thanked Miss Delphine once more and headed on over to my house. I let myself in and kicked off my shoes and dropped my backpack in the hall. I trudged on back to the kitchen and put the loaf of apple bread on the kitchen counter for Mama to find when she came in from work.

When I heard my mama come through the front door, I started getting antsy, scared she was going to sense with that sense that mamas have that I had played hooky from school all day. I thought maybe I should hide the apple bread. Hide my blue toenails. But it was too late. She was already in the kitchen.

"Hi, Briley," she said, giving me a half-hug and a kiss on my head. She put her empty salad bowl and her fork in the dishwasher and then went to the refrigerator and got herself a bottle of water. She stood at the kitchen window and drank from the bottle while she stared out at the back yard. I came and stood by her and stared out the window too.

"What'cha looking at, Mama?"

"Oh, nothing, Briley. Just thinking about Joe Bobby and wondering how he's doing."

Then she shuffled out of the kitchen and up the stairs to her bedroom.

She hadn't seen my bright blue toenails.

And she hadn't even noticed that I had helped bake apple bread for her.

Five

The wheels of justice move ever so slowly. It took the forensic experts forever and a day to analyze the evidence that the detectives had taken from Dr. Joe Bobby's house. We weren't expecting any surprises. It looked like Miss Libby Beth had put a gun to her own head and pulled the trigger, and we figured all the evidence would just confirm that. Then we'd just move on and forever wonder what could have been so bad in Miss Libby Beth's life to make her want to end it so abruptly and tragically.

Mama said, "What in the heck are those fools doing? The poor woman took her own life, for some sad, unknown reason. Why can't they just let her rest in peace?"

However, the evidence showed that what looked like a cut-and-dried case of suicide was anything but. When the experts gathered up all that data and went through it with a fine-tooth comb, they came to the conclusion that Libby Beth couldn't have possibly killed herself. They said that she would have had to stand behind herself with the gun to shoot a bullet at the angle it went into her head. And they were expert enough to know, for sure, that that just wasn't possible. Heck, even I was expert enough to know that just wasn't possible. Also, she'd have had to do that with her left hand. Miss Libby Beth was right handed.

Then who did it? And why?

The first suspect is always the spouse, for whatever reason. So much to nobody's surprise, Dr. Joe Bobby was called into the police station for questioning about the death of his wife of eighteen years. He went voluntarily and freely, anxious to clear his name, when, in fact, everyone in Bynum knew that it didn't need clearing at all. Why, he and Miss Libby Beth were the picture of happiness and marital bliss.

So we waited and waited for the interrogation to be done so Dr. Joe Bobby could come by the house and tell Mama and Daddy all the details of what the detectives had said to him. Of course, I'd get all the bits and pieces, too, 'cause I'd be sitting in the corner, minding my own business, pretending to read, all the while taking in everything Dr. Joe Bobby was saying.

But Dr. Joe Bobby didn't come, and he didn't come some more. Needless to say, Mama was frantic with worry.

"Well, where in the world do you suppose he is? Why, I've called over to the house about a dozen times, and the phone just rings and rings and rings and then goes straight to voicemail. Why do you suppose he isn't answering his phone, Kyle?"

"Bronwyn, perhaps Joe Bobby isn't at home?"

"But why not? Surely they finished with him down at the police station hours ago. Where do you suppose he could have gone?"

As Mama talked, her voice just got higher and higher until I was sure that pretty soon only dogs would be able to hear her.

Daddy was getting right exasperated with my mama's ranting, but, as I said before and will have reason to say again, he was slow to anger and real patient with my high-strung mama. He loved her to pieces and would have done just about anything for her.

"Bronwyn, it's not our job to keep tabs on Joe Bobby's whereabouts. He's a grown man and has a right to be any place he'd like to be, without consulting us first. Now, how about I fix us a glass of wine? Then we can relax and watch the news. Maybe they have some new developments that we just don't know about. Sound like a good idea?"

"I guess so, Kyle," Mama whined, wringing her well-manicured hands and heading to the living room in search of the remote.

While Daddy was in the kitchen pouring himself and Mama a glass of wine, Mama located the remote and was flipping through the channels for WSAV news. When she found it, we saw Kirby Kendall, yet another news reporter, standing in front of the county jail, microphone in one hand, iPhone full of notes in the other.

As he studied his phone screen, he said, "I am standing outside the Bynum County jail, where just over an hour ago Dr. Joe Bobby

Tisdale was arrested for the murder of his wife, Libby Beth Tisdale."

"Yiiiieeeeee!" my mama screamed at the top of her lungs. Her shrieks were so shrill, I was surprised all the wedding crystal in the china cabinet didn't shatter.

But I did hear glass breaking in the kitchen and my daddy thundering down the hall toward us.

"What in the world is going on in here? Bronwyn, have you lost your mind?"

"Kyle, they've arrested Joe Bobby! Do something!" she bellowed, flung herself into my daddy's arms, and sobbed uncontrollably.

"What do you mean arrested him?" Daddy said, prying Mama off of him and turning toward the television.

I'd put down my book and focused my full attention on the news.

"The police," Mama said through jerky sobs, "they arrested Joe Bobby. They seem to think he killed Libby Beth. That's absurd. Do something, Kyle. Do something!"

"What can I do, Darlin'? They must have had probable cause; otherwise, they wouldn't have arrested him. But once he can prove his whereabouts, show that he was up in Jacksonboro hunting at the time of the crime, he'll walk out of that place a free man. Now, calm down, and let the court system do its job."

"But, Kyle, we just can't let our Joe Bobby languish in that god-forsaken place for even one night," Mama wailed dramatically, throwing herself on the couch and holding a fringed throw pillow over her face.

"Bronwyn, how do you know that the county jail is a god-forsaken place?" my daddy asked. "How much time have you spent in the county jail?"

Flinging the throw pillow in Daddy's direction, she said, "None at all, Kyle, but that's really not the point now, is it?"

"No, Dear, you're right, as usual. It is not the point. Now, are you still interested in a glass of wine?"

"Well, of course I am, Kyle."

"Then as soon as I can get the broken glass cleaned up in the kitchen, I'll pour you a glass." Turning to me, he said, "Briley, you want something to drink? I think we can all use a drink, don't you?"

"Yes, sir, I most certainly do. May I have a glass of wine, please?"

"You most certainly may not, young lady."

Usually my daddy would have laughed at such a request, but, apparently, he was not in a laughing mood.

"All right, then, if I can't have any wine, I'll just have a Co-Cola. And I'll take that in a wine glass, please."

Well, Dr. Joe Bobby didn't get out of jail, because that murder charge stuck and he had to wait for his bail hearing. So there he sat in his cell, just waiting and waiting.

Mama dropped everything and said she just had to get right down to the jail house.

Daddy said, "Bronwyn, are you sure that's a good idea?"

"Well, Kyle, of course it is," she said, as if my daddy was an idiot to think that any of her ideas were anything but good.

Daddy said, "Well, Bronwyn, I have to go to work, so I won't be able to go with you to see Joe Bobby this morning. You think you can wait till I get home?"

"Absolutely not, Kyle. You know Joe Bobby is depending on us to stand by him, and I need to get down there and let him know that he can, indeed, depend upon us."

"But, Darlin', do you think a lady should go down to the jail by herself?"

Then dramatically putting the back of her hand to her head, she said, "Kyle, now is not the time to think about my safety or propriety. Our dear friend is alone and frightened. We must support him."

Knowing he would never dissuade my mama from visiting Dr. Joe Bobby in his jail cell, Daddy just sighed and said, "Do what you must, Bronwyn," and left for his office.

First Mama called her office and told Miss Gertrude, the office manager, that she wouldn't be able to make it in that morning, that she had a major crisis that she needed to tend to. Then she fluffed her hair and applied fresh lipstick, picked up her pocketbook and hung it on her arm.

"Well, I'll be on my way," she said, as if she were headed out for tea with the girls.

Backing her car out of the driveway, she headed toward town, stopping by Aunt Sal's Donut Shoppe just long enough to pick up a basket of blueberry muffins. For some unknown reason, Mama thought it was protocol to take a prisoner a basket of blueberry muffins. She must have seen that on some TV show. Surely she hadn't read it in one of her women's magazines, because I don't think those magazines have articles about what to do if a close family friend is in the county jail, falsely accused of murdering his wife.

We were having a teachers' workday at Bynum Central High, so all us kids were out of school for the whole day. I loved teachers' workdays so I could stay home alone and read and watch TV and drink Yoo-hoo all day long. After drinking Yoo-hoo with Miss Delphine, I convinced my mama that in spite of Yoo-hoo's insulting qualities, I'd really appreciate it if she'd allow several cartons into the house.

After mumbling, "Tacky, redneck soda," under her breath, she brought home two cartons of Yoo-hoo from the Piggly Wiggly. "Why, I was ashamed for Twila at the check-out to see that swill in my shopping cart."

Despite her embarrassment, Bronwyn Talmidge Beckwith showed that she could swallow her pride.

So it suited me just fine that Mama was going to go down to the jail house to see Dr. Joe Bobby and leave me to my solitary day.

Expecting her to be gone like forever, I was surprised to see her pull back into the driveway in just forty-five minutes, putting a major disruption on my plans for a day of shiftlessness. She brought the car to a screeching halt, got out and slammed the door, and stomped up the sidewalk, carrying the basket of blueberry muffins intended for Dr. Joe Bobby.

When she charged into the house and slammed the front door so hard the hallway chandelier jangled, I said, "What happened, Mama? Why are you back from seeing Dr. Joe Bobby so soon?"

"That twit, Sippy Holden, wouldn't let me see him. Said I had to come back at regular visiting hours. Doesn't he know that Joe Bobby's and my friendship isn't regular? That Sippy thinks just 'cause he has a badge, he can dole out orders and boss people around."

"Well, Mama, I believe he can."

"Oh, hush up, Briley. I'm in no mood for technicalities. I'm just so mad I could spit nails." Then she shoved her basket at me and said, "Here, go eat a muffin."

Blueberry muffins bounced out of the basket and rolled all over the floor. I crouched down to pick them up and headed back to the kitchen to eat a muffin and drink a Yoo-hoo. Mama went into the living room and flung herself face down on the sofa and screamed into a fringed throw pillow.

Soon her screams faded to whimpers and then completely disappeared. I heard her come shuffling down the hall, and when she rounded the corner into the kitchen, I noticed she looked all worn out and dejected. She'd been Dr. Joe Bobby's best friend all her life, and she was hurt to the core that she was being shut out when she felt he needed her most. The corners of her mouth were turned down, and her shoulders drooped like a woman defeated. She plopped down next to me at the kitchen table, pinched her lips together, and just stared into space.

"Want a muffin, Mama?"

"No thanks, Briley. This thing's bigger than a muffin."

"Oh, my lord, Kyle, come here quick," Mama yelled to Daddy, who was in the kitchen loading the dishwasher so Mama could watch the evening news on the big TV in the living room.

Daddy came down the hall, wiping his hands on a dish towel, and joined Mama and me on the sofa.

Squinting and pointing at the TV screen, Mama said, "Look at that. Isn't that Hey Boy Turner going into the jail?"

"Well, I believe it is, Bronwyn. You suppose he's come to Bynum to see Joe Bobby?"

"Well, who else? I'd say Joe Bobby is the only prisoner around who could afford the likes of Hey Boy."

Hey Boy Turner, whose real name is Heyward Boyd, is a big-time, big-shot lawyer from Atlanta who never takes a charity case and represents only real rich people who couldn't possibly be guilty of the crimes for which they've been accused. That's why he wins all his cases. So I guess it stood to reason that Dr. Joe Bobby would get Hey Boy to represent him, since Dr. Joe Bobby had lots of money and, of course, wasn't guilty.

Six

Judge Baxter denied Dr. Joe Bobby's bail. Hey Boy, who was indeed Dr. Joe Bobby's lawyer, protested loudly and publicly. The whole town, too, was outraged that such an upstanding citizen, someone they'd known all their lives, someone they all trusted, was being treated so shabbily.

But the judge wouldn't budge because he considered Dr. Joe Bobby a flight risk.

"A flight risk?" Mama screamed.

"A flight risk?" all of Dr. Joe Bobby's patients screamed.

"A flight risk?" all the men down at the lodge screamed.

"A flight risk?" the congregation down at Holier-than-thou Episcopal Church screamed.

"A flight risk?" Hey Boy screamed. "Why, Judge Baxter, where do you suppose Joe Bobby would flee? And why? He's got nothing to flee from. He's an innocent man. He wouldn't hurt a fly."

But Judge Baxter could not be swayed. Folks got wind that Dr. Joe Bobby's trial was being considered for TV, and everyone just figured the judge wanted to milk as much drama out of the case as he possibly could. So right there in jail Dr. Joe Bobby sat, incensing all of Bynum, especially best and oldest friend, Bronwyn Talmidge Beckwith.

Mama took a leave of absence from her nursing job. She wanted to be available to help her best friend since birth whenever he might need her; and once his trial started, she planned to be in the courtroom every time they opened the door to the court house. Daddy agreed with Mama on this particular issue. I guess he figured she wasn't fit for nursing, considering her agitated condition over Libby Beth's death and Dr. Joe Bobby's incarceration. He didn't want to open our family up to a malpractice suit, should Mama have her mind elsewhere and give somebody the wrong medicine.

It could happen.

The first morning of Mama's leave of absence, instead of dressing in her scrubs, she put on her lime green track suit and her Sketchers. She came skipping down the stairs and into the kitchen while I was reading and eating my morning Cheerios, her make-up in place and her hair just-so.

"You sure look pretty this morning, Mama."

"Why, thank you, Briley. I'm going down to the jail to visit Joe Bobby. I figure he doesn't want to see some disheveled, despondent somebody while he's being held in that ugly, dank old place. At least his best friend can be presentable for him to keep his spirits high."

"Well, you are definitely presentable, Mama," I said, as she scurried about, fixing coffee and packing a piece of chocolate layer cake to take to Dr. Joe Bobby.

"Will they let you take that cake in the jail, Mama?"

"Well, I should hope so," she said, real indignant-like. "It's not like it has a file in it or anything. What's more, I have an extra bribe piece for Sippy Holden."

"Well, that ought to work like a charm."

Sippy is known for his sweet tooth.

Day after day Mama got up and got dressed to visit Dr. Joe Bobby who was sitting all alone in a jail cell while I got up and got dressed to go to Bynum Central High School, my already-minimal interest waning by the day.

There was talk of moving Dr. Joe Bobby's trial to a different location, like maybe Savannah, where, it was figured, he could get a fair and impartial jury. In the end, though, somebody decided that the trial should just stay put right there in Bynum. Folks figured that Hey

Boy Turner, a man who apparently held lots of sway with the legal system, sweet talked the trial right back into Dr. Joe Bobby's home town, figuring the fine citizens of Bynum would surely give his client a fair trial.

The district attorney's office tried its darndest to find twelve jurors and three alternates who lived in Bynum and had never heard of Dr. Joe Bobby Tisdale. It seemed like an impossible task since Dr. Joe Bobby had doctored every woman in Bynum, delivered all the babies in a two-county area, was the President of the Lions Club, the Warden of the Vestry down at the Holier-than-thou Episcopal Church, and served on the City Council. Somehow, they managed. They must have scraped the outer fringes of town real good or gotten newcomers to Bynum, because they eventually came up with those twelve jurors and three alternates who swore beyond a doubt that Dr. Joe Bobby was a total stranger to them and that they'd never heard or read a word about the death of Mrs. Libby Beth Tisdale. Didn't they have a TV? Didn't they read the paper? Didn't they speak English? Were they from this planet?

So between jury picking and the trial, both the DA's office and Hey Boy set about preparing their cases, and Mama continued spending her days with her best friend, Dr. Joe Bobby Tisdale, to the complete exclusion of her one-and-only daughter. I seemed to be slowly fading from my parents' sight, as well as my grandmother's, whose complete concern was for her darling Bronwyn and her obsession with Dr. Joe Bobby's false incarceration. I no longer felt as though I didn't belong; I felt as if I were achieving invisibility.

I kept my tears to myself while Mama declared to Daddy and me, "Y'all understand, don't you? Joe Bobby has lost his wife to a heinous crime, which we all know he didn't commit, and he just has nobody. Miss Eulalee is just beside herself with grief and can't even lift a finger to help her only child. Why, I hear she's taken to her bed, lost her appetite, and is just dwindling away to nothing. So if he can't count on his best friend from birth, then who can he count on?"

And Daddy and I figured that to argue with that logic would be just down-right selfish.

Daddy even joined Mama and Dr. Joe Bobby in their waiting when he could get away from his job, 'cause Daddy and Joe Bobby went way back, even if they hadn't been friends since birth. But Dr. Joe Bobby had introduced Daddy to Mama when they were all students at Georgia Tech, so Daddy felt he owed a debt to Dr. Joe Bobby. Keeping him company in his jail cell was the very least he could do.

Now with absentee parents, I spent my time eating a lot of Cheerios and reading a lot of books, as well as perfecting my mama's signature. That came in handy for writing fake excuses for those days of school that I was skipping and spending with Miss Delphine. I had promised myself after that first day of playing hooky that it was just a one-time occurrence, but with my parents distracted the way they were and me worrying something awful about Dr. Joe Bobby, I had completely thrown my promise out the window and was ducking over to Miss Delphine's every chance I got.

Turns out Miss Delphine was funny as all get out, and I really needed a laugh along about that time. She entertained me with stories about her life up in New York City, and some of them were quite shocking. She said she'd tried just about everything at least once—and most of 'em twice—and had met some real important people, like Joe Biden, back before he was Vice President, John Travolta, Nathan Lane, and Bernadette Peters. I wasn't familiar with that last person, but Miss Delphine said she'd been quite the star in her day.

Miss Delphine also told me that she had been the understudy for Angela Lansbury one summer when she was starring in *Mame* on Broadway. But Miss Delphine said that Angela Lansbury was one tough cookie, 'cause she never missed a performance and Miss Delphine never got to fill in for her. And after learning every single one of Miss Lansbury's lines too.

On this particular morning, I was standing at the sink, drinking the milk out of my cereal bowl, when I heard the old grandfather clock in the living room chime seven forty-five, warning me that the bus would soon arrive. All of a sudden school seemed about the least important thing in my life. What good would school do when I could just end up dead one morning, face down on the bed in a pool of my own blood? Or accused of a heinous crime I hadn't committed? Why waste time on conjugating verbs and graphing equations, especially when I was never going to be a majorette or homecoming queen. I figured it would be better for me to be watching French movies and listening to opera with Miss Delphine and helping her bake apple bread. I reckoned those experiences would make for much more interesting contents for my Life Box, much more so than algebra. So, with that reasoning rattling around in my confused head, I decided I needed Miss Delphine more than I needed Bynum Central High.

I put my cereal bowl in the dishwasher and went upstairs to brush my teeth, 'cause I figured even if I was going to play hooky, I needed clean teeth and fresh breath. I put on my tennis shoes and jumped down the stairs, two at a time, and traipsed across our front yard, glancing in the directing of the bus stop where all my classmates were clustered together, giggling and posturing. I climbed Miss Delphine's front stairs and crossed her big porch to peck on her door. She answered in her bare feet, her gray hair pouffing out and settling around her shoulders, like a storm cloud. This morning she wore an orange lipstick that seeped into the creases around her lips.

"Hey, Briley. You okay?"

"Well, Miss Delphine, I guess I'm the usual okay."

"You need to come in?"

"Yes, ma'am, I believe I do."

So Miss Delphine stepped aside and let me pass. I made a bee-line to the parlor sofa, and she went into the kitchen to get me a cold Yoo-hoo from the refrigerator. When she returned, she handed me the drink and sat down beside me and lit up a Pall Mall filtered cigarette.

"You know, Briley, I don't mind you coming over here any time you'd like, if that's what will make you feel better."

"Yes, ma'am."

"But are you sure this is for the best? First time I invited you over, I thought you could just use a little diversion from all the chaos. I figured one day away from school couldn't hurt. But it seems we could end up making a habit of this."

"Yes, ma'am, I understand."

"Are you sure this is what you want to do?"

I looked up from bloodying my finger by picking at a hangnail, a habit I'd picked up since Dr. Joe Bobby's arrest and my mama spending her time down at the jail, to find Miss Delphine staring at me in an I-understand-what-you're-going-through sort of way.

"If you don't mind, Miss Delphine, I'd really like to stay. I feel like you're the only one who seems to care, seems to know what I'm feeling like on the inside. Fact is, you seem to be the only one who really sees me."

She took a long drag off her Pall Mall, blew two perfect smoke circles, and got a real far-off look, like she was pondering what I'd just said. When she took another drag and blew a slow, long line of smoke circles, I reached up and stuck my finger through each one of them, like I was threading beads on a necklace.

"Briley," she said, "I see you real good. You're a delight to see. If others don't see you, well, that's just their loss. And, Darlin', you are welcome in my house any time you need to be seen real good."

She blew one more long line of smoke circles, stubbed out her cigarette, and gave me a hug.

Seven

"Miss Delphine, I truly think that I have achieved the Power of Invisibility."

She and I were drinking a Yoo-hoo out on her front porch and watching the cars go by on Magnolia Street.

Miss Delphine stopped mid-sip, turned to me, and said, "Well, Briley, that can't be so 'cause I can still see you."

"Well, yeah, I know that," I said, "but I believe the day is going to come that even you won't be able to see me. I think my Power of Invisibility is a gradual thing."

"Whatever do you mean, Darlin'?" she said in that syrupy southern drawl that she hadn't, thank heavens, lost in her thirty-five-plus years up there in New York City.

"Well, like I've told you before, I've always been pretty much invisible at school. Kids just sorta look right through me. And Granny Evadelle—well, she doesn't see anything except her precious Bronwyn. She thinks my mama is the only thing worth her time and attention. And since Dr. Joe Bobby's incarceration and my mama's obsession with the case, my Granny Evadelle has become even more fixated on her darling daughter," I said in a not-too-sympathetic way.

"I see," Miss Delphine said in an ironic way, since my whole point was that people just weren't seeing me.

"And, Miss Delphine, I'd kinda come to accept that my Granny Evadelle and my classmates didn't see me. Can't say I liked it a whole lot, but you can get used to just about anything if it goes on long enough and becomes part of your life."

"I get that, Briley. And..." she said, knowing full well that I really hadn't gotten to the crux of this story.

"I believe my Power of Invisibility has gotten stronger 'cause my mama can't even see me anymore. And no matter how hard I try to get her attention, she just does that looking-right-through-me thing like my classmates do."

Miss Delphine gave me that you-poor-thing eyebrow scrunch and started stroking my arm, like she was petting a cat.

"And, you know, my daddy is so wrapped up in my mama's obsession with Dr. Joe Bobby being in jail, I kinda feel like I'm invisible to him too."

"I'm sure that's very painful for you, Briley," Miss Delphine said in a sort of sad and shuddery voice.

"Yes'm. Sometimes it hurts something awful, but I figure my invisibility sort of works to my benefit too."

"To your benefit?"

"Yes'm. You see, if I'm invisible, I can't be a failure."

"A failure?" she flat-out screamed. "Whatever do you mean, a failure? You are not a failure, Briley!"

"Yeah, I pretty much am, Miss Delphine. You see, my mama was a big success over at Bynum Central High School. She was head majorette and homecoming queen and a whole bunch of other stuff. Why, her picture and some of her majorette trophies are still in the trophy case right outside the principal's office. So if you're remembered for your achievements this many years down the road, then I'd say you're pretty much a success."

"Honey, you can't measure your success by another person's accomplishments. You have to find what you're good at and achieve success in your own way. Just be the best *you* that you can be."

I pondered that for a minute and realized Miss Delphine was probably right. It didn't feel right, but she was a grown-up, and grown-ups have a lot more years of experience with this sort of thing. So I told her, "I guess you're right," and I told myself I'd try to believe it.

But what was the best me? I really wasn't good at much of anything. I could read real well, but did that really make me a good me? Then I got stuck 'cause there wasn't a whole lot more to Briley Beckwith. But after a whole lot of thought, I came to the conclusion that what I did best was be invisible. So I figured I'd just have to work on being the best invisible girl that I could be.

I had left school in the middle of the day and ridden my bike down to the Rexall Drug Store. I had stopped riding the bus a while back when Mama got all caught up in Dr. Joe Bobby's plight and was no longer paying attention to what I did.

When I'd first asked if I could ride my bike to school, she'd said, "Absolutely not, Briley. Your daddy and I pay taxes, taxes that provide a school bus that drives right past this house to pick you up for school. We are not going to throw that service out the window for no good reason. You will ride the bus to Bynum Central High."

But buses and bikes were the least of her concerns, and I'd started riding off every morning on my bike, and Bronwyn was none the wiser.

The Rexall Drug Store was on Main Street, just four doors down from the First-and-only-one-that-matters Southern Baptist Church. I pulled up out front and dragged my bike up on the sidewalk, leaning it against a do-not-park-from-here-to-the-corner sign. I didn't even bother locking it 'cause I figured nobody would want a rusty old bike with a busted reflector light and a kick stand that hadn't worked in years.

When I was sure my bike wasn't going to tip over in the middle of the sidewalk, I went on into the drug store to pick me up a bottle of pink hair dye. Yes, I figured that dying my hair pink would be a good way of testing my Power of Invisibility. If folks continued to look right through me with my hair all bright pink, I'd believe I had truly achieved invisibility.

In my defense, I was fourteen years old, and fourteen year olds don't always possess astute powers of reasoning, even those who possess the Power of Invisibility.

There were many brands of pink hair dye. Having no idea which was best and how any of them worked, I just picked up the box with the model that sported the most shocking pink hair. Between the hair-dye shelf and the check-out counter, I felt myself getting right brave.

So when I plunked the box of dye down on the counter, I said, "And give me a pack of Pall Mall filters, please."

I'd been watching Miss Delphine blow those perfect smoke

circles, and I figured I needed to give smoke circles a try.

"Briley," Mr. Jensen, the pharmacist, said to me, "you know you're not old enough to be smoking."

"Oh, they're not for me, Mr. Jensen," I told him, starting to sweat a little on my upper lip. "I'm buying those Pall Mall filters for my mama."

"Now, Briley, I know very well your mama doesn't smoke. She's a nurse. She knows better," he said to me with squinty, accusatory eyes.

"Did I say Mama? I didn't mean Mama," I said, laughing nervously. "I meant to say Miss Delphine. Yeah, Miss Delphine said she'd run out of Pall Mall filters and would I pick up a pack for her when I came down here to get my pink hair dye."

Of course, Mr. Jensen wasn't buying it for a minute—and I was afraid he was going to call my mama—but it was too late to back down, even if my upper lip was sweating profusely. So I just reached into my jeans pocket and pulled out a wad of crumpled dollar bills and plunked them down on the counter. Mr. Jensen snapped a paper bag open and, still eyeing me suspiciously, dropped in my hair dye and a pack of Pall Mall filters. I refused to let him see my nerves. I just stood there looking all confident, smiling real big around my braces, sweat piling up on my lip.

Mr. Jensen straightened out my dollar bills, counted them slowly, and pushed them down into his cash register tray, locking them in place with a little silver bar. Then he scooped up fifty-seven cents in change and dropped it into my hand.

"Why aren't you in school, Briley?"

Without skipping a beat, I said, "Well, Mr. Jensen, we're having exams today, and since I have all A's, I placed out of my exams. So the teachers just said I didn't have to wait around for school to end, that I could just leave and go on home." Then I just shrugged my shoulders in a so-I-just-decided-to-come-on-over-and-buy-me-some-pink-hair-dye-and-cigarettes sort of way.

The lies were just rolling off my tongue so smoothly. The part about me getting all A's was true, but that other stuff I just made up on the spur of the moment. I found my creativity, well, creative.

Without taking his eyes off me, he said, "Now, you be real careful, you hear, Briley? You're a good girl. Don't want to see you getting into any trouble."

"I won't, Mr. Jensen. I promise."

Once outside the drug store, I hopped on my bike that I'd left leaning up against the do-not-park-from-here-to-the-corner sign and looked back once more through the front window. I could see Mr. Jensen still staring at me, so I threw up my hand, very confident-like, smiled real big, and raced for home. When I got there, I dropped my bike on its side under the magnolia tree. I raced up the porch steps, through the front door, and up the stairs to my bedroom, where I stashed my Pall Mall filters beneath the pink tissue paper in my Madame Alexander Cinderella doll box on the top shelf of my closet. When I'd caught my breath and realized for sure that I hadn't gotten caught with a pack of Pall Mall filters, I went to the kitchen to get the big scissors that Mama used to cut up chicken and cut open bags of frozen vegetables. I also grabbed me a great big yellow and red chip clip that said Piggly Wiggly on it. I ran back upstairs, picked up my bag of hair dye from my bed, and headed for the bathroom.

I looked at the clock in the hall. One thirty. I had plenty of time before Mama would get home from the jail and Daddy would get home from his office.

I pulled two towels from the linen closet. I spread one of them across the bathroom vanity and wrapped the other around my shoulders, fastening it under my chin with the red and yellow Piggly Wiggly chip clip. Then I picked up the big scissors, held my breath, and started chopping. I began at my right ear, just below my earlobe, cutting my hair at an angle around the back, ending at my left shoulder. It took me a good long while to get a nice, straight angular line, but eventually I had a respectable asymmetrical hairdo. I carefully removed the towel from around my neck and shook it over the trash can. Then with my hands I scraped up all the hair that had fallen on the floor and deposited it in the can, as well. I looked into the mirror and shook my head and watched my wispy hair fall back into place.

"Pretty cool," I said aloud.

Then I broke open the box of pink hair dye, pulled out the bottle, and uncapped it. Did I really want to do this? Wasn't the haircut enough? Nope. In order to test my Power of Visibility, I needed to go all the way. So I leaned my head over the sink and started to pour. The pink liquid was frigid on my scalp, and it made me shiver and shudder, but it soon warmed so that it was tolerable to my head.

When the bottle was empty, I set it aside and began massaging the dye into my hair, just as the instructions had told me to do. Once I'd finished, I stayed in my bent-over position so that the excess dye could drip off my head and down the drain. When the dripping stopped, I wrapped my clean towel around my head and blotted it well.

After waiting for fifteen minutes to let the color set, I pulled the towel away slowly, grimacing in anticipation of the finished product. When I turned toward the vanity mirror and saw my hair glowing bright pink, I actually screamed, "Yikes!" out loud. I had never heard anyone say the word *yikes!*—had only read it in comic books in a word balloon over someone's head. But that's just how shocking my pink hair was. And I hadn't yet dried it. I pulled out my mama's hair dryer, a contraption I'd never had need of, and fumbled with the switch. When it whooshed to life, I aimed it at my head, whipping my new do around my face. Once it was dry, I ran my fingers through my hair and let it fall into its new style.

"OMG!" I screamed, something else I had never said, because up until then I'd felt that *OMG* was reserved just for the cool, popular, vapid kids. But my hair wasn't just pink. It was shocking, OMG neon pink. The transformation was so outrageous—in a good way—that tears sprang to my eyes. I clapped my hands over my face and peered through my fingers at my reflection. Slowly a smile spread across my face, and I lowered my hands, ready to take it all in. I got out the hand-held mirror and examined the back, the sides, the top.

"Really cool! OMG cool!" I said to my reflection and let the one long side of my hair slither over my eye.

"No, Briley, absolutely not!" Mama whisper-screamed in frustration.

"But, Mama, you said I could have a book," I whined.

"Not that one, Briley. I said you could have a book, but not that book. It just isn't appropriate for a fourteen-year-old."

I was really testing the boundaries, as Dr. Phil would say, and I knew it. But with Mama totally obsessed with Dr. Joe Bobby's case, and Daddy busy with work and Dr. Joe Bobby and trying to reason with his obsessed wife, I just felt like I could use a little boundary testing. And they say that negative attention is better than no attention at all.

So there I stood in Barnes and Noble with my mother, who had offered to take me shopping for a book out of guilt for being an absentee parent since Dr. Joe Bobby's incarceration. Unlike my classmates, she had noticed my hair, and she was none too pleased.

"Briley, have you lost your mind?" she'd screamed at me. I didn't like having my mama scream at me, but like I said, screaming was better than ignoring. "What in heaven's name possessed you to color your hair like an Easter egg? And did you cut it with the lawn mower?"

Well, it was obvious my mother did not think my new look would pave my road to success, at least not to a successful stint as a Bynum Central High School majorette. But I had to be the best me, not the best Bronwyn, something only my mama could perfect. As I stood my ground for the first time in my life, confident that I had finally found the real, true me—an invisible girl with bright pink hair—Mama just threw up her hands in exasperation and figured my hair was just small potatoes compared to what her friend Joe Bobby Tisdale was going through.

So after a while of being exasperated and throwing up her hands, Mama just took to ignoring my new shocking-pink asymmetrical hairdo as best she could, accepting it as just a phase or a cry for attention. She could not ignore, however, the fact that I was asking her to buy me a copy of *Fifty Shades of Grey*. As I was holding the book aloft for all the shoppers to see, customers rolled their eyes and clucked their tongues at how disrespectful that Briley Beckwith was being to her dear mother who used to be three-time state champion twirler. Why, she was even belle of the ball. And no belle of the ball and champion twirler deserved to have a disrespectful daughter who would dye her hair that ghastly pink and wanted to read trashy novels. Especially when her mother's best friend had been arrested for murder.

Pink hair aside, I bet you a dollar every last one of those tongue cluckers had read *Fifty Shades of Grey* while their husbands were at work. Fact is, I was in the library once, my nose in a book, as usual. Ms. Delores Sherman and Ms. Sadie Cromwell, both of them well beyond their prime years, were in the stacks, talking about *Fifty Shades of Grey*. They were chatting like I couldn't even hear them, which was one of my very first indications that I was, indeed, invisible.

Ms. Delores said to Ms. Sadie, "You know, Sadie, I read that book *Fifty Shades of Grey.*"

Ms. Sadie said, "Hush your mouth, Delores. You did not read that trash."

"I most certainly did. And you know what?"

"What?"

And then sort of whispering, but still loud enough for me to hear, Ms. Delores said, "Well, Sadie, reading that book made me realize that I still have a hormone."

Ms. Sadie snorted so loud all the librarians turned around and scowled at her, and Ms. Delores said, "Sh, sh, sh."

So I figured those old biddies in Barnes and Noble should just keep their tongue clucking to themselves 'cause I just might say real loud, "How'd you ladies like this book?"

"What about this one?" Mama said, ignoring the stares and my behavior and holding up *The Hunger Games*, a book I'd read—and rather enjoyed—several years earlier. In fact, I'd read the entire trilogy.

Shaking my pink hair for effect, I said, still loud enough for all to hear, "So you're saying, Mama, that it isn't all right for me to read about sex, but it's acceptable for me to read about kids fighting to the death for food?"

"What?" Mama whisper-screamed again and made her big old eyes bug out like one of those shocked cartoon characters.

"That's right, Mama. That's what *The Hunger Games* is all about—kids fighting to the death for food. And there's even sex in that book."

"Well, I never," she said dramatically, dropped the book like it was on fire, and headed for the door, as if that one bad apple had spoiled the whole bunch.

And I really didn't mind that Mama hadn't bought me a book. I'd recently gotten an Amazon gift card from Granny Evadelle. I assumed it was also a guilt gift because it had come out of nowhere, something that Granny Evadelle had never done before. And she said she was giving me a gift card instead of an actual gift so I could pick out what I wanted. My grandmother added that she just didn't know what to do with the likes of me anymore and had no idea what else to buy a pink-haired teenager who was going through a phase or crying for help.

I'd show Granny Evadelle just what kind of phase I was going through. I'd use her gift card to download a copy of *Fifty Shades of Grey*.

Eight

At nine o'clock on the morning of June 14, 2016, Jimbo Stimson, Bynum's district attorney, began his opening statement. His given name is James, but everybody just calls him Jimbo. His kids, Becky and Bernard, are in my class at Bynum Central High. Becky and Bernard are twins. But Becky and Bernard, and the fact that they are twins, had absolutely nothing to do with Dr. Joe Bobby's trail. So I promise that this is the last time I'll mention either Becky or Bernard.

Mr. Stimson said, "On Saturday, October 17, 2015, Mrs. Bertha Ransom arrived at the home of her employers, Dr. and Mrs. Joe Bobby Tisdale. When Mrs. Ransom let herself in, she called out to Mrs. Tisdale, as she did each morning when she arrived to clean the Tisdales' home. When Mrs. Tisdale, that would be Libby Beth, did not respond to Mrs. Ransom's call, the domestic went looking for her employer. She searched the downstairs of the Tildales' home and found no one. She then climbed the stairs, by now concerned that there was no response to her calls. It was upstairs in the master bedroom of Dr. and Mrs. Tisdale's home that Mrs. Ransom found Libby Beth lying face down in her blood-soaked bed, a gunshot wound to her left temple, a Smith & Wesson .357 Magnum Revolver in her left hand. Forensic evidence indicates that Mrs. Tisdale had been dead approximately seven hours."

Hadn't we heard this—well, most of it, anyway—the morning Miss Libby Beth's body was discovered? Didn't Andrew Morton from over at WSAV stand right there in front of Dr. Joe Bobby and Miss Libby Beth's house, by that yellow crime tape, and say that very same thing? Well, maybe Mr. Stimson figured some of the people in the courtroom hadn't been watching Andrew Morton that morning. But they'd been saying it over and over for months on end. But, then, I guess he had to bring all those jurors up-to-date, 'cause they'd all sworn under oath that, oh no, they didn't know a single thing about this case and had never heard of Dr. Joe Bobby Tisdale or his wife, Libby Beth.

"At first glance," Mr. Stimson went on, "it appeared that Mrs. Tisdale had committed suicide, yet evidence ultimately concluded that Libby Beth had, indeed, been murdered. The trajectory of the bullet indicated that Mrs. Tisdale could not have inflicted the wound to her temple, that someone else had to have pulled the trigger. Furthermore, Mrs. Tisdale was right-handed, yet the gun was found in her left hand, the wound in the left side of her head."

It was along about here that the whole courtroom started to fidget nervously and wish this would all just go away and that we could get on back to normal, back to when Miss Libby Beth was still alive and Dr. Joe Bobby wasn't accused of murdering her.

Mr. Stimson continued over the fidgets and sighs, "There was no forced entry at the home of the Tisdales. Therefore, it is apparent the crime was committed by someone with easy access.

"The fingerprints on the gun belonged to only two people, Mrs. Tisdale and her husband, Dr. Joe Bobby Tisdale. Though the prints of Dr. Tisdale were clean, the prints of Mrs. Tisdale were smudged, as if someone had placed her hand upon the butt of the gun, attempting to make the murder appear to be a suicide.

"On the Thursday before the murder, Dr. Tisdale traveled by automobile to Jacksonboro, South Carolina, where he and three companions were to dove hunt over the weekend.

"The prosecution will prove, ladies and gentlemen of the jury, beyond a shadow of a doubt, that Dr. Tisdale did, on Friday night, October 16, 2015, leave his companions in Jacksonboro, South Carolina and return to Bynum, Georgia, where he did, in cold blood, murder his wife, Mrs. Libby Beth Tisdale. Once he had shot his wife, Dr. Tisdale staged the scene to appear as if Libby Beth had committed suicide, by placing the murder weapon in her hand and leaving her dead body in their bed. Dr. Tisdale fled the scene, returning to his hunting companions in South Carolina on the morning of Saturday, October 17, 2015."

My mind started to wander with all that repetition, and I looked around the courtroom to find that plenty of other folks had their minds elsewhere too. Mr. Clarkson was dozing away, his chin on his chest, just like he did every Sunday during the sermon down at the Holier-than-thou Episcopal Church. Ms. Juneleigh was reading a paperback book, and Mrs. Robinette was reading her Bible, which she carried with her everywhere she went. I even saw Miss Mercelene Tibideaux knitting something bright orange, her needles clicking away. I pulled out my book and started reading until I heard Mr. Stimson's voice get real loud to make his final point. Once he had made that point and decided he was through, he eyed Hey Boy warily, nodded his head, and claimed his seat at the prosecution table.

Hey Boy stood, looking every bit the stereotypical big-city lawyer. He wore a perfectly tailored dark suit, a starched white shirt, and a dark print tie paired with shiny black lace-up shoes. He was mighty intimidating looking, not like the district attorney, Mr. Stimson, who was skinny as a rail with an Adam's apple that hopped up and down in his neck when he talked. Also, Mr. Stimson wore a shiny green suit he probably got at J.C. Penney, over at the Oglethorpe Mall between Bynum and Savannah.

Facing the jury, Hey Boy's face slid into an oily grin, and he began to address the court in his thick southern drawl: "Now, y'all all know Dr. Joe Bobby Tisdale, the very pillar of this community. You also know that he and his lovely wife, Libby Beth, were married happily for over eighteen years, with nary a single spat."

Didn't sound like lawyer talk to me, but I figured Hey Boy knew how to work a crowd.

"Throughout this trial we will show that Dr. Joe Bobby Tisdale was in Jacksonboro, South Carolina with three hunting companions at the time of his wife Libby Beth's death, and that it would have been impossible for him to have driven to Bynum, Georgia, all the way from Jacksonboro, South Carolina, committed the crime, and returned to Jacksonboro, South Carolina, in a single night without being detected by his hunting companions. We will show, with the help of character witnesses and concrete evidence, that Joe Bobby Tisdale had no motive and was incapable of harming his wife, Mrs. Libby Beth Tisdale."

I'd gotten another chapter read, and Miss Mercelene had knitted what looked to be a big orange sleeve before Hey Boy finally took a deep breath and wrapped things up.

And then the trial of Dr. Joe Bobby Tisdale officially began.

"Mr. Stimson, please call your first witness," Judge Baxter said, making sure his good side was facing the camera, because the murder trial of Dr. Joe Bobby Tisdale was indeed being televised. It had all the makings of good TV, and Judge Baxter wanted to be sure he was looking his best and judging better than he'd ever judged before. Who knew where this stint on the television might lead? Why, Judge Judy may be on the verge of retirement and in need of a replacement.

Mr. Stimson said, "The prosecution would like to call Mr. Mitchell Kibbons Beaumont to the stand."

With that the doors to the courtroom swung open and crazy old Kibby Beaumont came striding down the aisle, his rotund belly beating the rest of him to the witness stand by a good foot and a half. Once he'd stepped into the witness stand, he hiked up his khakis real good and gave his red suspenders an audible snap.

The bailiff stepped to the witness stand, extended a Bible toward Kibby, and said, "Sir, will you please place your hand on the Bible and state your name for the record."

Placing his left hand on the Bible and raising his right, Kibby said, "My name is Mitchell Kibbons Beaumont, but everybody just calls me Kibby."

"Mr. Beaumont," the bailiff said, refusing to be lumped in with everybody by calling the witness Kibby, "do you swear the testimony you are about to provide this court is the truth, the whole truth, and nothing but the truth?"

"Sure," Kibby chirped.

"Mr. Beaumont, please respond 'I so swear' or 'I do,'" the bailiff ordered him in his most no-nonsense voice.

So Kibby said, "I believe I'll say *I so swear*, 'cause I ain't never swore in court. I've swore just about everywhere else but never in court."

He guffawed, and so did everybody else in the courtroom, except the judge, the attorneys, and Dr. Joe Bobby. Dr. Joe Bobby just shook his head and looked toward heaven, for divine help, I supposed. Judge Baxter's head snapped up and he looked out at all of us and squinted his eyes real sternly. Everyone in the room quieted down because Judge Baxter had already warned us about making noise and told us he'd throw us all out if we didn't behave with decorum. And none of us wanted to be thrown out.

When he was relatively certain we were all going to behave ourselves, he said, "Mr. Beaumont, you may be seated."

After Kibby plopped himself into the witness chair, he looked at Judge Baxter and said, "Hey, Jasper, how's it goin'?"

The whole courtroom busted out laughing, and Judge Baxter, once again, glared at everybody.

"Kibby," Judge Baxter said, "this is a courtroom, not Gert's Diner. Please show respect."

Kibby grinned real big and said, "Sure thing, Judge…I mean, Your Honor."

That old fool suppressed a giggle while Jimbo Stimson took one last look at his notes on the yellow tablet on the table in front of him, stood up, gave his shapeless, shiny green jacket a quick yank, and strode toward the witness stand.

"Mr. Beaumont, do you know the defendant, Dr. Joe Bobby Tisdale?"

"Sure do. Me and Joe Bobby go way back."

"Just how far back do you and Dr. Tisdale go, Mr. Beaumont?"

"Honest, Jimbo, you really don't need to call me Mr. Beaumont. You know nobody calls me Mr. Beaumont. It's just plain old Kibby."

It's darn near impossible to be formal in a small town like Bynum.

"Okay…Kibby. Please answer the question."

"Um, will you please repeat the question? I forgot it."

More giggles came from the spectators, and Judge Baxter narrowed his eyes at us all again. I figured at the rate Kibby was going, he'd be on that witness stand a month, and we'd never get out of that courtroom and set Dr. Joe Bobby free.

"How long have you known Dr. Tisdale?"

"Let me see if I can get my math right. I'm going on forty-five now, and me and Joe Bobby met when we started first grade down at Bynum Elementary School. So forty take away six, 'cause we'd have been six years old in first grade…"

Mama was sitting next to me and whisper-hissed, "Idiot!"

Folks started to giggle again, all except my mama who found nothing amusing about that idiot Kibby Beaumont. A quick beady-eyed look from Judge Baxter quieted all the gigglers. I guess we figured we were getting real close to riling him enough to make him throw us out like he promised.

And just as Kibby held up all his fingers and started counting backwards from forty-five, Mr. Stimson said, "Close enough. So you've known Dr. Tisdale since first grade. That's a long time, wouldn't you say?"

"I'd say that."

"And did you and Dr. Tisdale become immediate friends when you met in the first grade?"

"Oh, no, Joe Bobby was a townie and hung out with the rich kids. I was just a old farm boy," Kibby said.

"You mean Dr. Tisdale wouldn't befriend you because he was rich and you were a farm boy?"

"It wudn't nothin' like that. It was just a given that the townies stuck together and the country kids stuck together. Easy as that."

"But you and Dr. Tisdale became friends at some point, right?"

"That's right."

"Just when did you and Joe Bobby Tisdale become friends, Mr....Kibby?"

"I'd say," Kibby said, glancing over at Dr. Joe Bobby, "about seventh grade."

"And what happened around seventh grade to make you and Joe Bobby become friends?"

"We both discovered hunting and shooting guns about that time," Kibby said, glowing with the memory of their shared interest and smiling real big over at Dr. Joe Bobby.

"Kibby, tell us about the friendship with Joe Bobby. What did you boys do together?"

"Well, me and him would go out in the woods up 'hind my daddy's farm, and we'd shoot squirrels, lots of squirrels, 'cause that's about all there was to shoot back up in them woods."

"Is that all you and Joe Bobby would do together, Kibby?"

"No, me and him would go over to Neville Holcomb's shooting range and practice shooting at targets. Sometimes we'd shoot targets for four, five hours at a time."

"That's a lot of shooting practice, wouldn't you say, Kibby?"

"Your honor," Hey Boy bellowed and made me jump, "I object. Question calls for a conclusion."

Judge Baxter, resting his chin on his fist like this whole thing was boring him to death, said, "Sustained. Watch it, Jimbo."

"Yes, Your Honor," Mr. Stimson said.

"Kibby, was Dr. Tisdale a good shot?"

"Oh, yeah, Joe Bobby could shoot better'n any of us. Could hit a bull's eye a hunnert yards away nine out of ten times. He was cracker jack shot. Still is."

"So, Dr. Joe Bobby is quite the marksman, you'd say?"

"Yes, I would say that."

"You say, Kibby, that you and Dr. Tisdale hunted squirrels and went to a firing range when you were school boys. When did the two of you begin going on weekend hunting trips together?"

"Um, let me see…I guess that would be about thirteen years ago, when Joe Bobby and Libby Beth moved back here for Joe Bobby to set up his medical practice."

"And have you gone on a hunting trip every year for the past thirteen years?"

"Yes, me and Joe Bobby and Bayless Bramble and Mayhew Farmer have been going up to Jacksonboro—that's up in South Carolina—every year."

"Now, Kibby, how far is it from Bynum, Georgia, to Jacksonboro, South Carolina?"

"Oh, I'd say it's about a hour and a half. Yeah, that sounds about right."

"And how far would that be in miles, Kibby?"

"I'd say about eighty, give or take a few."

"Now, do you all ride up to Jacksonboro together when you go on your hunting trips?"

"Funny thing is, we usually do. This year, though, me and Bayless and Mayhew drove up on Thursday, around noon, like always, but Joe Bobby drove up by hisself later on that afternoon."

"And just why didn't Dr. Tisdale ride up with the rest of you, as he had in the past?"

"Well, Joe Bobby said he had some patients he needed to tend to late Thursday afternoon and that he just couldn't get away till late. We told him we'd be glad to wait till he was done with his patients, but he told us, no, to go on ahead without him and he'd catch up to us."

"Kibby, don't you think Dr. Joe Bobby could have rescheduled his patients, seeing as how this annual hunting trip was such a special occasion?"

"Objection, Your Honor!" Hey Boy shrieked and slammed his fist down on the table. "That question calls for speculation."

Judge Baxter, still resting on his fist, said, "Sustained. You know better, Jimbo."

"Yes, Your Honor," Mr. Stimson said and glanced over at the jury and shrugged his shoulders.

This was going awful slow, but Kibby seemed to be getting real comfortable on the stand, all reared back with his right ankle resting on his left knee, his right arm slung over the back of the witness chair. He looked like he was an old pro at testifying and was enjoying all the attention.

I looked around the courtroom. Mrs. Robinette was still reading her Bible, and it looked like Miss Mercelene was making real good progress on her orange sweater sleeve.

"So, Kibby," Mr. Stimson continued, "you and Mr. Farmer and Mr. Bramble drove up to Jacksonboro early Thursday afternoon and set up camp. Setting up camp, that's what you call it, right?"

"Yep, that's right."

"Kibby, what does setting up camp entail?"

"Well, first we clear the site of sticks and brush and rocks, get it all level, you know. Then we pitch our tents and set up our cook stove. That's pretty much it. Then we spend the rest of the afternoon scouting the area and getting our gear ready to hunt."

"You say you pitch your tents. So you don't all sleep in one tent?"

"Well, no, four guys in a tent would be a might too friendly, if you know what I mean," he said, waggling his eyebrows and chuckling, his round belly hopping up and down.

Before anyone could laugh at Kibby's foolishness, Judge Baxter's squinty eyes darted out toward the courtroom. No one made a peep.

"So, how many do you sleep to a tent?"

"Usually, we sleep two to a tent, me and Bayless in one and Joe Bobby and Mayhew in another."

"You say *usually*. What do you mean by *usually*?"

"Well, this year Joe Bobby and Mayhew didn't share a tent."

"And why didn't Joe Bobby and Mayhew share a tent this year, Kibby?"

"Joe Bobby bought this new light-weight, single-person tent over at REI in Savannah, and he wanted to try it out."

"So on the most recent hunting trip, Dr. Joe Bobby Tisdale slept alone in a new tent for the first time in all your thirteen hunting trips?"

"That is correct," Kibby said, glancing over at Dr. Joe Bobby with sort of an apologetic look on his face.

Even I knew that this was starting to look kind of bad for Dr. Joe Bobby, and I peered over at him just in time to see him shake his head and put his face in his hands.

Mr. Stimson looked toward the jury and made sure that had sunk in before he went on.

"Kibby, would you like a drink of water before we continue?"

"No, thanks, I believe I'm good. I'll let you know, though, if I change my mind," Kibby said, regaining his composure after that last line of questioning.

"Gentlemen," Judge Baxter said, "it appears we are at a stopping point. I say we recess for lunch." Looking at his watch, he said, "It's a few minutes past noon. Court will reconvene at 1:30 sharp."

And with that he stood up and strode to his chambers, his long, black robe flowing out behind him.

"You want a ham sandwich, Briley?" Mama asked as she pushed my pink hair out of my eye and hooked it over my ear. "We can go over to the Bread Basket and get us a ham sandwich. Sound good?"

I unhinged my hair and let it slither back to cover my face and said, "Yes, ma'am, I'd like a ham sandwich. I'm real hungry."

Ignoring my imperfection as best she could, which was real hard for my mama, she cooed to my daddy, "Kyle, Honey, you gonna be able to join us for lunch? We could have us a ham sandwich over at the Bread Basket."

"Thanks, Sugar," Daddy said, "but I really need to get to the office. Mary Beth and Bryce can hold down the fort for just so long. Y'all take notes this afternoon, and I'll see you girls at home for supper."

So Daddy kissed my mama on the cheek, patted me on the back, and rushed on out of the courtroom. Mama and I walked across the street with a fairly large group of courtroom gawkers and found ourselves a two-topper bistro table at the Bread Basket back by the kitchen.

"I really do hate eating by the kitchen—all that traffic and all those smells. But I guess it's the best we can do, under the circumstances."

She added that it was like eating with the help, a remark I found awful pretentious, seeing as how Mama hadn't lived in a family with help since she was a little girl.

Sarah June Slattery came to the table and said, "Hey, Miz Beckwith," and, glancing my way, just said, "Hey." Then she asked Mama, "What can I git y'all to eat?"

Mama said, "I'll have a ham sandwich with mayo and lettuce and a Co-Cola, Sarah June. And give me some chips with that, please."

And without moving her pencil from her pad or even turning her head in my direction, she cocked her eyes at me and waited for me to give her my order.

"I'll have the same, please, Sarah June," I said, and, without another word, our waitress disappeared into the kitchen to get our sandwiches and chips.

"Well, what do you think?" Mama said, as if I were an expert at analyzing courtroom testimony.

"I don't know, Mama." I said and grimaced. "Kibby is making Dr. Joe Bobby sound like a really shifty character."

"I know, Briley, I was thinking the very same thing. And I don't like it one little bit. But there are plenty of character witnesses who will vouch for Joe Bobby, will tell that court there's nothing shifty at all about him."

"Yeah, I guess you're right, Mama."

"'Cause we all know Joe Bobby is innocent," she said, confidently.

"Yes, we do, Mama. Yes, we do."

Sarah June brought us our ham sandwiches and chips and Co-Colas, and we ate in silence. When we finished and Mama dabbed her lips with her napkin, she reached into her pocketbook for her Revlon Fire and Ice lipstick. She pooched out her lips, swiped them red, and rubbed them together, back and forth. Dropping her lipstick back in her pocketbook, she glanced at her watch. It was just a little past one o'clock, but she said she didn't want to wait too late and lose our prime seats right behind Dr. Joe Bobby.

"He needs to know we are there, Briley, needs to feel our presence. We must continue to be a constant in his life," she said, placing her hand over her heart very dramatically.

We made our way back across the street and filed into the courtroom, finding that our prized seats behind the defense table were still vacant. While we waited, I pulled my book out of my backpack and began to read. Mama pulled her nail file out of her pocketbook and began to file her nails. Waiting and filing her nails is Mama's idea of multi-tasking.

"Court is now in session," the bailiff bellowed. "All rise for the Honorable Judge Baxter."

I slipped my book into my backpack, and after making one last grating swipe across her left hand, Mama dropped her fingernail file into her pocketbook as we joined the rest of the courtroom in standing. Judge Baxter entered and sat behind his big, tall desk.

Then the bailiff bellowed once more, "All be seated."

Nine

While everyone shifted and squirmed, getting comfy for the afternoon, Kibby Beaumont, having caught his second wind, returned to the witness stand.

"Mr. Beaumont, I mean Kibby, when Dr. Tisdale reached the campsite alone late on Thursday, October 15, what did your group of hunters do?"

"We ate supper and drank liquor," Kibby said and laughed out loud, looking around to make sure everybody else saw the humor in what he was saying. "Then after that we went to bed to sleep it off."

"So after eating and drinking, you climbed into your respective tents and went to sleep," Mr. Stimson repeated.

"That's about it," Kibby said.

"And when you awoke the following morning, Kibby, what did you do?"

"Well, since Mayhew provides the cook stove, I volunteer to cook. So I fixed bacon and eggs and pancakes for all of us. And a pot of coffee."

"So you ate breakfast, and then what?" Mr. Stimson said in an impatient tone, like he just wanted Kibby to spit it all out without him having to ask what came next.

"Well, we cleaned up after ourselves and went hunting."

"And how successful was the hunting?"

"Not very. Just a couple doves, which was a surprise, since we usually brought back a whole passel. But we come up pretty dry that day."

Even I was getting bored with all this, so I could well imagine how Mr. Stimson must have felt. But I fought to keep my eyes open and pay attention, just in case Kibby was to say something real interesting and important. But I had my doubts about this, considering how things were going, so far.

Then Mr. Stimson said, "So when you finished your relatively unsuccessful hunt that Saturday, what did you and your friends do?"

"We went back to our campsite."

"And just what did you do, Kibby, when you got back to your campsite?"

"Well, first off we cleaned our guns and stowed them away. Then we cleaned the couple of doves we'd shot and put 'em in a cooler. Then we just sorta sat around and drunk a few beers while Joe Bobby cooked us some steaks he'd brought up in his cooler. And once they was done, we ate 'em, of course."

"Of course. And after supper what did you and your friends do?"

"Well, we was so tired, we just decided to turn in."

"You mean you got into your tents and went to sleep?"

"Yep, that's what I meant by turn in."

"Did all of you get into your tents and go to sleep?"

When Mr. Stimson said that, Kibby looked over at Dr. Joe Bobby in a very helpless manner.

"Kibby, you don't need to consult Dr. Tisdale before you answer the question." Then stepping between Kibby and Dr. Joe Bobby—I'm guessing so they couldn't see each other and send some sort of signals, 'cause that's what they do on TV court cases—Mr. Stimson repeated, "Did all of you get into your tents and go to sleep?"

And then Kibby said real quiet, so quiet we could hardly hear him, "No."

"Kibby, please speak up so the court can hear you," Mr. Stimson said.

"I said no, not all of us got into our tents and went to sleep."

"Well, then, who didn't get into his tent and go to sleep on the night of Friday, October 16, 2015?"

"Joe Bobby," Kibby all but whispered.

Raising his voice, Mr. Jimbo said, "You say that Joe Bobby Tisdale, the defendant, did not retire to his tent when you, Mr. Bramble, and Mr. Farmer did?"

"That is correct."

"Kibby, what did Dr. Tisdale do while you and Mr. Bramble and

Mr. Farmer slept in your tents?"

"I object!" yelled Hey Boy. "Calls for speculation."

"Sustained. Jimbo, don't make me keep saying that," said Judge Baxter, stifling a yawn.

"Yes, Your Honor. Kibby, was Dr. Tisdale in his tent when you awoke the following morning, Saturday, October 17, 2015?"

"No, sir."

"Well, was he at the campsite at all?"

"No, sir."

"Did Dr. Tisdale ever return to the campsite?"

"Yes, he did."

"At what time, Kibby, did Joe Bobby Tisdale return to your campsite?"

"I'd say it was around seven o'clock in the morning."

"And, Kibby, where do you suppose…strike that. Where did Dr. Tisdale say he had gone when he left the campsite sometime during the night of October 16, 2015?"

"Joe Bobby said that he'd been restless and couldn't sleep. So he decided to drive over to Folly Beach just to cruise around a bit and look at the ocean and the stars. Dr. Joe Bobby and his mama and daddy used to vacation up at Folly beach, and he says the place is very near and dear to his heart."

"Kibby, do you know how far Folly Beach is from Jacksonboro?"

"I believe it's about a hour away, give or take a few minutes."

"So it's about as far from Jacksonboro to Folly Beach as it is from Jacksonboro to Bynum, right?"

"Well, Bynum's a little bit farther away."

"But close, right?"

"Yeah, close, maybe…"

"And Dr. Tisdale didn't return from," and here Mr. Stimson cleared his throat, "Folly Beach until seven o'clock on the morning of Saturday, October 17, 2015?"

"That's right. Joe Bobby said he finally got tired while he was over at Folly Beach and just fell asleep in his car, looking out at the ocean. Didn't wake up till the sun was coming up."

"So you're saying that from shortly after supper on Friday, October 16, 2015 until seven o'clock on the morning of Saturday, October 17, 2015, you are not certain of Dr. Joe Bobby Tisdale's whereabouts."

"Well, he said he went to Folly Beach to look around and just fell asleep. I ain't got no reason not to believe him."

"That'll be all, Mr. Beaumont," Mr. Stimson said, as he turned and nodded at the jury on his way back to his table.

Then Judge Baxter turned to Hey Boy and said, "Mr. Turner, you may cross examine the witness."

Kibby shifted in his seat and looked kind of sheepishly at Dr. Joe Bobby while Hey Boy made a big production of shuffling papers, clearing his throat, and adjusting his cuffs, for dramatic effect, I assumed.

"Mr. Beaumont," he bellowed in his best, good-old-boy southern drawl.

And then he proceeded to ask Kibby basically the same questions that Mr. Stimson had asked. He just asked them louder and more southern-sounding. Don't know if he thought he could make Kibby change his answers with his accent, but, if he did, he was wrong. Kibby stuck to his story and made Dr. Joe Bobby look guiltier 'n sin.

Finally Hey Boy just shook his head and wandered on back to where Dr. Joe Bobby was sitting. Once he reached the defendant's table, he braced his hands on the back of his chair and said, "That will be all, Your Honor."

You could hear a pin drop when Kibby left the witness stand, looked over at Dr. Joe Bobby real sorry-like, and left the courtroom.

When Kibby was all the way out of the courtroom and the door had closed behind him, Mr. Stimson said real loud, "The court calls Mr. Bayless Bramble to the witness stand."

I turned in time to see Mr. Bramble stride into the courtroom and head down the aisle toward the witness stand. I've always liked Mr. Bramble. If my grandfathers had lived long enough for me to meet them, I'd have wanted them to be just like Mr. Bramble. He's always reminded me of Mr. Rogers. He wears bow ties and cardigans, except in summer, when he wears just a short-sleeve button-down shirt. He used to teach fourth grade back before he retired, and he talks real quiet and gentle, I guess so he won't scare kids. I can't, for the life of me, imagine Mr. Bramble drinking liquor and hunting, or hanging out with the likes of Kibby Beaumont, for that matter. But he does, and that's why he was called as a witness to testify about the hunting trip with Dr. Joe Bobby.

Mr. Stimson asked the exact same questions, in the very same order, that he had asked Kibby Beaumont. And Mr. Bramble answered those questions almost verbatim to what Kibby had said, only quieter and with a little better grammar. There was just no disputing it as gospel. After several hours of being questioned and cross examined, Mr. Bramble was excused and Mr. Farmer was called into the courtroom.

The bailiff swore him in, Mr. Stimson asked him the very same questions he'd asked Kibby and Mr. Bramble, and Mr. Farmer's recollections of the hunting trip up in Jacksonboro, South Carolina, sounded just about the same as Kibby's and Mr. Bramble's.

Hey Boy didn't even bother cross examining Mr. Farmer.

The whole thing just made my stomach turn over with nervousness and made my mama gasp and shudder and dig her freshly-filed nails into my arm.

Mrs. Robinette kept on reading her Bible, her lips moving while she read, and Miss Mercelene was knitting so fast she looked like she might just set her knitting needles on fire.

Just when I thought Mr. Stimson had called all the witnesses he could round up, he said, "The prosecution calls to the stand Mr. Blake Warwick.

"What in the world does Blake have to do with this, Mama?"

"Shhh, we'll find out soon enough, Briley."

Blake Warwick was a Bynum Boy who'd come back home after college. Why, I can't imagine, but, then, he didn't consult me. He'd graduated from the University of Virginia and had returned to marry his high school sweetheart, Jennie Mae Loving. We went to their wedding down at the First-and-only-one-that-matters Baptist Church and then out to the Bynum Country Club for their fancy reception, with lobster and an orchestra and dancing. I did not dance. I did eat some lobster, though. With money his granddaddy had left him, he and Jennie Mae built a house down by the river. He'd started his own insurance business and opened an office in the old Sears catalogue store down on Main Street.

Now, Blake was in direct competition with my daddy, Bynum's favorite insurance agent, but Blake's intrusion on his territory didn't seem to bother my daddy at all.

"Glad to have Blake back home where he belongs. He's a fine boy, a smart boy, and there's plenty of insurance business to go around. The Bynum population is aging, and we need young blood like Blake to carry on."

What Daddy said didn't surprise me. Daddy had always liked Blake, 'cause Blake really was a fine boy. He was even nice to me, a little old squirt who had a crush on him. Also, his mama and daddy were in my mama and daddy's bridge club. Come to think of it, Dr. Joe Bobby and Miss Libby Beth were also in their bridge club. And, of course, they were all members over at the Bynum Country Club.

But what in the world did he have to do with Dr. Joe Bobby's murder trial?

When Blake came striding in the courtroom, I realized why I'd always had a crush on him. He was so handsome, with blond hair and big blue eyes and a year-round tan. He used to wear his hair long and shaggy, like a surfer, but since he was a grown-up businessman, he'd cut his hair short and combed it over to one side, like my daddy's. But he was still cute, and I still sort of blushed when I saw him approach the stand.

"Please place your right hand on the Bible and state your name."

"Blake Lawton Warwick."

"Mr. Warwick, do you promise to tell the truth, the whole truth, and nothing but the truth, so help you God?"

"I do," Blake said. He apparently didn't feel the need to say *I so swear* like Kibby.

Mr. Stimson stood up and walked toward Blake. He was holding the lapels of his cheap jacket. It looked like something he'd learned from Hey Boy. It didn't suit him. Looked like he was play acting.

"Mr. Warwick, do you know the accused, Joe Bobby Tisdale?"

"Yes, I do."

Blake was not cutting up and playing it for laughs, like Kibby. He was just answering the question.

"And how do you know the defendant?"

"Well, I was born here in Bynum and have known Dr. Joe Bobby and his family all my life. He and Miss Libby Beth were good friends of my parents. Fact is, Dr. Joe Bobby delivered my younger brother and sister."

"Mr. Warwick, what is your line of business?"

Mr. Stimson knew very well what line of business Blake was in. Everybody in Bynum knew. We'd all seen him remodel that old Sears catalogue store and move his desks and computers right in. But Blake answered Mr. Stimson's question anyway.

"I'm the President of Warwick Insurance."

"So you sell insurance policies."

"That is correct. I am also a certified financial planner and a certified estate planner."

"Is Dr. Joe Bobby Tisdale a client of yours?"

"Yes, he is."

I looked over at Mama, who had a very quizzical look on her face, and said, "Mama, I thought Daddy was Dr. Joe Bobby's insurance agent."

Mama just held that quizzical look and put her hand on my leg to silence me.

"Mr. Warwick, are you Dr. Tisdale's estate planner?"

"No, I'm not."

"His financial planner?"

"No."

"Well, Mr. Warwick, did you sell Dr. Tisdale medical insurance?"

"No, I didn't."

"Then, Mr. Warwick, just what sort of services did you offer Dr. Tisdale?"

All eyes went to Dr. Joe Bobby, and we could see that he had turned white as a sheet.

"Well, Mr. Warwick…?"

"I sold Dr. and Mrs. Tisdale two life insurance policies."

"Two life insurance policies," Mr. Stimson repeated. "Would that be one policy on the life of Dr. Tisdale and one policy on the life of Mrs. Tisdale?"

"That is correct."

"And what was the value of these life insurance policies, Mr. Warwick?"

"They each bought two-million-dollar policies."

"So both Dr. Joe Bobby and Mrs. Libby Beth Tisdale bought two-million-dollar life insurance policies. Does that mean if one should die, the other would collect two-million dollars?"

"That is correct."

"And when did you sell Dr. and Mrs. Tisdale these life insurance policies?" Mr. Stimson asked, looking from Blake to Dr. Joe Bobby to the jury.

"September 10, 2015."

"So what you are saying, Mr. Warwick, is that you sold the

defendant, Dr. Joe Bobby Tisdale, and his wife, Mrs. Libby Beth Tisdale, life insurance policies on September 10, 2015, approximately one month before the death of Mrs. Tisdale. Is that correct, Mr. Warwick?"

"That is correct."

The courtroom started buzzing and rumbling, but Judge Baxter banged his gavel before the whole thing could get out of hand and told us all to quiet down. And I believe it could have gotten out of hand in no time, 'cause this news about the life insurance policies was a big shock to everybody.

When the buzz settled down, Mr. Stimson continued. "Mr. Warwick, are you aware that Dr. Tisdale and his wife have always relied on Mr. Kyle Beckwith for their insurance needs?"

"Yes, I am. Dr. Joe Bobby and Kyle and Bronwyn are the best of friends. It makes sense that he'd do business with Kyle."

"Why, then, do you suppose he came to you when he wanted to take out an insurance policy on his wife's life…just one month before her death?"

"I object!" screamed Hey Boy, as he leapt from his chair and pounded his fist on the table.

"All right, Jimbo," said Judge Baxter. "Now, that was way, way over the line, and you know it."

"Yes, Your Honor." Then with a sly grin and a glance over at the jury, Mr. Stimson said, "I have no further questions for this witness," and strode back to his chair.

He shouldn't've said it, but there was no taking it back. 'Cause what's said is said.

Then Hey Boy stood up, took the deepest breath I've ever heard anybody take, and walked slowly toward Blake.

"Mr. Warwick, why do you suppose Dr. Joe Bobby Turner came to you when he wanted to purchase life insurance policies for him and his wife?"

Now it was Mr. Stimson's turn to jump up and scream that he objected. But after that last little shenannigan he'd pulled, Judge Baxter just held up his hand and said, "Cool it, Jimbo. Maybe Blake can repair the damage you just did. Now, sit down."

Mr. Stimson's face turned sorta red, and he sat back down, like Judge Baxter had told him.

"So, Blake, did Dr. Joe Bobby tell you why he had come to you for insurance when he ordinarily dealt with Kyle Beckwith?"

Blake looked straight at Dr. Joe Bobby and said, "No, not in so many words. It's just that Dr. Joe Bobby is the kindest person I know, the kindest person I've ever known. I'm certain he bought insurance from me just to help me out, to do me a favor. That's just the sort of man he is. He's known me all my life, and he has been kind to me all my life. When I was a kid, he'd buy band candy and magazines and whatever else I was selling. Heck, he'd buy whatever any Bynum kid was selling. He was just generous and kind to all us kids. I believe he still sees me as a Bynum kid, and he just wanted to help me get my business off the ground."

Then Blake folded his hands in his lap and just stared at them. He looked like he was going to cry.

Maybe what Blake said was true.

But the damage had been done.

Ten

One by one the Court called the crime scene investigator, the entomology expert, fingerprint experts, the county pathologist, and the medical examiner. They painted a gruesome picture of a bloodied crime scene and a dead woman who couldn't have possibly shot herself. They presented the murder weapon and pointed out that there were only two sets of fingerprints on that gun—a smudged set belonging to the deceased and a very clear set belonging to the accused, Dr. Joe Bobby Tisdale. The pathologist and medical examiners also said there wasn't any evidence at all of gunshot residue on either of Libby Beth's hands, which made them believe it couldn't have been a suicide. Next, they presented pictures of Libby Beth's body, making the entire courtroom squirm and grimace and look away. Then, without flinching, they gave graphic descriptions of her injuries. It went on for two days—two exhausting, cringe-worthy days. I'd rather have listened to Kibby Beaumont babble some more.

Then the prosecution rested its case, and it came time for Hey Boy to call character witnesses, those folks who would testify to Dr. Joe Bobby's goodness and would, surely, convince a jury of his peers that the good doctor was above reproach and incapable of anything as heinous as murdering his own wife.

"The defense calls Ms. Lyda Upchurch to the stand," said Hey Boy, still southern drawling, his chest all puffed out, his thumbs hooked in his suspenders with American flags marching up and down them.

He was wearing a blue-and-white-striped seersucker suit with black-and-white wingtip shoes, and he had a straw hat resting on the chair next to him. Up until then he'd worn just a dark suit and black shoes. But on that day he looked like a caricature of a backwoods southern lawyer. Guess he figured with the outcome of Dr. Joe Bobby's case not as sewn-up as he'd like for it to be, he needed to play the part of a good-old-boy backwoods lawyer, since he was in backwoods Bynum, Georgia. Well, the crowd just wasn't buying the act. You could feel the eyes rolling all over the courtroom.

"Who the hell does he think he is? Clarence Darrow? Atticus Finch?" said Mr. Austin. He was sitting three rows behind me, but I could hear him plain as day.

Judge Baxter put on his stern face and squinted at Mr. Austin, but he didn't say a word.

The courtroom doors opened, and Ms. Upchurch, the one-and-only, hired-for-life librarian for the Bynum public schools, waddled down the aisle, wearing the same green sweater I'd seen her wear every day since I'd begun my career as a student in the Bynum public school system. And I bet she'd been wearing it a long time before that. She had her pocketbook hooked in the crook of her left arm, while she carried her ever-present umbrella in her right hand.

"I'm always prepared," she said, though Bynum, Georgia is not known for sudden bursts of showers, and our rainy season is pretty predictable. But that thing was permanently fused to her right hand. "I'd rather have it and not need it than need it and not have it," she explained.

Well, she may have been prepared for rain, but she certainly wasn't prepared for testifying in a murder trial.

"Ms. Upchurch, do you know the accused, Dr. Joe Bobby Tisdale?"

"Why, my goodness, yes. Everybody in Bynum knows Joe Bobby," she said, as she looked in Joe Bobby's direction and gave him a motherly smile.

So far it was going pretty good, but she didn't just stop at that.

"You see, Joe Bobby's mama, that would be Eulalee, and I go way back, way, way back. She and I were in the same Sunday school class down at the Episcopal Church, as well as Wednesday night Prayer Ladies Bible Study. But Eulalee and I met way before Sunday school. We got to know each other in tenth-grade library science class when my daddy was transferred from Skokie, Illinois, to

Savannah with the Baker Shoe Company. Course, my daddy didn't want to raise his family in the city—didn't think it was safe for his young'uns—so he settled us here in Bynum. Now, he had quite a commute over there to Savannah every day, but anything for the family, you know. Now, where was I?"

But before she needed to be reminded where she was, she refreshed her own memory and continued, "Oh, yes, Joe Bobby. Joe Bobby and I go way back, as well. Why, I've known him since the day he was born, but I guess you'd say our first personal interactions came when he was in kindergarten. That little boy could read like a champ even then. He loved coming into my library, picking out books. Why, he'd stay for hours, poring over the shelves, especially the mystery and adventure sections. So I just sorta watched Joe Bobby grow up."

I thought to myself, *Good lord, if everybody goes on like this, I'll be graduating from college before Dr. Joe Bobby is declared innocent and sprung from his god-forsaken jail cell.*

And what in the world was Ms. Upchurch proving? That Joe Bobby could read when he was five years old? Well, how could that information help prove that he didn't murder his wife?

"Character witness, Briley. Ms. Upchurch is attesting to Joe Bobby's character," my mama said when I'd rolled my eyes and wondered out loud what purpose that particular testimony was serving.

Ms. Upchurch apparently wasn't near done with her pointless-to-my-way-of-thinking testimony, but when she took a deep breath and before she could keep on about her life-long relationship with Dr. Joe Bobby and Miss Eulalee, Hey Boy held up his hand and said, "Ms. Upchurch, all you need to do is answer yes or no."

"Okay, then," Ms. Upchurch said, "ask me the question just one more time, please."

"Ms. Upchurch, do you know the accused, Dr. Joe Bobby Tisdale?"

So she said, "Yes," even though we already knew her answer.

The character witnesses came in droves, most of them characters, in their own rights. And just when I thought Hey Boy had searched under every rock and scoured every corner of Bynum for everybody who had ever come in contact with that saint, Dr. Joe Bobby Tisdale, Hey Boy bellowed, "The defense calls Katherine Suellen DuBois to the stand."

The courtroom doors swung open, and down the aisle pranced Miss Kitty Sue, her tiny feet teetering on towering red high heels. Miss Kitty Sue had been in Mama and Dr. Joe Bobby's class in school from Miss Minnie's Preschool for the Privileged Progeny of Bynum all the way through Bynum Central High School. Mama said she was right pretty in the day but that the years had not been kind to her.

Then Mama added, "But if I'd had to put up with that crazy mama of hers, my pretty would've worn off too. Bless her heart."

I don't know if Mama was blessing crazy Mrs. DuBois's heart or the unpretty-with-age Miss Kitty Sue's heart. Either way, Mama was following southern protocol by canceling out an insult with a *bless her heart.*

Anyway, Miss Kitty Sue wore her bleached white hair all teased up real tall—a hairdo mama said went out of style way back in the '60's. I, however, found it hard to believe that such a monstrosity had ever been in style.

When she passed by Mama and me on her way to the witness stand in her short, tight red and black print dress, I heard my mama cluck her tongue and felt her roll her eyes before she hissed, "Do, lord, her mama must have poured her into that frock. It'll take a shoe horn to get her out of that thing. And it looks like she put her make-up on with a trowel. Why, I ought to go over to her house and give that poor thing a lesson or two on fashion and whatnot and invite her into the twenty-first century."

That's so like my thoughtful mama—always thinking of ways to improve others. But she didn't even end the offer with a *bless her heart.*

Several people around us gave Mama a *shhhhhh,* and Judge Baxter glared at her real stern-like over his glasses. She just huffed, like it was her right to critique all the witnesses.

"Please place your hand on the Bible and state your name," the bailiff said.

Miss Kitty Sue pursed her pouty red lips and dramatically placed one hand on the Bible, the other high in the air. "My legal name is Katherine Suellen DuBois," she said, pronouncing her last name

DuBwa, even though everybody else in Bynum, including her own family, pronounces it D*uhBoze*.

"Pretentious!" Mama would say, and, in fact, said it often.

Then Miss Kitty crinkled up her eyes and added, "but y'all can just call me Kitty Sue, same as everybody else."

Ignoring his witness's pretentiousness, the bailiff said, "Miss DuBois, do you swear to tell the truth, the whole truth, and nothing but the truth, so help you God?"

Placing her right hand over her heart and closing her eyes, Miss Kitty Sue said real dramatically, "I do so sway-uh."

Mama's eye roll was nearly a scream.

Miss Kitty Sue told the court how she and Dr. Joe Bobby had been the very best of friends and that they had dated when they were students at Bynum Central High School.

I could feel my mama puff up in a rage at the mention of Miss Kitty Sue and Dr. Joe Bobby being the very best of friends. Nobody was the very best of friends with Dr. Joe Bobby except Bronwyn Talmidge. And as for Joe Bobby and Miss Kitty Sue's dating, Mama spat, "Dated, my butt. They went to the Sadie Hawkins dance because she invited him. Joe Bobby was just too polite to refuse. But dated? I don't think so!"

Once Miss Kitty Sue started praising Dr. Joe Bobby and his perfectness, I sort of lost track of who said what 'cause it all sounded pretty much the same. But I guess Hey Boy wanted the world—and the court—to know that everybody knew that Dr. Joe Bobby was the pillar of goodness and could never have murdered his wife in cold blood.

So after a parade of why-yes-I've-known-Joe-Bobby-all-his-life witnesses testified to the best-doctor-in-Bynum's wonderfulness, I was surprised that there wasn't a halo on Dr. Joe Bobby's head and that the Pope hadn't appeared to bestow sainthood upon the man.

But what good would it do to have all your friends say you were a great person? Well, we'd see.

"The jury is in," Andrew Morgan yelled into his microphone and, turning, began running in the direction of the courthouse, along with dozens of other reporters. Judge Baxter had allowed the reporters to remain in the courtroom but insisted they keep their lips zipped during the trial.

"I will not have my courtroom turned into a circus, media or otherwise. There will be complete decorum, everyone behaving civilly and professionally."

For the most part, the media had behaved most professionally, remaining quiet, texting discreetly, only faint tick-ticks heard over the proceedings.

But as I watched the reporters running in a herd toward the courtroom, looking anything but professional, I felt my stomach clench in a tight knot and my mouth go dry as a wad of cotton balls.

Mama and Daddy had left for the courtroom early that morning, so that they could be assured their seats directly behind Dr. Joe Bobby and Hey Boy. Each morning Mama had taken up her post behind her friend, certain of his innocence and incensed that the system was subjecting him to this indignity when he was grieving the loss of his wife. It was down-right heartless. Daddy, of course, had to work most days, but this day, Verdict Day, was different. Daddy wouldn't have missed Verdict Day for the world.

Even though, after much whining, my mama had agreed to let me sit in on the trial, I had chosen not to be present for the reading of the verdict. I had sat through weeks and weeks of brutal testimony, the prosecution dragging out the most intimate details of Dr. Joe Bobby's life, misguided events of his otherwise-innocent childhood and thoughtless teenage indiscretions that mortified Dr. Joe Bobby in the telling. Jimbo Stimson twisted the witnesses' words and accentuated the absurd until I could hardly look on Dr. Joe Bobby's embarrassment. But regardless of how Mr. Stimson and his helper-lawyers parsed the testimony, I knew, all of Dr. Joe Bobby's friends knew, that he was a kind man, an innocent man, a man who would never have shot his own wife, or anybody else, for that matter.

But did the jury know that? Throughout the trial I had watched the jurors' faces, observed their demeanor. They wore poker faces, would not show their hands. Perhaps, as they'd promised, they really didn't know Dr. Joe Bobby and hadn't heard a word about the case. I just didn't feel that I could be there when they told the court what they thought of my mama's best friend. I needed to be somewhere by myself, to shout with joy real loud or cry with anguish real hard.

So when the jury was excused to deliberate, I kissed my mama and daddy good-bye and ducked out of the courtroom. I found my crippled bike right where I'd left it—leaning up against a do-not-litter sign—hopped on, and pedaled toward home. The streets were deserted. Folks were either in the courtroom, waiting for the verdict, or at home watching their televisions, waiting for the verdict. When I got to my house, I dropped my bike beneath the magnolia tree and made my way to the kitchen to make myself a peanut butter sandwich. I took my lunch to the living room and turned on the TV, hoping I hadn't missed anything about Dr. Joe Bobby's trial. And there I sat, for three hours, on the edge of our sofa, all by myself, watching people mill around the courthouse while reporters blathered on aimlessly, all waiting for the verdict.

So when Andrew Morton, the reporter who started this whole thing, yelled, "The jury is in," and turned and ran toward the courthouse, I clenched my teeth and my fists and held my breath. When it took longer for the verdict to be announced than I could hold my breath, I let it out in a raggedy rasp and tried to compose myself.

My heart was pounding in my throat and I was still clenching all over when I heard, "We, the jury, find the defendant, Joe Bobby Tisdale, guilty of murder in the first degree."

So I cried real hard.

I knew that my mama would be crying real hard. And my daddy too.

And I cried real hard for them, as well as for Dr. Joe Bobby. And for me.

"It's going to be all right, Honey."

I was clinging to Miss Delphine, crying into her neck. I hadn't even heard her come into the house. But as soon as she'd heard the verdict, she'd run to me, let herself in. That's just the way Miss Delphine is.

"That's okay, Sweetie. You just cry it out."

So I did. I sobbed and cried, like I'd never sobbed and cried before. I'm normally not a crybaby, but this was different. And Miss Delphine just held me, not saying a word, and let me cry it out.

When I finally exhausted myself and took a deep breath, she reached into her pocket and pulled out a wad of Kleenex and handed it to me.

"Here, Briley, dry your eyes, and we'll go over to my house and get a Yoo-hoo."

"Okay," I said, mopping my face and blowing my nose. I dropped the wet blob of Kleenex on the coffee table and clicked off the TV, silencing the courthouse mayhem. "I think I could use a Yoo-hoo about now."

Miss Delphine just smiled, took my hand, and pulled me up from the sofa. Then she put her arm around my shoulders and walked me over to her house, where she got me a real cold Yoo-hoo.

I sat at her kitchen table and took a long draw on the bottle, burped, and said, "'Scuse me."

Even at my most distressed, I couldn't forget the manners my mama had taught me.

"You're 'scused," Miss Delphine said, patting my hand and smiling.

After a long silence, I said, "How did that happen, Miss Delphine?"

"I don't know, Briley, I just don't know."

"But we know Dr. Joe Bobby," I said. Then thinking about that, I said, "Don't we?"

"Of course, we know Joe Bobby, Briley," Miss Delphine said, rather indignantly.

"But if we know him, we know he didn't kill his wife. Why, then, didn't the jury know that?"

"Like I said, Briley, I just don't know. I'm as confused as you are. I was certain he'd be found innocent," she said, letting out a real heavy sigh.

Pondering our confusion and not knowing where to go with it, we sat there in silence for a good long while. All I could hear was her grandfather clock ticking in the parlor and a bird singing real happy outside the kitchen window. Didn't he know there was nothing to be happy about? Hadn't he heard the news about Dr. Joe Bobby? And while I sat there wondering how a bird could be happy at such a tragic time, I realized I needed to be with my mama and daddy.

"Miss Delphine, I think I'm going to go on home now."

"All right, Briley, but I don't want you to be alone over there, you hear?"

"Yes, ma'am, but I just need to be at home when my mama and daddy get there."

"I understand, Sugar."

I gave Miss Delphine a hug, and we held onto each other real tight. When I finally broke away, I headed for her front door and let myself out. I jumped off the side of her porch and was happy to see that Mama and Daddy hadn't beaten me home. I wanted and needed to be there to greet them after the tragic news about Mama's best-friend-since-forever.

I waited and waited, wondering where they could possibly be for so long. But I didn't leave my post at the door, because I wanted me to be the first thing my mama and daddy saw when they came in the house, wanted them to know that I was there for them.

When they finally got home, Mama was crying big, wet tears that were dripping off her chin and splashing onto her pink silk blouse.

"Mama," I said, and reached out to touch her arm.

She pulled away from my touch, and, without even looking in my direction, she ran up the stairs and into her bedroom and slammed the door with an ear-splitting crash.

Daddy just pursed his lips and squinted his eyes and headed on upstairs to tend to Mama. On his way he said over his shoulder, "Your mama is distraught, Briley."

Well, any fool could tell that my mama was distraught.

Then he added, "And Joe Bobby is going to need her more than ever. You're just going to have to fend for yourself for a while. You understand, don't you?"

I looked down and watched myself fade away to nothing.

Eleven

There's just no hiding grief. It can figure a way to escape and ooze through the best-insulated walls. That's what Mama's grief did late, late into the night—every night. I'd be sleeping real soundly when I'd hear that grief creeping from Mama and Daddy's room and making its way through the wall into my bedroom.

And though there was just no denying that it was grief, I could not make out what the grief was saying. The voices of grief were just muffled sounds. I could imagine what was being said by the inflection in my parents' voices. Mama would be crying and wailing over her best friend's false conviction, and at first Daddy would make clucking, consoling sounds. But when his consoling failed to calm my mama, my father's sounds would turn to frustration. Frustration would give way to exasperation. By the time his mood reached anger, my head would be buried beneath the pillow, a futile effort to block out the oozing noises.

One afternoon when I came home from school, I became aware that what my mama was experiencing was much more than just grief. That's when I realized that she had, as my Granny Evadelle would have put it, gone off her ever-lovin' ga-zip. As I climbed the stairs to the front porch, the steady thump, thump, thump crept up my legs toward my insides. When I opened the front door, the bass thrummed so loudly that I couldn't even hear myself yell, "Mama, I'm home!"

I was certain my mama couldn't hear me either.

I followed the unsettling pounding up the stairs, stomping in cadence to the beat. I realized when I reached the upstairs hall that the sound was coming from the attic. I yanked the perpetually-swollen-from-humidity attic door, and John Philip Sousa hit me with a force that made my heart feel as if it would explode right through my chest. Covering my ears but unable to protect my throbbing heart, I crept up the stairs till I was eye level with the attic floor. Peeking cautiously over the edge, I found my mama decked out in her yellowed-with-age and frayed-at-the-seams Bynum High School majorette uniform. It still fit Bronwyn Gail Talmidge Beckwith perfectly, except where it strained a bit across her boobs. Guess boobs tend to grow somewhat from sixteen to whatever age Bronwyn admitted to being on any given day.

Mama was wearing her parade boots, the short white ones with the gold tassels, not the knee-high white patent ones that she said were strictly for performance. I have no idea where she performed in knee-high white patent leather boots. She liked her short boots best because the tassels swayed and bounced with each high step. And on that day those tassels were bouncing with joy because my mama was flat-out marching. And twirling.

She had a shiny silver baton in each hand, and as she tapped her heels on the wooden floor and spun round and round, she'd throw one baton into the air and then the other, catching one and then the other with each rotation: throwing and spinning and catching, throwing and spinning and catching. Don't know how she managed to spin that way and stay upright because it was making me dizzy just watching her. But her beautiful, long, perpetually tan legs kept her upright, just as she commanded them to do.

Mama's legs are legendary here in Bynum. Once I was down at Bertie Slocum's Conoco station pumping up my bike tires at the do-it-yourself air pump when Skeeter Hickman came sauntering over and just stood watching me, picking his teeth with a grimy-with-grease fingernail. I thought he should help me pump up my tires since he was employed by the Conoco station, but, apparently, he didn't think so.

Instead, he just took his fingernail out of his mouth and wiped it on the leg of his stained jeans, sucked real loud on his teeth, and said, "You Bronwyn Talmidge's young'un, ain't you?"

My mama had been Bronwyn Beckwith for a good, long time, but to all of Bynum of a certain age, she would forever be Bronwyn Talmidge.

I said, "Yes, sir, I'm Briley."

"You don't look nothin' like your mama," he said, as if I didn't already know that.

"No, sir, I don't," was all I said.

He looked down at my scrawny legs which were sporting fresh scabs, the result of a recent bike spill I'd taken when I'd careened at an excessive rate of speed around that sharp corner on Azalea Place. That turn isn't called Collision Corner for nothing. I wanted to hide my unsightly legs, but that was impossible, considering I was wearing my cut-off jeans.

After eyeing my scabby legs and my skinny physique and weirding me out until I had goose flesh, he sucked again real loud and said, "That Bronwyn's quite a looker. Got legs that just go on forever."

I agreed with what Skeeter was saying, but I didn't think it was appropriate for him to be saying those things to Bronwyn Talmidge Beckwith's daughter, so I just said, "Yes, sir," flung the air hose back in the direction of the pump—I didn't care whether my tires were full or not—jumped on my bike, and headed out of the Conoco parking lot without even looking right or left for traffic.

So there was Bronwyn, prancing around on the objects of Skeeter's affection, seemingly oblivious to the ear-splitting, chest-exploding music. And her daughter.

I climbed the rest of the way into the attic, crossed over to Mama's old boom box, and flipped the switch on Mr. Sousa.

"Briley! Lord, you scared the puddin' out of me. Don't you ever sneak up on me like that again!"

"Mama, I didn't sneak. I stomped and screamed. You just couldn't hear me over your loud music."

"Oh, well, no harm done. Come on and join me," she said, flipping her long, chestnut ponytail from side to side and assuming the traditional majorette stance—boots at attention, back erect, chin in the air, baton in each hand perched on hip.

"Thanks, but I think I'll pass," I said to my beautiful, erect, perky mother who still wanted to believe that I was majorette material.

Relaxing her stance and screwing her face into a grimace of dissatisfaction, she whined, "Briley, you're just no fun."

I had lived with the woman for fourteen years, and she was just figuring out that I was no fun.

But instead of going there, I said, "Mama, are you all right?"

"Why, of course," she said. "Why would you think I'm not all right?"

Well, if my mama could march in the attic and twirl her batons in her high school majorette uniform to ear-splitting music and wonder why her daughter would think something was wrong, I figured something was really wrong. I knew it had to do with Dr. Joe Bobby—lately everything had to do with Dr. Joe Bobby—but I sure didn't know how to fix whatever was wrong with my mama.

So I just said, "Mama, why don't you just come on downstairs now?"

"Yeah, I probably should. I believe I've practiced long enough."

Practiced for what?

"I guess I ought to be getting back to the news."

I was hoping she guessed she should be getting back to her nursing job and fixing her daughter after-school snacks, like normal mothers did.

But I'd come to accept that normal mothers don't practice majorette routines in the attic. But as unsettling as her majorette practice was, her middle-of-the-night wailing was just more than I could bear.

So early one morning, around four or four-thirty, I'm guessing, when my mama's grief was showing no sign of abating and I was showing no sign of being able to block it out, I crept from my bed, put on the clothes that I had tossed on the floor just hours before, picked up my shoes, and headed for the hall that separated my parents' bedroom door from mine. I tiptoed down the stairs, careful to skip the eighth step, the one with the pitiful, mournful squeak that Daddy had tried but failed to quiet. But the mournful step was really no competition for my mournful mother.

Once I'd cleared the house, I stepped into my tennis shoes, hopped to the ground from the edge of the porch, and picked up my bike, lying on its side, playing dead.

I jumped on and pedaled out of the yard, to where I had not yet decided. This was a spur-of-the-moment trip, and I hadn't had time to devise a plan. I pedaled across the front yard and out onto Magnolia Street, where I took a left and picked up speed, still not sure where I was going. I soon found myself out in the country on the lonely, two-lane road that went past Mr. Tillman's tobacco farm and not much else. It was still dark out, but I could tell that Mr. and Mrs. Tillman were already up because I could see the light through the kitchen window. Mrs. Tillman was at the stove, I assumed making breakfast for her and Mr. Tillman. Mr. Tillman was sitting at the kitchen table, reading something. I figured they didn't even see me riding by, peering in their window.

I rode and rode, faster and faster, no destination in mind, till my calves were hard, cramped knots and my legs burned like fire. And as the pain grew from my calves up to my thighs and I refused to buckle under, the tears began streaming down my cheeks—for legs that were on fire and for a mother who was drowning in grief and was unreachable.

Just as daylight began to peer over the horizon, I found myself at the edge of Yamasee Lake, named for the Yamasee Indians who had once inhabited the area. I've been told that there is an Indian burial ground somewhere nearby, although I've never seen it. I have, though, with the help of my daddy, dug up many an arrowhead right on the banks of the lake.

The popular kids come out to Yamasee Lake in the summertime to swim and swing on the big old rope that is attached to a huge live oak that hangs out over the water. The popular kids also drive out to Yamasee at night to park and make out. I've never been to the lake with the popular kids—to swim or to make out.

I laid my bike on its side and climbed up on the enormous rock that sits at the north edge of the lake.

It had been nearly forty years since my Uncle Riley had toted his seven-year-old sister, Bronwyn, on his bike out to Yamasee Lake. He'd helped her climb the big old rock, the very same one that I was sitting on, and told her, "You wait right here, Bronnie. I'm gonna go swing off the rope. Now, you watch, and you can swing off the rope when you get to high school."

Bronwyn had watched as her brother Riley sprinted around the edge of the lake and shimmied up the ancient oak tree, his feet clamped on the sides of the trunk, boosting him upward toward the branch that held the big knotted rope that would send him sailing out over the lake. He reached the branch and inched his way toward the rope. Once there, he gathered it hand over hand, eventually reaching the knot at the end. Wrapping his legs around the rope, he sat on the knot and gave the branch a shove, propelling himself in a wide arc over the crystal clear lake. He rode the rope for several more exhilarating arcs before it snapped, sounding like the crack of a rifle.

The last words Bronwyn heard Riley scream were, "Holy shit!"

They found Bronwyn right where Riley had left her, high atop the big old rock.

"I watched, just like Riley told me," was all she said.

Once the authorities pieced together what had happened to her brother, my mama never mentioned Riley again, except to sort of name me after him.

And as I sat on that big old rock and thought about my seven-year-old mother watching her only brother disappear under the water of Yamasee Lake, I kicked off my shoes, gathered my legs close to me, and tried to knead the fire-hot knots out of my calves and thighs.

I noticed that the morning was quickly turning warm and humid—an indication that we were in for a scorcher. By ten o'clock all the locals would be at home or taking refuge in the Piggly Wiggly because the Piggly Wiggly had the best air conditioner in Bynum. In addition to the encroaching heat, there wasn't a hint of a breeze, and the area was shrouded in fog, a fog that would blanket the lake until the sun rose over the scrub pines to burn it away.

As I sat on the big rock, motionless and silent, listening to the cicadas chirr and something I was hoping wasn't a snake rustle in the underbrush, a small lizard, the kind that changes colors for camouflage, scurried over the edge of the rock and headed in my direction. It ran fearlessly toward me, crawled up onto my foot, and peered out over the foggy lake. As it sat perched on my red, blue, and yellow striped sock, its body turned red, blue, and yellow striped, as well. Its tail, long and skinny and still draped across the rock, remained granite gray. I sat transfixed, fascinated not only by the lizard's transformation but by unquestionable proof of my previous supposition: I was, without a doubt, invisible, just like a lizard that changes colors to blend in with its surroundings. I was just a part of the huge rock. Or the landscape. Nothing and no one could see me, and that was for the best. If no one could see me, then no one could hurt me. Murder and grief and madness could swirl around me, but it couldn't touch me if I were invisible.

While I was sitting there marveling at my invisibility and watching the little lizard's colors become my vivid sock colors, I heard a loud *awwwrrrkk*. I looked up just in time to see a great blue heron swoop just mere feet over my head and touch down noiselessly in the water at the edge of the lake. And there it stood, as motionless as a statue, for a good ten minutes, I guessed. Then in the slowest of movements, he lifted one leg, leaned forward several inches, and placed his foot soundlessly back into the water. He repeated this slow-motion dance over and over, nearly lulling me to sleep. Just when I was about to nod off, that great bird struck the water with his beak—struck so fast his head was a blur. When he came up for air, he was holding a big, flapping fish in his beak. Now that his breakfast was secure, he lifted into the air and flew back in the direction he had come, his dangling feet trailing droplets of water as he disappeared over my head.

As the sun began shining through the scrub pines, I figured I'd better head on home before Mama and Daddy figured out I was gone. I gently lifted the lizard from my foot and placed it on the rock beside me. It didn't move but just continued to stare out over the lake. I watched as its red, blue, and yellow stripes turned to gray. I put on my shoes, slid off the rock, and picked up my bike.

I returned to Bynum, comforted by my Power of Invisibility.

When I got home, I found my mother sitting on the sofa in her nightgown, her hair all tangly and hanging in her face. Her eyes were glued to the morning news on TV station, WSAV. Was she hoping for some new developments in Dr. Joe Bobby's case? Did she think that watching the news would somehow make Dr. Joe Bobby innocent?

As I stood in the door of the living room, she looked up and slurred sleepily, "Good morning, Briley. I didn't hear you get up."

I had been gone for hours, yet my mother hadn't even missed me.

"Where's Daddy?"

"He left for the office long ago."

It was Saturday morning, a morning my daddy usually stayed at home. But Mama didn't notice that it was Saturday and that her husband would rather put on a suit and go to an empty office than stay at home and deal with his wife's encroaching madness.

"Want some breakfast?" she asked.

I smiled at the notion of my mama fixing me some breakfast. Anticipating pancakes and bacon or maybe some scrambled eggs with cheese, I smiled at her and said, "Sure would, Mama."

"Well," she said, returning her attention to WSAV, "I think there are some Pop-Tarts in the pantry."

Trudging down the hall toward the kitchen, I told myself, *I can't be hurt because I'm invisible.* But that stabbing pain in my heart told me that exercising my Power of Invisibility was going to take a lot of practice. And I decided that the best time and place to practice was every morning at Yamasee Lake.

Twelve

Dr. Joe Bobby's conviction was appealed, just as every first degree murder conviction is appealed. Didn't do any good, though. He was pronounced guilty beyond a shadow of a doubt and transferred from the county jail to the state penetentiary, where he was to serve a life sentence for killing Mrs. Libby Beth Tisdale, his wife of eighteen years.

How could they have gotten it so wrong? Twice! But did they get it wrong? Maybe I'd gotten it wrong. But didn't I know Dr. Joe Bobby just about as well as anybody? Why, he was the doctor who had delivered me. If you can't trust the doctor who delivered you not to kill his wife, then just who can you trust? I was so certain he was innocent; then all that evidence made my head spin with confusion. It was enough to make a girl welcome her Power of Invisibility.

Following Dr. Joe Bobby's second and final and you-don't-get-any-more-chances conviction, Mama began a quest to prove her best-friend-since-birth's innocence. She set up her laptop and her printer on the dining room table and began accumulating file folders of research data that she was certain would fit all together into one big puzzle which, once assembled, would make the Court cry, "Hallelujah!" and carry Dr. Joe Bobby from his cell on shoulders, amid cries of praise and abject apologies.

Each morning when I'd come downstairs—or from Lake Yamasee—for breakfast, I'd find Mama hard at work on her research. She'd be wearing the same nightgown she'd worn for the past two weeks and had, somehow, forgotten to wash. Her unkempt hair became flatter and greasier by the day, and the bags under her eyes grew darker and puffier as time went on.

With her nose nearly pressed to the computer monitor, she'd mumble-read article after article about convicted felons being proven innocent. As she read, she'd scribble pages of illegible notes. When she'd accumulate a good stack, she'd make copies, stuff them in a box, put her coat on over her nightgown, and head down to FedEx to ship her research off to The Innocence Project. She was confident that between her and that team of hotshot lawyers, they'd have Joe Bobby freed in no time.

But for all her research sharing, she never heard from The Innocence Project. But that didn't deter my mother.

She wrote to Alan Dershowitz, that well-known lawyer who had helped get O. J. Simpson cleared, when everybody in creation knew he had murdered his wife. Now, this all happened way before I was born, but who doesn't know all about that case? Why, they're still writing books and making movies about it. Mama just knew that Mr. Dershowitz was the answer to Dr. Joe Bobby's innocence. Well, she didn't hear from Mr. Dershowitz either. Guess he couldn't read her scribblings that she called research.

"I don't need their help," she said, her back straight and defiant, her research spilling from files across the dining table and onto the floor. "I know that Joe Bobby didn't kill Libby Beth, and I'm going to prove it—or die trying!"

At the rate she was going, she just might die trying—and take her mama and my daddy and me along with her. Her dedication to her new obsession was wearing on all of us.

Daddy suggested, in his oh-so-gentle-and-soothing voice, that he find her some help.

"Help? Why do I need help? I'm working as hard as I can! Aren't I all the help that Joe Bobby needs? I don't need the Innocence Project. I don't need Mr. Alan I'm-a-big-hotshot-lawyer Dershowitz. I'm very capable of handling this all by myself."

She clearly misunderstood what Daddy was trying to get at 'cause he said, "Not help for Joe Bobby, Bronwyn, help for you."

"For me? Why would you get help for me? I'm fine!"

"Bronwyn," my daddy said real softly, so as not to spook my mama, "you are distraught, overwrought by Joe Bobby's conviction. I understand that, but, Darlin', you haven't bathed or washed your hair in I-don't-know-how-long. And you haven't moved from that computer, even to sleep or eat. I thought it might help if you spoke with Father Caleb or, perhaps, a counselor."

"A counselor?" she shrieked. "You think I'm crazy? The only thing I'm crazy about is crazy with grief over our best friend's false conviction. And if that makes me crazy, then so be it! Now, if you'll excuse me, I have research to do. At least someone cares about our dear friend."

And with a huff she returned to her computer, clacking and scribbling.

Thank goodness for Miss Delphine. God sends us angels when we're most in need, and I truly believed God had sent Miss Delphine to me just in the nick of time. I was sorry he'd had to kill Miss Delphine's mama to get my angel back to Bynum, but I was ever so grateful that she was living next door when my mama succumbed to her madness.

"Miss Delphine, it's getting bad over there," I said when she answered the door. Without saying a word, she just opened the screen door and invited me in, her soft hand of comfort on the small of my back.

I headed straight to the kitchen where I heard some opera singer's screechy voice coming out of Miss Delphine's old radio. Needless to say, opera had not begun growing on me, as Miss Delphine had so hoped it would. I reached into the fridge for a cold bottle of Yoo-hoo, for which I'd acquired quite a taste. Miss Delphine got me the bottle opener from the utensil drawer, and I popped the top and took a long draw.

Wiping my mouth on the back of my hand and plopping down at the kitchen table, I said, "Miss Delphine, I just don't know what I'm going to do. I feel like my mama is just going mad right in front of my eyes, and I don't know how to fix it. And my daddy seems helpless too. I can hear him through the wall every night, trying to reason with her, but it just isn't doing any good. Mama is certain that Dr. Joe Bobby is innocent, and she just isn't going to give up until she has cleared his name in the Courts.

"Well, Briley, your mama has lost her oldest and dearest friend. Nobody knows Joe Bobby the way Bronwyn does. Why, those two were practically joined at the hip from birth, and she is certain that he didn't kill his wife. She probably feels that everyone has turned their backs on him and that it is up to her to protect him and prove that he is blameless. What she is doing is admirable. Friends don't give up on friends."

After thinking about what Miss Delphine had said and knowing that it made all the sense in the world, I said to her, "I know that's the truth, Miss Delphine, and I do admire Mama for sticking up for her best friend. But me and my daddy need her too. We're not her friends, but we are her family."

Putting her arms around me when she saw that I was getting ready to cry, she said, "I can only imagine how hard this must be on you and your daddy, Briley. Would you like for me to talk to your mama?"

"Well, me and my daddy haven't had any luck trying to reason with her, but I'd sure appreciate it if you'd say something. It may not help at all, but I don't think it could hurt, either," I said, my voice trailing off in resignation.

"Come on," she said, pulling me up from the table. "Bring your Yoo-hoo. You can finish it at home."

Taking my hand, she walked me over to my house, smiling at me and squeezing my hand for reassurance. When we let ourselves in the front door, we could hear my mama tapping away on her keyboard, talking to herself, gathering her data. As we approached the dining room, I was torn between sadness and embarrassment at my mother's condition. My normally perfect mama looked disheveled and smelled rank with body odor and greasy hair. My heart ached for her and feared for me.

"Mama, look who came for a visit," I said, my voice quavering.

Mama looked up from her work, her eyes all hollow and sunk in, and smiled at Miss Delphine. "Hey, Delphine. I didn't hear you come in. Guess I was just so busy with my research."

"That's all right, Bronwyn. I just wanted to drop over for a chat," she said to my mama. Then to me she said, "Briley, why don't you fix your mama and me some tea while we talk."

"Yes, ma'am, Miss Delphine," I said and ran to the kitchen to turn the burner on under the tea kettle, which was always full and on the stove. Then I ran back to the hall so I could hear what Miss Delphine and Mama had to say.

"Mind if I sit here while you work, Bronwyn?"

"Oh, no, Delphine, I don't mind a'tall," Mama said, returning her attention to her computer screen.

"You know, Bronwyn, Briley is concerned about you."

"Really? Why is that?" Mama asked without looking Miss Delphine's way.

"Well, she says that you spend all your time here in the dining room."

Turning slowly to face Miss Delphine, Mama said, "Well, Delphine, how else am I supposed to prove Joe Bobby's innocence? It takes research, you know."

"Yes, that's true, Bronwyn. But must you spend all your time researching? Perhaps you could allot a number of hours a day to your research, after you've cared for your child."

"But Briley understands the importance of my research. She wants Joe Bobby out of prison, just as I do."

"Yes, she does, Bronwyn. But she also needs her mother."

Before my mother could respond to Miss Delphine, I heard the tea kettle screaming in the kitchen. I ran to remove it from the burner and to drop some tea bags into mugs for Mama and Miss Delphine. I poured the boiling water over the tea bags and carried the mugs to the dining room, where I found that my mother had returned to her research. And from the look on Miss Delphine's face, I figured that she had accepted defeat.

I tiptoed carefully into the dining room, trying not to slosh tea as I walked. Miss Delphine took both mugs from me and said, "Here, Bronwyn, Briley has made us some tea. Wasn't that nice of her?"

"Why, yes, Briley is such a kind, thoughtful daughter," Mama said, taking the tea and smiling at me. My heart leapt with the first accolade I'd gotten from my mama in a good, long while. She took a sip, said, "Mmmmmm," placed the mug on the table by her computer, and returned her attention to her research.

Miss Delphine took my hand and walked me toward the front door. She hesitated, getting a far-off look in her eye, before she put her arms around me and said, "Briley, my door is forever open. You'll always have a safe place with me."

I thanked her, but it was not what I wanted to hear. I did want to believe that Miss Delphine's door was open and that she was a safe place for me. But, mostly, I wanted to believe that she had shook some sense into my mama.

Thirteen

"Mama, you want a bologna sandwich?"

"Thanks, Briley, but I think I'll pass. You go on and fix yourself some lunch. I'll get something later."

I knew she wouldn't get something later. She never got something later. I couldn't figure out what was keeping my mama alive. She seemed to be subsisting on adrenaline and air—and stale old house air, at that. 'Cause she sure never went out of the house. I knew there was no sense in arguing with her, so I wandered down the hall to the kitchen and reached in the fridge for the bologna and Duke's mayonnaise. Only Duke's will do for a bologna sandwich, or a tomato sandwich, for that matter. I opened the bread box and pulled out a fresh loaf of Wonder Bread that I'd gotten at the Piggly Wiggly the day before.

I picked out two slices, closed the loaf back up real tight, and stuck it back in the bread box, 'cause if you don't close your bread real tight in our hot and humid climate, it'll get all moldy in a heartbeat. And nothing makes me madder than to be looking forward to a bologna or tomato or peanut butter and banana sandwich and discover the bread has turned all blue and gross.

But my bread was fresh and soft and yeasty smelling, so I spread my Duke's on real thick, making sure I smeared it out all the way to the edges. Then I put on two slices of bologna, 'cause I was extra hungry. I returned the bologna and Duke's to the fridge and got myself a Yoo-hoo while I was in there. Since Mama had turned the grocery shopping over to me, I made sure the fridge was always stocked with Yoo-hoo.

It was a nice, sunny day, so instead of eating at the kitchen table alone, I decided to take my lunch to the back yard, where I would still be eating alone.

I headed for my old swing set, rusted from age and neglect. I eased myself down into a swing—a swing that had fit my butt the last time I'd used it but now squeezed my cheeks together.

I had just bitten into my sandwich when a scruffy little dog, about the size of a Chihuahua but of some indistinguishable breed, came charging through a gap in the cypress hedge row that divided my house from The Other Side of the Tracks. The actual tracks are two miles west of our house, but everybody calls the neighborhood behind ours The Other Side of the Tracks because most of the houses are single-wide trailers, and the yards are mostly dirt, littered with beer bottles and old car parts.

It's amazing the difference a cypress hedge row can make.

The dog charged right at me, stopping just a few feet away, and barked a loud, snarly bark, which was surprisingly frightening coming from a dog his size. And as it barked and snarled at me, its body trembled with rage. Why it was so angry with me for swinging on my own rusty swing in my own back yard, I'll never know. I paused mid-bite, afraid to move, fearful of what the scruffy little dog with the menacing bark would do to me. I knew, for sure, he could do a number on my ankles, if nothing higher.

Just as I was attempting to plan an escape, a kid I'd seen before squeezed through the gap in the hedge row and bellowed, "Quit yer yappin', Maude!"

That little mutt cut off its tirade like it'd been slapped, ran to the boy, jumped into his arms, and started licking him all over his face. Then it settled down, resting its head under the boy's chin, its little stub of a tail flipping back and forth with glee. I couldn't believe it was the same dog that had, moments before, acted as though it wanted to rip me to shreds.

"You Briley, ain't you?" said the boy from The Other Side of the Tracks.

"Yeah, I'm Briley, and you're Carl, right?"

Everybody knew Carl. Or, at least, everybody knew about Carl.

"He's bad news," folks would say.

Carl was dingy looking, like his skin was permanently colored gray, and he had dirt caked underneath his fingernails. His hair was long and greasy and stuck tight to his head.

Carl was a little hard to understand, 'cause he had a profound lisp. Legend has it that he'd jumped out of a tree one time. When he hit the ground, his legs buckled, and his chin whacked against his knee. And if that wasn't bad enough, he had his tongue stuck out when he landed. Bit it clean off. The doctor sewed it back on, but he must have reinstalled it crooked. Thus the lisp. At least that's the way the story goes.

"You in high school, ain't you?"

"Yeah, I'm gonna be in tenth grade come September," I told Carl.

"I'm still in middle school. Don't think I'll make it to high school. I'll be sixteen in November. Think I'm just gonna drop out. Don't like school too much. School don't like me too much either."

Carl had been held back three years. People called him stupid or, at best, mentally challenged. I didn't think that Carl was stupid or mentally challenged. I thought, maybe, he just learned different from other kids. I'd seen some of the intricate pencil drawings Carl had made—of dragons and dinosaurs and even people's faces—and I was certain no one who was stupid could make such beautiful art. I hoped that some teacher would recognize that Carl wasn't stupid at all, but that he just learned different. But that teacher would have to hurry, because she probably wouldn't get a chance after November.

"Why'd you name your boy dog Maude?" I asked Carl.

"Weren't my choice. My little sister named him Maude. But he don't care. I could call him Queen Elizabeth, and he wouldn't know no difference. It's just a word to him."

"Well, Maude sure does like you."

"Yeah, me 'n him's buds."

Just then I heard a bellow coming from the other side of the hedge row. "Carl, wher you at? You git yer ass home raht now, you hear?"

Carl looked kind of sheepish and embarrassed and said, "Well, Maude, looks like Ma done tracked us down again. Guess we'd best git on home."

With that Maude wagged his stub and shimmied all over, just 'cause Carl had acknowledged him. And then the two of them disappeared through the gap in the cypress hedge row.

Maude didn't care that Carl had bitten his tongue off or that he may or may not have been challenged or that he lived in a single-wide with a dirt yard littered with car parts. He loved Carl—just 'cause.

I wanted to be loved the way Maude loved Carl. I wanted someone or something to shimmy all over with the sheer joy of seeing me. I wanted someone or something that understood me the way Maude seemed to understand Carl.

I ate my bologna sandwich and drank my Yoo-hoo, all the while listening through the hedge row to Carl and Maude being buds. Carl would coo, "Good boy, good boy," and Maude would yip with glee. I could imagine his little stubby tail wagging and his scruffy body shimmying. I rocked back and forth on my rusty swing, listening to it complain *skronk, skronk, skronk.*

When I'd finished my lunch, I headed back to the house, dropping my Yoo-hoo bottle in the recycle bin by the back door. A chipmunk darted out from behind the bin, scaring the crap out of me and making me squeal like a little girl. Now, chipmunks are cute as all get out, but not when they jump out at you when you're not expecting them. When I'd recovered from my chipmunk panic and my heart had settled to its normal rhythm, I stepped into the kitchen and headed for the dining room, where Mama was still glued to her computer.

Without any preparation or lead-in, I got straight to the point. "Mama, can I have a dog?"

I figured she was so engrossed in her research that she'd just say "Um hum," and I'd hold her to it when the time came.

But I was wrong. Guess the word dog got her attention. "Good grief, Briley! Of course not! Have you lost your mind?"

It sounded like a relatively reasonable request to me, but my mama acted as if I'd gone temporarily insane or maybe had asked for a pet crocodile.

"Why not, Mama?" I asked.

"Why not? It'd be easier to tell you why, because there is absolutely no good reason in the world to get a dog. For starters, they smell. Yuck! Wet blankets. They smell like wet blankets!"

"I'd bathe it, Mama," I promised.

"Wouldn't do a bit of good. That wet-blanket smell is built in. And don't get me started on dog breath. And that's just the tip of the icebeg, Briley. Dogs shed hair all over the place—on the floor and on the furniture and on your clothes." And again she said, "Yuck!" That appeared to be her favorite word when describing dog ownership.

But she wasn't through. "And you have to walk a dog and feed a dog. And you have to carry a plastic bag around with you to pick up a dog's poop! Yuck!" There was that word again. "Where do you put a bag of dog poop? Not in my trash can, I'll tell you that!"

"But Mama," I said, but she wouldn't let me finish. Actually, I couldn't remember what I was going to say, but I doubt whatever it was would have swayed her one bit.

"Now, Briley, if you can find yourself a hairless dog that bathes itself, brushes its own teeth, picks up its own poop, and, oh yeah, wipes its own butt, it's all yours."

And, with that, Mama went on back to whatever she was doing—twirling her baton or researching how to get a convicted felon out of prison.

So, feeling ever so sorry for my dogless self, I chose to take my sorrow next door to Miss Delphine.

"Miss Delphine, you ever had a dog?"

"No, Honey, never did. Always wanted one when I was a kid, but my mama was allergic. Or so she said."

"How 'bout when you grew up and moved to New York City? Did you get one then?"

"If you'd seen my apartment, you wouldn't be asking such a question."

"Why's that, Miss Delphine?"

"Briley, when I was in New York City, I lived in an isosceles triangle on the sixth floor of a six-floor walk-up…with no elevator!"

"A what?

"My room—and, yeah, I lived in one room—was triangular shaped. The longest wall had a sleeper sofa and a little chest of drawers, while the opposite wall had a hot plate and fridge about big enough for a quart of milk and a package of lunch meat. In one corner was a bathroom, hardly big enough to turn around in. It had a corner sink and a toilet and a shower head that came out of the ceiling and sprayed all over the place. So there was hardly enough room for me, let alone a dog.

"And, as I said, I lived on the sixth floor and had to walk up and down those six flights of stairs whenever I wanted to go out and come back in. Can you imagine me having to run down those stairs every time a dog had to pee? Why, I doubt we'd have ever made it. So, no, I did not have a dog, for all the above reasons."

"Wow, I can't imagine living in a place like that."

"Wasn't so bad, 'cause I didn't go to New York for an apartment. I went to New York for an adventure."

"But if you could have had a dog—like, say, you lived in a big apartment on the first floor—would you have gotten one?"

"Probably not, Briley. My life was way too busy. I just wouldn't have been able to give a dog the attention it would need."

"What about now, Miss Delphine?"

"Now what, Briley?"

"Why don't you get a dog now?"

"Well, I just never gave that any thought."

"Miss Delphine, your life isn't busy now. You could give a dog all the attention it needed."

"But, Briley, I'm not real sure that's how I want to spend my waning years."

"But I'd help. I promise."

Then Miss Delphine said the one thing that made me know she—and I by association—would not be getting a dog.

Miss Delphine said the dreaded, "We'll see…"

When an adult says, "We'll see…," you know your request is dead in the water.

I wouldn't be getting a dog. Or even part ownership of a dog.

I continued to pout and feel sorry for myself because of my lack of a dog that would love me unconditionally and shimmy with glee by my mere presence. No one seemed to notice, though, so my pouting was a waste of my time and my energy.

Then along came the fourth of July, probably the only day of the year that could temporarily take my mind off being denied a dog.

Fourteen

The Fourth of July, Independence Day, is the only day anything ever happens in Bynum, Georgia. If a Bynumite wants excitement on the other 364 days of the year, he has to go to Savannah. In the past I'd loved the Fourth of July because of the parade and the food vendors and the bluegrass bands in the city park and a whole bunch of other stuff. Anybody who has the measliest amount of talent is welcome to show it off at Bynum's Fourth of July celebration. So the festivities go on all day long with whistlers and jugglers and twenty-pound watermelons and pigs dressed up in pink tutus. There's something for everybody.

Plus, something unexpected always happens at the Bynum Fourth of July celebration. And that's primarily the reason I look forward to the festivities.

One year the reigning Miss Bynum was riding on her float, crown on her head, her big bouffy yellow dress spread out all around her. She was waving to all her subjects, smiling real big, and a bee flew in her mouth. She swallowed the thing, but not before it stung her on the tongue. It swelled up before she even realized what had happened, 'cause, come to find out, Miss Bynum was severely allergic to bee stings. The parade stopped dead in its tracks until an ambulance could come get her and whisk her away to the hospital. Once they were sure Miss Bynum was in good medical hands, the officials resumed the parade, but there was nobody left on the Miss Bynum float, except the two runners-up. And nobody comes to a parade to see runners-up. Why, those girls didn't even have crowns.

Then there was the time the Grantham boys from out on

Highway 57 lobbed firecrackers at the lead parade horse. It was carrying Mr. Peegram, our driver's ed teacher, but on the fourth of July he was dressed up like a Civil War general carrying a great big confederate flag. Of course, the horse got spooked, reared up, and threw Mr. Peegram right down in the middle of Main Street. The fall broke Mr. Peegram's leg and dislocated his shoulder, but the horse didn't even notice. That thing took off through the park, trampling the Baptist ladies' biscuit stand and making Miss Ina June scream and cry her eyes out.

Stamping her foot, her fists all balled up, she cried, "We plan and plan and plan all year long, and a damn horse, of all things, just screws it all up! Well, shee-it!"

She didn't sound too Baptisty to me.

After trampling the Baptist ladies' biscuit stand, that horse galloped on out the back of the tent and made a bee-line for the Mortons' annual picnic, which was set up on a red checked tablecloth right by the statue honoring Jeremiah Theodore Bynum, for whom Bynum, Georgia, is named. It kicked fried chicken all over the place and stepped right in Mrs. Morton's bowl of red-skin potato salad. Traveling at full speed, it sailed in one side of the bandstand and out the other. The last time anybody saw that horse, it was traveling west on Old Sutter Road, heading toward the Oconee River.

I was hoping nothing or no one would destroy the Baptist ladies' biscuit stand—'cause my mouth was watering for one of their country ham biscuits—but I was sure hoping some excitement would ensue.

'Cause my mama was going crazy, and I couldn't get a dog.

"Mama, what time are we leaving to stake claim to our spot in front of Mr. Jensen's drug store?"

Mama and I would take off early every year so we could be up front and center when the parade started. That way Mama could coach the Bynum High majorettes from the sidelines, whether they wanted coaching or not. I'm thinking they did not. But I guess being crowned state champion twirler three years in a row makes you think you have a life-time obligation to tell other twirlers what to do and how to do it properly. We would take our places along the sidewalk on Main Street, right in front of Mr. Jensen's Rexall drug store, and we could hear the band start up even before it left the football field at Bynum Central High School, five blocks away. The music would get louder and louder as the band drew near, and by the time the majorettes rounded the corner at Azalea Street and Main, Mama would already be critiquing in her head. And as they'd draw up alongside us, Mama'd join in step, barking orders.

"Michelle, chin up, eyes forward! Sue Ellen, smile! This isn't a funeral! Mary Beth, knees up! Sarah Katherine, you need to lay off those Snickers bars!"

She'd follow them about two blocks before she'd leave them to their own devices, claiming she'd done all she could do.

But when I asked my mama when we were going to leave for the parade, she looked up from her computer, the dark circles under her eyes growing darker, days—or maybe weeks—of tangles in her hair. I knew before she answered that she wouldn't be claiming our spot in front of Mr. Jensen's drug store and that she wouldn't be instructing the Bynum Central High School majorettes. But how else would those majorettes know how to lift their chins, smile real big, and lay off the Snickers?

"Briley, Honey, you're going to have to go on without me this year. This research is just taking more of my time than I ever imagined it would."

More of her time? How about all of her time?

"But here, Sweetie," she said, digging into the pocket of her bathrobe—her everyday uniform—and pulling out of wad of bills. Thrusting them at me, she said, "Now, you treat yourself to all the funnel cakes and Baptist ladies' biscuits you want, you hear?"

I took the money from her and crammed it in the pocket of my shorts, giving my mother a half-hearted "Thanks."

She was back to her computer by the time I reached the front door. I didn't even bother telling her good-bye. I doubt she'd have noticed if I had.

I jumped off the porch and headed for Miss Delphine's. She wasn't Mama, but maybe she'd keep me from going alone to the Bynum Fourth of July celebration.

"Miss Delphine, you home?" I called through the screen door. I could hear the kitchen opera as I opened the screen and let myself in.

"Hey, Briley, what you up to?" Miss Delphine said, coming out of the bathroom in her bare feet, rubbing her wet hair with a towel.

"Just stopped by to see if you'd like to go with me to the parade and the festivities in the park."

"Don't believe I do, Briley. I'm just not big on parades and Fourth of July hoopla."

"You sure, Miss Delphine? The Baptist ladies have mighty good country ham biscuits."

"You mean they're still selling those biscuits?"

"They sure are. Come on and get one with me."

"Thanks, Sweetie, but I think I'm going to have to pass. Gatherings of Bynumites just ain't my cup of tea. Never have been."

"Okay," I said, understanding what she meant but still not liking that she'd said it.

I crossed back over into my front yard and grabbed my bike that was resting on its side by the gardenia bush. The gardenias were in full bloom and smelled so sweet and fragrant. Mama says there's nothing more southern than the smell of gardenias in bloom. She'd always snip a bouquet to take along to work with her and would put one of those fragrant flowers behind her ear. But Mama no longer worked and probably didn't even know that the gardenias were in full bloom.

I climbed on my bike and headed for town, passing lots of folks walking along with their picnic baskets and checkered tablecloths. I saw the Elmore kids, all seven of them, in their front yard, decorating their bikes for the parade. They'd attach colored streamers to the handle bars and would stick playing cards in their spokes, so that their bikes would make that clicking noise when the wheels turned. Once they had their bikes all tricked out, they'd jump into the parade with the Shriners, the marching bands, the floats full of beauty queens, the horses, the pigs in tutus, and all the other zillion kids with their decorated bicycles.

I passed Mr. Grimm, who lives up to his name. He was washing his car and glaring at the passers-by. He had absolutely no intention of participating in the Fourth of July activities and made sure everybody knew it. Before the evening was over, though, someone would have TP'd his yard and egged his house. Tormenting Mr. Grimm was just one of those long-standing Fourth of July traditions.

I waved and said, "Hey, how ya doin', Mr. Grimm," but his scowl told me exactly how he was doing.

"Hey, Miz Walker," I called, when I passed by the mom pushing a stroller with her twins, Sasha and Sidney.

"Hey, Briley, where's your mama?"

"She can't make it this year, Miz Walker," I called, trying to put some distance between us so I wouldn't have to explain why my mama couldn't make it this year.

"Well, who's gonna tell the majorettes what to do?" she called, a chuckle in her voice.

I laughed over my shoulder and waved, swerving to keep from hitting a bunch of Bynum High football players who were pushing and shoving each other all over the place—another tradition, one not reserved just for the Fourth of July.

I was at cruising speed when I reached Aunt Sal's Donut Shoppe and cut a hard right onto Main Street. The sidewalks were already lined with people four deep, and Mama's and my spot in front of Mr. Jensen's Rexall drug store was already occupied by a big country family, in town just for the festivities. Bet my mama could have made a spot for us, just by clearing her throat. Since I didn't have Bronwyn's charm for getting her way, I gave up on my spot and rode on off to find me a place to watch the parade.

I pedaled on down Main until I reached Daffodil Way, near the head of the parade route. I could already hear the band warming up, so I just anchored myself at Daffodil, planning to view the parade from my bike seat.

I could hear it coming, the faint sound of Dixie getting louder and louder by the minute. And around the corner came a beautiful chestnut horse, so tall and stately. It strutted, its hooves clopping along the paved street, its snow white tail swishing back and forth to the beat of the marching music coming from the Bynum Central High band. Mr. Eggleston sat atop the beautiful horse, decked out in his gray confederate uniform, the same one he wore for Civil War battle reenactments. As the horse pranced by, no one tossed firecrackers or spooked it in any way, and it just clopped on down the street, looking like the regal leader that it was.

Then came the Bynum High majorettes. Michelle's chin was up and her eyes were forward, and Sue Ellen was smiling broadly. Mary Beth was strutting her stuff, and Sarah Katherine looked fine to me. She must have laid off those Snickers, just like Mama had told her. I know they were happy that my mama wasn't there to bark orders at them. But I wasn't. As embarrassing as my mama could be at times, going to the parade without her just wasn't fun at all. I felt like I was trying to clap with one hand. So instead of waiting around to get waved at by Miss Bynum and Miss Georgia State Fair and Miss Georgia Peach, I cruised on over to the park, where the vendors were putting the finishing touches on their tents and tables and carts. I was pleased to see the Baptist ladies were open and already doling out biscuits.

I rode my bike right into the Baptist ladies' tent and up to the table piled high with wax-paper-wrapped ham biscuits.

"Sure does smell good, Miss Ina June. I can tell you been working hard."

"You got that right, Sugah," she said to me. "Been baking biscuits all night long, just like Reba and Esther Lynn and Gretchen over there. But we gotta make 'em at the last minute, so's they'll be nice and fresh for all y'all."

"Yes, ma'am. I've been waiting all year for this, Miss Ina June. You s'pose you got a great big one over there with my name on it?"

"Why, yes, Briley, I've been saving the biggest, flakiest ones just for you and your mama. Say, where is your mama? She get tied up with them majorettes?"

"No, ma'am, Mama couldn't make it this year. She said to give you her regards, though."

"Well, that's awful nice of her, Briley. I hope she's okay."

"Oh, she'll be fine, Miss Ina June. Thanks for asking, though. But I'll just have one biscuit this time."

"Coming right up, Briley," Miss Ina June said, as she handed me a wrapped biscuit still warm from the oven, country ham hanging out all around the edges.

I reached into my pocket and pulled out two dollars, the cost of a Baptist ladies' biscuit and handed it over.

Miss Ina June gently cupped my hand and pushed it away, saying, "This one's on me, Sugah. Now you go have yourself a good ole time today, you hear?"

"You sure, Miss Ina June? I got money."

"I know, Briley, but this is my treat."

"Well, thanks, Miss Ina June. That's awful nice of you."

"Bye now, Sugah. You just go tell everybody that the Baptist ladies have the best ham biscuits in town."

"I'll do that, Miss Ina June," I said, as I climbed on my bike and rode off to find the very best spot to eat my Baptist ladies' biscuit.

I pulled up under the swooping branches of the 100-year-old oak beside the grandstand and dropped my bike to the ground. Then I sat down, crossed my legs, and leaned up against the massive trunk. I opened my biscuit, the biscuit I'd been waiting on for a whole year. I took a bite. And I waited. I waited for my mama to say the same thing she said every year when she took her first bite of her Baptist ladies' biscuit.

Closing her eyes, she'd inhale real deep, grab my arm, and say, "Good lord, Briley, how can anything on earth taste this wonderful! If heaven had a taste, it would taste like a Baptist ladies' biscuit."

And then we'd both laugh real hard, like she'd never said it before. Then we'd eat our biscuits in silence, except for the moans of delight coming from my mama.

Instead, I just ate my biscuit in silence. It was delicious, the biscuit so flaky and light, the ham juicy and salty. But it just wasn't the same. The occasion just needed my mama. When I finished my biscuit, I balled up the wax paper and stuffed it in my pocket. I looked around at the teeming crowds, women setting out picnics, men playing horse shoes, some folks playing cornhole, little kids riding piggy back on big kids' backs. A bluegrass band was getting set up on the bandstand; soon the park would be full of music, people singing along, clapping and dancing on the lawn.

Mama liked to dance on the lawn to the bluegrass band. Daddy would go over to the school to help set up for the parade and direct who goes where, so he couldn't watch the parade with us from the sidewalk in front of Mr. Jensen's Rexall drug store. But after the parade was over, he'd join us in the park, so he could laugh and dance and hold my mama real close. I guess Daddy hadn't helped with the parade. I think he just went on down to his office.

He'd been going to his office a lot lately.

When the people started crowding around and I was afraid I was going to get stepped on, I stood up, brushed the biscuit crumbs off my shirt, and picked up my bike. I pushed it across the park toward the funnel cake vendor. I had funnel cake money, so it wouldn't have been right not to eat a funnel cake, even though I was still full of Baptist ladies' biscuit.

I loved watching Mr. Crowder make funnel cakes. He'd drip the batter in a long, thin string into the hot grease, and the string would go round and round, making a sort of web, until it turned into a funnel cake, bobbing around in the grease, getting golden brown.

Then he'd pick it out with long tongs and sprinkle powdered sugar on top of it—and, in my case, on both sides.

"Hey, Mr. Crowder," I called and waved, as I pushed my bike through the grass.

"Well, hey, Briley," he said. "I hardly recognized you with that pink hair.

"Yeah, just needed a little change, that's all."

"I like it. It makes quite a statement."

"Thanks, Mr. Crowder."

"One made-to-order funnel cake, powdered on both sides, right?" he asked, grinning and showing me his new teeth. They were startlingly white and big as piano keys. Just the white keys, not the black ones. And he sure seemed real proud of them.

"That's right, Mr. Crowder. I like to see my funnel cake coming to life."

So Mr. Crowder scooped my batter out of the vat and dribbled it into the grease, and I watched it bob and spin round and round, taking shape, turning golden brown. When he figured it was done, he fished it out and gave me a double dose of powdered sugar. Handing it to me over the counter, he didn't refuse my money when I reached to pay.

"Thanks, Mr. Crowder. See you later."

"Bye, Briley. Don't take any wooden nickels."

"Okay, I won't, Mr. Crowder."

I have absolutely no idea what *don't take any wooden nickels* means, but Mr. Crowder always said that to me, and I always assured him that I wouldn't.

I wandered around, eating my funnel cake, powdering my shirt with sugar. I saw the football players, still tussling, and the spirit girls giggling at their antics. Folks were laying tablecloths end-to-end, and ladies were arranging picnics for their families and friends. Occasionally someone would speak and ask after my mama, but I didn't want to explain that my mama had gone off her rocker and spent her every waking hour sitting at home in her bathrobe, her rancid body odor, and her tangled hair, glued to a computer that was not going to get her best friend out of prison. So I'd just say, in passing, that she wasn't up to coming to the Bynum Fourth of July festivities but that I'd sure tell her they'd asked about her, and then I'd just move on real fast.

Soon I was so exhausted from trying to dodge all the where's-your-mamas, and there wasn't anything I wanted to do without my mama, so I climbed on my bike and headed on back home. Though I was full of Baptist ladies' biscuit and Mr. Crowder's funnel cake, I had a real lonely, sinking feeling in my stomach, a feeling that even a runaway horse couldn't fix.

A dog sure would have been mighty comforting.

Fifteen

I almost got caught!

I had dressed without making a peep. I'd become quite impressed with my level of stealthness. I had crept quietly down the stairs, missing the squeaky step, of course. Just as I reached the downstairs hallway, I heard my parents' bedroom door open and someone cross the hallway to the stairs. I ducked behind the wall that divided the living room from the entry and listened for footsteps on the stairs.

I was certain it was my dad. My mom would come down the stairs with a despondent, defeated sound. My dad would come down with a frustrated and, at times, an angry sound. That morning his steps just sounded frustrated, like he'd been up all night with my mama and just didn't know what to do with her. I could understand his frustration. Nobody knew what to do with my mama.

I was hoping he wasn't going to come into the living room to watch television because I'd have a hard time explaining why I was fully dressed, plastered up against the living room wall. But, now that I think about it, that sounds sane, compared to all the craziness that was going on in our house. He didn't stop by the living room to watch TV, but, instead, went on back to the kitchen to make himself some coffee.

While he was back there clattering around, I crept across the entry, eased open the front door, stepped out onto the porch, and closed the door behind me. I tiptoed across the porch, jumped to the ground, and grabbed my bike. I was hoping that Daddy was still in the kitchen and didn't see me take off out the yard and pedal down Magnolia Street. Once I was out of sight of the house, I realized I'd been holding my breath. I let it out in a ragged whoosh and gasped for air.

The celebration of the day before hadn't been too celebratory for me. No mama instructing the majorettes. No daddy coordinating the band. No mama and daddy dancing to the bluegrass band. It was just biscuits and funnel cake and no one to share it with.

And I didn't have a dog.

So I rode hard, rode hard toward the lake.

As usual, Mr. and Mrs. Tillman were already up and eating breakfast. They looked like a Norman Rockwell painting, bent over the table in their cozy kitchen, frilly white curtains framing the two of them. I bet Mrs. Tillman had a teapot collection or maybe a bunch of ceramic chickens displayed on a shelf above her kitchen window. I noticed that the Tillmans' cows, about ten of them, had wandered out of the back pasture and were lined up along the front fence by the road, as if they had come out to greet me.

"Morning," I said, but they just stared as I passed by.

Guess they weren't there to greet me, after all.

I made it to the lake at sunrise, just as I did every morning. It was the only constant in my life, and I wanted to make sure it stayed that way. I dropped my bike and climbed up onto my rock, where I waited for my friend to appear. I gazed out over the lake, so quiet and peaceful, except for an occasional dragonfly lighting on the surface, making concentric circles spread out across the water. Then out of the corner of my eye, I saw him peer over the top of the rock, look from side to side, and then scurry my way and climb onto my hand. I watched him turn from slate gray to flesh. We sat for a while, just enjoying the morning and each other's company.

Then I reached into my pocket and pulled out my box of colored pencils. I eased them out of the box, one by one, careful not to startle my friend. I placed the pencils side by side, in rainbow order: red, orange, yellow, green, blue, indigo, violet. I slowly lifted my hand and gently laid the lizard across the colored pencils. Then I watched my friend turn into a rainbow of color, except for his head and the tip of his tail, which were hanging off the sides of the pencils onto the rock. They turned slate gray.

"I'll call you Joseph," I whispered, "because you have a coat of many colors."

As soon as I had given Joseph a name, a fly touched down on our rock, directly in front me. Joseph eyed it but remained motionless. Then, in a flash, he struck and grabbed that fly in his mouth and disappeared over the edge of the rock, his rainbow fading to gray as he scampered away.

Alone again, I eyed the huge rope hanging from the giant live oak. Many ropes had hung from that tree since my Uncle Riley had swung out over the water and disappeared beneath Yamasee Lake. I slid down the side of my rock and kicked off my shoes. I walked through the dewy grass bordering the lake until I reached the base of the tree. I had never been this close before. I ran my hand across its rough coat, wrapped my arms around its trunk, and rested my cheek on its bumpy surface. Then I straddled the base, clamping my bare feet to its sides. Inch by inch, I boosted myself upward. Perspiration broke out on my face, and adrenaline raced through my body, propelling me toward the rope. I didn't dare look down, for fear of fainting from fright and falling to the ground. Instead, I kept my eyes on the rope ahead.

Just twenty more feet, I told myself. *Just fifteen more feet. Just ten now. Almost there. Just five more feet. That's less than my height. I can make it. Just a few more feet, and one swift heave and a swing out over the water, and, with luck, the rope will snap and it'll all be over. I'll never again have to watch my mama sink deeper into her madness. I'll never have to hear my daddy come down the stairs, angry and frustrated because he feels helpless. And hopeless.*

When I reached the rope, I grabbed it and held on tight. It was huge, bigger than my arm. But I could hang onto that rope with both hands and swing out over that lake, and the hurt I was feeling would be all over.

But my mama's hurt would go on. And on. And I would be heaping more hurt on top of her hurt. And as crazy as my mama had gotten, she didn't deserve any more hurt. And my poor daddy didn't do a thing, and he was already angry and frustrated enough, without having hurt heaped on top of that. And I knew my Granny Evadelle loved me, even if I sometimes found it hard to see that love. But she'd already lost her only son to that big old rope. Didn't seem fair to make her lose her only grandchild to that rope too.

So I let go of the rope and watched it swoop out over the lake and then swoop back. I watched it till its swoops got narrower and narrower, and eventually it just hung limp over the water. Then I inched my way backward down the trunk of the old oak tree, pausing at the bottom to hang on tight and commit this experience to memory. 'Cause I never planned to scale that tree again.

I unclasped my feet, jumped to the ground, and headed back through the still cool, wet grass to my rock. I climbed back up and lay flat on my stomach. Then I took my colored pencils and on my rock drew a perfect rainbow: red, orange, yellow, green, blue, indigo, violet. Underneath, in red, I wrote my initials, BGB. I tried to draw Joseph, all rainbow striped, but I had overestimated my artistic abilities. So I just spit on partially-drawn Joseph and erased him with the heel of my hand.

I returned my pencils to the box, slipped them in my pocket, and slid off my rock. I stepped into my shoes and picked up my bike. Then I headed back home to deal with whatever the day was planning to throw at me.

Sixteen

I never dreamed I could be happy for summer to end and for me to return to Bynum Central High School. But that summer when I was fourteen was one for the books, a you-just-can't-make-this-stuff-up sort of summer. It began with Dr. Joe Bobby going to trial for the death of his wife—a mere formality, since everybody and his brother knew full well that Dr. Joe Bobby was innocent as could be and would be out of jail just as soon as all the nonsense could be straightened out.

But, of course, that's not the way it happened. Dr. Joe Bobby was found guilty of premeditated murder and was sentenced to life in prison. Then my mama went off her ga-zip and started spending her every waking moment trying to prove that the courts were made up of utter and complete idiots and that they had gotten it all wrong.

And nothing and no one could convince her otherwise. Not Miss Delphine. Not my daddy. And certainly not me, 'cause, by then, I was completely invisible, with no powers of persuasion whatsoever.

That first morning of school, I woke up and realized that Mama had forgotten to take me on our annual shopping trip over to Savannah. Every year, right before school started in the fall, she'd take me into Savannah to buy my new school clothes and shoes. She'd let me have just about anything I wanted—within reason—and then we'd go to K&W cafeteria for lunch. I loved going to K&W because of all the choices, but each visit I'd get the same thing: fried chicken drumstick, shrimp cocktail, and green Jell-O. I had picked this for my lunch the first time Mama and I had gone school-clothes shopping, back when I was five years old. It was such a wonderful memory—my mama and me shopping just for me, me having my mama's undivided attention—that I decided year after year to eat the same lunch, in order to replicate our adventure. And it had worked—until the year my mama went mad.

I'd gone through a growth spurt over the summer, a spurt that had gone unnoticed by everyone, including me—until I started dressing for my first day of tenth grade. My jeans rode above my ankles and were hard to zip, and my tee shirt strained across my chest. My tennis shoes still fit, but they were fraying at the toes and in terrible need of a trip through the washing machine.

So I dressed for school that first day, making a note to myself to discuss a shopping trip with my mother, just as soon as she returned from wherever she'd gone.

I found Mama already at the computer when I went downstairs for breakfast. There'd be no first-day-of-school pancakes, just another Pop-Tart. And as much as I'd always loved Pop-Tarts and would have taken them over pancakes any day, they were really starting to wear on me. But I'd taken to drinking Yoo-hoo for breakfast, so there was a bright spot to my morning meal.

After eating my breakfast in the sterile kitchen, with the tick-tick of Mama's computer as background music, I headed upstairs to brush my teeth and grab my backpack.

"Bye, Mama," I said at the dining room door.

"Are you going somewhere, Briley?"

"Mama, school starts today. I'm in tenth grade now, remember?"

"Oh, my, Briley, time does fly," she said with a real far-off, wistful look on her face. Then recovering and smiling real wide, she said, "Now, you remember to find out about majorette tryouts."

Before I could assure her that I would, indeed, find out about majorette tryouts, she had returned her attention to her computer.

When I picked up my bike from where it had been resting under the magnolia tree, I noticed that my tires were getting mighty squishy. But it was better to ride on squishy bike tires than to have to ride the school bus with Kurt and all the spirit girls. I was sure that all the spirit girls had gone to Savannah with their mothers for their first-day-of-school outfits and had eaten a lunch at the K&W that they'd never forget. And I was certain that they'd be full of what-I-did-over-the-summer stories, stories that didn't include sitting through a murder trial and watching their mamas spiral into madness. So I'd endure my half-flat bike tires until I could stop by Conoco to pump them back up on my way home from school. I was just hoping I wouldn't run into Skeeter Hickman. I didn't need to hear him talk about my mama's legs, legs which, I was confident, Granny Evadelle never allowed to go to Bynum Central High School in above-the-ankle jeans.

I made it to school just in time to hear the first bell ring, signaling us to hightail it to homeroom. I slipped my bike into the last slot in the bike rack and joined my classmates as they made their way into the building. No one seemed to notice that I was wearing last year's clothes, which probably had something to do with my Power of Invisibility, but I noticed all their cute skinny jeans and fashionable tops from Forever 21 and H&M, over at Oglethorpe Mall. Still hoping Mama would remember that I needed clothes, I figured what difference did it really make, when no one would even see them? And then I started feeling guilty for thinking about something as superficial as clothes with my mama grieving so.

I headed to Mrs. Hatcher's homeroom, where, much to my angst, I found Kurt and most of the spirit squad. I took a desk in the middle of the classroom, that spot where you just blend in and never get called on. If you sit up front, you're the teacher's pet and answer every question without even being asked. If you sit in the back, the teacher notices and calls on you all the time. As I found my seat and waited for Mrs. Hatcher to give us our locker assignments and class schedules and pass out our books, I listened to the conversations swirling around me.

"Can you believe they sent him to prison?"

"Who would have thought that Dr. Joe Bobby would kill Miss Libby Beth?"

"Do you think they'll ever let him out on good behavior?"

"Even if they let him out, could he still be a doctor?"

"Well, if he could be a doctor, I sure wouldn't ever let him examine me!"

And all the girls squealed and said, "Euuuwwwwwwwww!"

I couldn't wait to escape summer and my mama and talk of Dr. Joe Bobby's trial and return to school. For what? More of the same?

I put my fingers in my ears and sang *la-la-la* in my head until Mrs. Hatcher said, "Sit down, everybody, so I can take roll."

Everybody scuffled and dodged for seats, as if they were playing musical chairs. When they finally settled all around me, I felt as if the walls were closing in and I was suffocating. I couldn't see how I was going to be able to endure an entire year of suffocation and talk of Dr. Joe Bobby and a school full of perky classmates in fashionable clothes.

But at least I was invisible.

Seventeen

"Hey, Miss Delphine."

"Hey, Briley. You doing okay?"

"Yes'm, I guess so. I just got home from school."

"Yeah, I know. I just saw you pull up on your bike."

"You want to come in for a Yoo-hoo?" I asked her.

It felt funny, me inviting Miss Delphine in for a Yoo-hoo. It was usually the other way around. But there stood Miss Delphine on our front porch, and Mama had always taught me that it was polite to invite visitors in and offer them a beverage. And since Yoo-hoo was Miss Delphine's and my beverage of choice, and since Mama had given in to that tacky drink and was keeping a stock of Yoo-hoo on hand for me, I figured it was the appropriate beverage to offer Miss Delphine when she came to visit.

To be honest, Mama hadn't really stocked my Yoo-hoo for me. Fact is, Mama didn't stock anything anymore, 'cause Mama had just given up on grocery shopping—along with anything else that didn't have to do with getting her best friend out of prison.

Instead, I'd just say, "Mama, we need some new food," and she'd say, "Then go get some money out of my pocketbook," without even looking up from the computer and probably not even realizing that she'd told me to take money out of her pocketbook. I could have taken all her money, and she probably wouldn't have even noticed. But I wouldn't have done that.

And since Daddy and I didn't know our way around the kitchen and had never taken the time to learn how to cook, I just stocked up on bologna and bread and cereal and Pop-Tarts. I'd get frozen pizza and Kraft mac and cheese—those things we did know how to cook—and, of course, Yoo-hoo. I'd buy four cartons of Yoo-hoo at a time, 'cause that's how many I could fit in my bike basket, and as much food as I could fit in bags to hang off my handle bars. It wasn't fine dining, but it kept my daddy and me fed. Sometimes we could even get Mama to eat a little something. She kinda liked Kraft mac and cheese.

"No, thanks, Briley, I think I'll pass on the Yoo-hoo," Miss Delphine told me.

"Then, do you want to come on in?"

"No, I didn't come to visit. I just came to see if you'd like to go to Savannah with me tomorrow. I haven't been out of town since I moved back here to Bynum, and I'm itching to do some shopping and eat lunch in the city. Maybe even do a little sightseeing."

"Wow, Miss Delphine. I'd really like that. Mama and I usually go over to Savannah to do my school-clothes shopping, but Mama has sorta been under the weather this year, you know."

"I figured your mama just wasn't up to a shopping trip this year, and every girl needs a trip to the city every once in a while," she said and winked at me. "Now, you ask your daddy if it's okay and let me know if you're in."

"I'll do that, Miss Delphine."

Going shopping and to lunch with Miss Delphine wasn't exactly like going with my mama, but I figured it would be right nice—certainly better than no trip to Savannah at all.

When Daddy came in from work, I said, "Daddy, Miss Delphine asked if I could go to Savannah with her tomorrow to shop and eat lunch. And maybe do a little sightseeing. You think that would be okay?"

"Sure, sure, Briley," Daddy said, already heading for Mama and sort of half listening to me.

I could have said that Miss Delphine had asked me to go on a cross-country trip to California and would it be okay, and he'd have probably said, "Sure, sure, Briley," all the while worrying about my mama.

But he had said I could go, so I ran over to Miss Delphine's house and banged on the door.

"I can go!" I told her, more excited than I expected I'd be, and said, "When you want me to come over?"

"What you say we leave around nine-thirty. That way we can get to Savannah shortly after the stores open and make a day of it.

"Sounds great!" I said and rushed back home to find something to wear on our shopping trip.

I ran up to my room and began rummaging through my closet. I thought about wearing my dress, but if I wore my dress, I'd also have to wear my flats. And there was just no way I could traipse all around Savannah for the day in those uncomfortable shoes. I'd end up with blisters the size of quarters. So I pulled out my least frayed and least high-water jeans and a yellow tee shirt with no stains. I looked down at my pitiful tennis shoes but decided they would have to do since they were my only choice, other than my pinchy flats.

I headed for the laundry room and dropped my jeans and tee shirt in the washer. Then I pulled off my grungy tennis shoes and added them to the drum. Then I poured lots of soap in and turned on the machine. At least I'd be clean for Miss Delphine's and my trip to Savannah.

I found Daddy sitting beside Mama, still wearing his suit and tie, stroking her arm and talking in a gentle voice. Guess he didn't want to spook her. She'd gotten right fragile.

"Daddy?" I said.

Looking up at me with his worried eyes, he said, "What is it, Briley?"

"I'm going to go fix us something to eat. Would you like pizza or some mac and cheese?"

"How 'bout you make that decision. Either is fine with me." I turned toward the kitchen, and Daddy said, "Briley?"

"Sir?"

"Thank you, Honey, for taking care of us. You're doing a great job."

"Thanks, Daddy," I said, nearly skipping to the kitchen, swallowing back the tears.

I decided on a pizza so that Daddy and I could eat it on the sofa in front of the TV. I'd fix us both a glass of sweet tea and set the coffee table with place mats and napkins and silverware. Then I'd turn on reruns of The Andy Griffith Show, about the only thing that could make my Daddy smile—and sometimes laugh—anymore.

When I was little, I'd watch The Andy Griffith Show with my daddy, and he'd laugh so hard at silly old Barney Fife. He'd throw his head back and laugh a great big belly laugh and pat me on the leg and say, "Briley, isn't that Barney Fife the funniest thing?"

I decided when our pizza was done, I'd sit real close to my daddy on the sofa, and we'd eat our pizza and watch The Andy Griffith Show. Maybe my daddy would laugh and pat me on the leg and say, "Briley, isn't that Barney Fife the funniest thing?"

But Daddy didn't laugh or pat me or say anything about Barney Fife. We just sort of ate in silence and let Barney be silly all by himself.

About halfway through our pizza, I said, "You know, Daddy, Mama usually takes me to Savannah every year to buy me some school clothes. Guess she sort of forgot about it this year, what with all her grief over Dr. Joe Bobby."

"Briley, I didn't know that...," he said, not sure what he was supposed to do about my mama's neglect.

"That's okay, Daddy. But you think I could have some money to get some new jeans and stuff when I go to Savannah with Miss Delphine?"

"Oh, sure, how much do you need?" he asked me, reaching for his wallet.

I had no idea how much I'd need. I'd never paid for school clothes, had no idea how much jeans and stuff cost.

So I said, "I just don't know, Daddy. I've never done my own buying before."

"Well, then," he sputtered and reached into his wallet. He pulled out his credit card, handed it to me, and said, "You just take this and get what you need."

I took my daddy's credit card from him, not quite sure how to use it. I'd never been trusted with a credit card either.

Noticing my discomfort, Daddy just smiled and said, "Briley, it's time you learned how to buy on credit."

"Okay," was all I said.

"You just swipe this through the machine when you make a purchase and sign where the clerk tells you to. And bring me all your receipts."

"Thanks, Daddy, I'll do that."

"And, Briley, if anyone gives you any trouble about using my card, you just tell 'em to call me, you hear?"

If there's any trouble, just call my daddy.

Yes, I can just call my daddy.
Call my daddy.
Call Daddy.

I could hardly sleep. Miss Delphine and I were going on an adventure, and I had my very first credit card to buy new school clothes. She and I were going to eat lunch in Savannah, and I was hoping that lunch was going to be at K&W.

And I could call my Daddy if there was any trouble.

I was up early, early enough to shower and wash my hair. After using my mama's hair dryer for the second time in my life to whip my shocking pink hair all around my head, I squeezed into my jeans and tee shirt and stepped into my frayed-but-clean tennis shoes. I headed to the kitchen for a Pop-Tart and a Yoo-hoo. When I passed the dining room, I found Mama hard at work at the computer.

"Hey, Briley. Is it bedtime yet?"

"Bedtime? Mama, it's eight o'clock in the morning. Haven't you gone to bed yet?"

"Oh, silly me," Mama said, "guess I just lost track of time. Of course, I went to bed last night. I just got up."

My mama was making no sense at all, but she hadn't made sense for a long time. There was nothing I could do about it, and I wasn't going to let her lack of sleep ruin my adventure with Miss Delphine. Daddy was home for the day, and as selfish as it may seem, I decided to let him figure out how to handle Bronwyn Gail Talmidge Beckwith.

I sat on the swing on the back porch and ate my Pop-Tart and drank my Yoo-hoo. There was a fall morning crispness in the air, and the birds were chirping and singing like crazy. I knew that Indian Summer, that sweltering September spell that sneaks back and blasts you just when you're settling into fall, would soon be upon us, but I was going to enjoy this glorious glimpse of fall while it lasted.

I watched a squirrel shimmy up Daddy's squirrel-proof bird feeder and stuff his cheeks with sunflower seeds before sliding back down the pole and racing for the base of the live oak tree. He scratched his way back up the trunk and disappeared among the branches. I could hear him up there, rustling around, probably so proud of his morning theft. But Daddy knew that old squirrel had unlocked the combination to his bird feeder, so he'd always put out extra seed for that pesky little critter.

"Oh, he's a crafty one, isn't he, Briley?" Then my daddy would laugh and shake his head, not at all sorry that that rascal had outfoxed him.

When I'd finished my breakfast, I headed on back inside to brush my teeth and find my wallet—with Daddy's credit card tucked safely away in a side zipper pocket. At nine thirty on the dot, I kissed Mama good-bye and hugged my daddy, who had just emerged from his shower and was heading for his morning coffee.

"See y'all this afternoon," I said, as I headed for the door.

"Bye, Briley. Y'all be careful," Daddy said as Mama just kept on working.

I jumped off the porch just as Miss Delphine backed her mama's 1976 Orange Chrysler LeBaron out of the garage. That 40-year-old boat was in mint condition and had just 18,000 miles on it since Mrs. Dudley drove it only to church on Sundays and to the Piggly Wiggly on Tuesdays, because Tuesday is Senior Day at the Piggly Wiggly. That's the day when everybody over 65 gets 5% off their entire purchase and a free quart of Sealtest ice cream—a flavor of their choosing.

I hopped onto tufted white leather seats and said, "Hey, Miss Delphine."

"You ready for our adventure?"

"I'm ready, and I have a credit card burning a hole in my wallet."

Miss Delphine laughed. It felt good to hear Miss Delphine laugh. I hadn't heard any laughter in my house since, well, that day we woke up to yellow crime tape all around Dr. Joe Bobby's house.

"Then let's not waste another minute. And since we're driving this big old gas-guzzling car, I think you need to find us some old music on that radio."

So I spun the dial till I found Cyndi Lauper singing "Girls Just Want to Have Fun."

"You think that's old enough?"

"Sounds pretty old to me," she laughed.

Then we rolled down our windows, cranked up the volume, and sang with Cyndi all the way to Savannah, my neon pink hair whipping about my face.

I couldn't remember the last time I'd been so happy.

We made it to Savannah in just a little over thirty minutes, 'cause as Miss Delphine says, "Why, Savannah is just down the road."

We spotted a parking space about two blocks from Needham's Department Store, and Miss Delphine, after a lot of backing and forthing, maneuvered her mama's big old orange LeBaron into that parallel parking spot.

When she finally got us all straightened out and close enough to the curb to call it quits, Miss Delphine turned off the engine and said, "That darn near wore me out. I haven't parallel parked since I left Bynum for New York City all those years ago. Why, I didn't drive a car the whole time I lived in the City. Whew!"

I decided right then and there that when I finally got my driver's license, I'd never parallel park. I'd always look for a parking lot.

We hopped out and made our way to Needham's Department Store, where we found that we had jumped feet first right into the middle of their biggest sale of the year. I've never seen so many people pushing and shoving over four-dollars-off bras and two-for-one neckties. I started to get my daddy two neckties, but I just didn't think I could tolerate the shoving.

Hanging onto my hand, Miss Delphine threaded me through the crowd and said, "Follow me. I'll find the jeans department."

Guess she had noticed my high-water britches.

I was grateful to find that there was very little shoving in the teen department, and I was able to make my way to the jeans without incident.

I figured two new pairs would do, but Miss Delphine thought different. "I think you better make that three. You just never know when we'll get back, and a girl your age needs some back-up."

So after trying on several styles and settling for low-riding, straight leg, we made our way to blouses. Miss Delphine talked me into five, one for each school day of the week. I got two tee shirts, two dressier knit tops, and one cotton blouse. After getting a new pair of tennis shoes and a pair of comfortable flats—another of Miss Delphine's suggestions—I said, "I think I'm all set, Miss Delphine."

"I think you did well, Briley. Look at all you saved coming to this grand, once-a-year sale."

And although I'd never paid much attention to the cost of clothes, even I knew I'd gotten some mighty sweet deals. I couldn't wait to tell daddy that I'd saved him a bunch of money.

"You getting hungry, Briley?"

"Yes, ma'am. Shopping can sure work up an appetite, can't it?"

"That it can," agreed Miss Delphine. "Any suggestions about where we ought to eat?"

"Miss Delphine, if it's all the same to you, I'd like to eat at the K&W? It's just up the street a ways."

"Why, I think that sounds wonderful, Briley. I've always loved the K&W. My daddy would always treat me to the K&W when he'd have to come into Savannah on business and would ask me to ride along. I have very fond memories of the place, and of those trips to Savannah with my daddy."

We wound our way through the crowds that had gathered on the sidewalk. When we reached the K&W, we found that all the sale shoppers had the same idea that we had: to eat lunch at the K&W.

"We have all the time in the world," Miss Delphine said. "Let's just enjoy our time together while we people watch."

So we made our way through the long, winding line and finally arrived at the food in around thirty minutes. By that time my stomach was growling and wanted one of everything. But I didn't get everything. Instead, I got the same thing I always got when my mama and I went school-clothes shopping in Savannah: a fried chicken drumstick, shrimp cocktail, and green Jell-O.

When Miss Delphine saw what I'd chosen and I told her the story behind my choices, she said, "It surely does look so delicious, I think I'll get the same."

We carried our trays to a small table at the back of the cafeteria and unloaded our plates and bowls. As we ate, Miss Delphine asked me all about my shopping trips with my mama. As I talked, I recalled the fun things my mama and I had done and the funny things we had said—those private jokes that only Mama and I would understand. But I told Miss Delphine anyway, and, like a true friend, she laughed at all the right places and pretended to be interested. One thing I told her was about the time Mama and I tried on a bunch of great big hats in Needham's Department Store and talked to each other in British accents. It was real funny, and Mama and I laughed until we were doubled over and could hardly catch our breath. I was happy to be with Miss Delphine, but, as hard as I tried, it just wasn't the same. She just wasn't my mama, the one who was supposed to help me pick out school clothes, the one who was supposed to make memories that only she and I would appreciate, the one who was supposed to eat at the K&W cafeteria with me, the one who was supposed to laugh with me until we couldn't catch our breath.

Even the food didn't taste as good as it did when I ate it with Mama.

When we finished our lunch, Miss Delphine folded her napkin and placed it by her plate and said, "I don't know about you, Briley, but I'm a little weary. Can I take a raincheck on the sightseeing?"

"I was hoping you'd say that, Miss Delphine, 'cause I'm kinda pooped myself."

"Then let's just head on back to Bynum, what do you say?"

I told her that sounded like a great idea.

We hauled all my bags back to Miss Delphine's car and loaded up her trunk. Then she had just about as much trouble jockeying out of that parallel parking spot as she'd had getting into it. But she finally broke free, much to the gratitude of the lady waiting for Miss Delphine's spot and all the cars backed up behind her.

As we whizzed down the highway toward Bynum, I said, "I really appreciate the shopping trip, Miss Delphine."

She reached over and patted my leg.

"It was my pleasure, Briley. I had a great time. You're an excellent shopping companion."

And it wasn't until then that I realized Miss Delphine hadn't looked at or bought a single thing for herself. That's when I understood that the trip was, and always had been, all about me.

Miss Delphine pulled up in her driveway and killed the engine. She hopped out, popped the trunk, and started loading my arms with shopping bags.

"You need some help, Briley?"

"No, ma'am, I think I can take it from here."

"Then I believe I'm going to head on in and take me a nice, warm bubble bath."

As I thanked her for the trip, she climbed back in her car and headed on down the driveway to her garage. I clutched my bags and headed on home.

"Hi, Mama," I said when I came into the house and saw my mother bent over her research.

"Hi, Sugar. Did you have a good day at school?"

"Mama, it's Saturday. I didn't go to school today. Miss Delphine took me to Savannah to shop for school clothes."

"That was nice of her," she said, as I backed out of the dining room and headed upstairs to unload my packages.

I hung my clothes in my closet, smoothing the fold wrinkles with my hands.

Then I reached in my back pocket and pulled out my phone and dropped it on my dresser. It sprang to life, and I noticed the date glowing on the screen: September 10.

My fifteenth birthday.

Eighteen

The Monday after Miss Delphine's and my shopping trip, I jumped up, ready for school. Well, not the school part, but the getting-dressed-in-my-new-clothes part. I'd never been much for new clothes—just got them because I outgrew my old ones and Mama said it was time to buy some new ones. But these new clothes were different. Miss Delphine had made a special trip to Savannah just for me, where we bought clothes and had lunch at the K&W, my very favorite place. She even ate my very favorite meal, just for me.

It was kind of like a birthday present.

On Sunday night, while Mama was hard at work on her research to free Dr. Joe Bobby from prison and Daddy had gone out in the dark for a very long run, I picked out the outfit I'd planned to wear the next morning and laid it out on my bed. Then I bit off the tags with my teeth, something my mama screeched about every time she saw me do it.

"Briley, you are going to ruin your teeth biting off those tags, and your daddy and I did not invest in those braces just to have you ruin your teeth."

But I was too lazy to go downstairs to the kitchen and get the scissors, and Mama would never know that I'd bitten off the tags.

It felt so good to put on a pair of jeans that fit. They slid right on, and I was able to zip them up without sucking in my breath and holding it real hard. And the hems even came down to my ankles, just like they were supposed to. And instead of a skin-tight, stained tee shirt, I wore one of my new blouses that fit real good and even made my boobs look a reasonable size for my age. Once I got dressed, I turned around to check out the back view in my full-length mirror. I actually blushed when I realized that my butt had gotten kind of round, like the other girls in my class. When had that happened? Guess I was just too busy thinking about my mama and Dr. Joe Bobby to notice.

I reached into my closet for my new tennis shoes and then decided, *Nah, my new outfit deserves new flats.*

So I stepped into my new flats and, for the first time in a long time, skipped down the stairs for breakfast.

"Hey, Mama," I said when I reached the downstairs hallway and found my mother already—or still—working away at her computer.

"Hi, Darlin'. Did you sleep well?"

She reached out her arms to me.

My heart raced with happiness that my mama was acting normal and in anticipation that the normal would last.

"Yes, ma'am. How about you?"

I walked into her arms.

"Oh, Briley, I slept like a baby."

I was so happy that my mama had slept like a baby. She needed a good night's sleep. She needed to hold her daughter in her arms. I needed to be comforted by her arms.

"That's good, Mama. Then how about some pancakes this morning?"

And just when I thought I had my mama back, she released me and said, "No, thank you, Sweetie, I couldn't eat a thing. I'm onto something this morning, and I just can't possibly take a break. But you go ahead, you hear?"

Then I asked her, "Mama, where's Daddy?"

"He left for his office long ago. Said he had a day full of clients."

She told me this without looking up from her break-through.

I checked the time. It wasn't even seven o'clock in the morning. My daddy didn't open his office until 8:30. My poor daddy. He'd done all he could do to help his oozing-from-reality wife, and the only thing he knew to do was escape. I just wished he could take me with him.

I trudged down the hall to the kitchen, where I did not make pancakes but, instead, grabbed my usual Pop-Tarts and Yoo-hoo.

When the time came to leave for school, I found my backpack and headed to the dining room to tell my mama good-bye.

"Bye, Mama, I'm leaving for school," I told her as I leaned down to give her a hug. I felt as if I were wrapping my arms around a bunch of bones. She hadn't eaten since I don't know when, and she had lost so much weight and had gotten terribly frail. And my mama, who always smelled like gardenias, smelled rank and unwashed. But she looked up and smiled, her eyes ringed in purple, her lips dry and cracked.

"Bye, my Darlin'. I love you."

I had to run for the door, so she wouldn't see me cry. I leapt off the porch and grabbed my bike from the ground. I jumped on and careened out of the driveway, barely missing Kurt and the spirit squad, who were waiting for the school bus. Don't think they even noticed. How could they? I was invisible.

Somewhere between home and Bynum Central High School, I lost interest in my new curves and new clothes. I still appreciated Miss Delphine's kindness, but life just seemed heavier and more complicated than new clothes. And as I picked up speed, the tears blew out of my eyes, disappearing behind me.

I went through the motions of classes and lunch, sitting alone in the cafeteria, trying to choke down a pimiento cheese sandwich. After lunch I went to P.E., a class I barely tolerated. I went to the girls' locker room, where I found all my classmates prancing around in their bras and panties, preening and posing. I don't know who they were trying to impress. It's not like the rest of us hadn't seen bras and panties before. I located my locker and pulled out my gym uniform. After changing my clothes, I headed for the gym, where I found that we were going to be playing dodgeball. I hated dodgeball. I was a good dodgeball player, but why would I want to deliberately hit someone with a ball? It seemed so inhumane.

When class officially started and all the rest of the girls dribbled out of the locker room, Coach Gail yelled, "Step on it! Class has started. If you don't want detention, you better line up, two teams." After my classmates jockeyed and jostled to be on the team with their besties, Coach Gail said to me, "Beckwith, you're up!" and tossed me the ball.

As I said, I didn't like throwing a ball at people, but that morning something just seemed different about dodgeball. Something felt different about me. I couldn't put a name to it, but something had just shifted inside me. When all the players on the other team started jeering at me, saying I couldn't hit 'em, calling me names like weakling and klutzy, something snapped. Now, trash talk is just part of playing dodgeball, and I've even dished out my share of trash. But, like I said, something felt real different that morning. And when that something inside me snapped, it snapped so hard I could almost hear it go *boing*. I could feel the heat rising in my face and my heart beating in my ears. My teeth were clenched so hard it was making my jaw hurt, and my eyes were stinging from holding back tears.

Angela Joyner is a big girl with a big mouth, and she was louder than the rest of the class that morning. She jeered and twisted up her face at me, and when I heard that thing snap and go *boing* inside me, I just don't quite know what happened. But I lost it, and I reared back with all my might and let that ball fly with all the force I had in me, aiming straight for Angela Joyner's nose. That ball was soaring so fast that she didn't have time to dodge or duck, and my shot found its mark, dead center.

Angela crumbled to her knees, and I did the same. Blood exploded from her nose as she grabbed her face and wailed. Her teammates gathered around her as she toppled over and rolled around on the gym floor, the blood oozing from beneath her hands. Then I heard a high-pitched keening, which I naturally assumed was coming from Angela.

But then everyone was crowded around me, and Coach Gail was saying, "What happened, Briley? Are you okay? Calm down, Honey. It's all right. Breathe, Briley, breathe."

But that keening just wouldn't stop. It just went on and on, getting higher and louder, while the faces of my classmates started to swirl and blur above me.

I woke up in the nurse's office. There was a cold compress on my head, and Miss March, the school nurse, was taking my blood pressure.

"You okay, Briley?" she asked me when she saw me open my eyes.

"I don't know. What's going on?"

"You tell me. What happened in the gym?"

"I don't know, Miss March. Can I go, please?"

"Briley, you need to stay here until we're sure you're okay, until you tell us what provoked your outburst."

"I don't know. I guess just all the screaming and heckling…"

"Now, Briley, you know that's part of the game."

I didn't say a word because I knew that to be true. It was so much more than that, but I wasn't willing to go there. I was afraid if I started talking, I'd just fall down a hole, a deep, dark hole, and I would never be able to climb back out.

And then my daddy was there and I was crying in his arms and he was saying, "It's okay, Honey, it's okay." And he just let me cry and cry, for as long as I wanted. When I finally slowed to a snuffle, he reached into his back pocket and pulled out his handkerchief. He handed it to me and said, "Now, you dry your eyes and blow your nose while I go talk with Miss March. Okay?"

"Okay, Daddy."

I watched him leave Miss March's office and saw them meet up out in the hall. I could tell my daddy was talking real serious-like to the school nurse, and she shook her head knowingly and looked toward me with a pitying look in her eyes. I looked away real quick, anger creeping up the back of my neck. I didn't want to be pitied. I didn't want people to know about my mama's research, didn't want them to know that she had gone batshit crazy. I didn't want people to know that my daddy was leaving for his office hours early, just to get away from the craziness at our house.

Finally Daddy and Miss Marsh came back in the office, phony grins pasted on both of their faces.

"Well, Briley, looks like it wasn't too serious," Daddy said, "and Miss March says you're free to go. How'd you like a chocolate soda? Just you and me."

I just shook my head and said, "How's Angela?"

Miss March smiled real sweet and said, "She's going to be just fine, Briley. I'll let her know you asked."

"Thanks. Please tell her I'm real sorry."

"I will."

"Then let's go get that soda," my daddy said, real cheery, like I hadn't just bloodied my classmate's nose with a dodgeball.

"I gotta go get my clothes and my backpack."

"Okay, Briley, I'll wait out front for you."

I hustled to the gym locker room, my eyes trained on the floor. I was certain people were staring at me and whispering that I'd gone berserk in gym. So I ducked in the locker room, grabbed my clothes out of my locker and stuffed them in my backpack, and headed for the door, still wearing my gym clothes.

I found Daddy waiting by the front door.

He headed toward his car, and I said, "Daddy, I have to get my bike."

"Your bike? I thought you rode the school bus."

"Not for almost a year."

"Oh," was all he said.

So we wrestled my bike into the back of Daddy's car, and we headed for The Soda Shoppe, which is an original name, if there ever was one. We both ordered chocolate sodas, our favorite, the flavor we always got on Sunday afternoons when he and I would go to town for a soda. But we hadn't been to town for sodas on Sunday afternoon in a very long time, probably not since that day they found Miss Libby Beth dead in her bed.

"I'm so sorry, Briley," Daddy said, but I was just too spent to respond. And maybe I was just too sad and too mad and too confused to accept his apology.

We drank our sodas in silence and walked to his car without even looking at each other.

"Hop in," he said.

"No, thanks, I'll take it from here," I said and started dragging my bike out of the back of his car.

He helped me haul it to the ground and said, "You sure?"

"I'm sure."

I hopped on and rode off in the direction of home. And during my ride, I came to yet another realization: my outburst had destroyed my invisibility shield. In order to maintain my Power of Invisibility, I'd have to try not to make any sudden moves, keep my mouth shut, and ignore that *boing* when it went off inside me.

When I got close to our house, I could see my mama standing out beside the mailbox at the end of our driveway. She was wearing her nightgown.

I pulled up alongside her and said, "What you doing out here in your nightgown, Mama?"

"Waiting for the mailman."

"What are you expecting from the mailman?"

"A letter from the Innocence Project."

"Okay," I said and rode my bicycle into the yard, dropped it under the magnolia tree, and went on in the house to take off my new clothes and hang them up to wear for another special day.

Nineteen

I woke up Saturday morning and realized the sun was up. I'd slept right through my going-to-the-lake time. That whole week I'd been so tired from the dodgeball incident, that I'd gone to bed real early each night and had slept real hard. The night before I'd gone to bed without my usual bedtime snack, and I was paying for it with a grumbling, ravenous stomach. I needed Cheerios. Or Pop-Tarts. Maybe both.

I stepped out of bed, and without even peeing, washing my face, or brushing my teeth, I grabbed my book and headed downstairs to the kitchen. I had gotten as far as the landing at the top of the stairs when I heard my mama and daddy talking.

"But, Kyle, I have to."

"Why, Bronwyn. What happened?"

"Kyle, nothing has happened. It's just destiny. It was meant to be. Don't you understand?"

"No, Bronwyn, I don't understand. You're my wife."

"But Joe Bobby is my soulmate," she wailed. "Always has been."

"Bronwyn, I know that you and Joe Bobby have a special bond, that you've been best friends all your life. But I believe your judgment is being clouded by your emotions. Joe Bobby is in prison for murdering his wife," Daddy said, trying to reason with her.

As if reasoning with Bronwyn Talmidge Beckwith was an option. Since Dr. Joe Bobby had been convicted of murdering Libby Beth and been sent over to the penitentiary at Reidsville, my mama had lost all sense of reason, had slipped off the edge of the earth into the abyss. She spent Sunday through Friday sitting at the computer doing her research and Saturdays visiting Dr. Joe Bobby in jail. She'd fill notebook after notebook with illegible scribbling, which she swore was the key to her best friend's freedom. She'd then take her files to the penitentiary to show him just how hard she was working on his behalf.

Daddy and I continued to eat bologna sandwiches, pizza, or mac and cheese for supper while Mama refused to eat much of anything and, instead, chewed her nails down to the quick, drawing blood, and clacked away on her computer keyboard, putting together the puzzle that would spring her dearest friend from his lifetime of incarceration. She became a shadow of her former majorette self, and Daddy threatened to put her in the hospital if she didn't eat something and didn't stop her obsessive research.

"Kyle, there is absolutely nothing wrong with me. I am merely helping Joe Bobby. You and I both know that he is innocent of killing Libby Beth, and I'm going to prove it."

"But, Bronwyn, you just can't keep on going like this, not eating, not bathing, not sleeping. Why, Darlin', I'm afraid you're going to die if you don't take care of yourself," Daddy said, so much pain in his saying.

But my mama didn't die. Instead, she decided that she needed to leave my daddy so that she could devote her entire life to freeing Dr. Joe Bobby. And there was just no changing her mind.

"But, Bronwyn, where will you go?"

"I'll be moving into Joe Bobby's house, of course."

"Does he know about this, Bronwyn, or are you just inviting yourself into his home?"

"Certainly he knows, Kyle. And why wouldn't I be moving into his home?"

"For one thing, Bronwyn, it doesn't belong to you. And, for another, this is where you live."

"But, Kyle, this won't be my home after Joe Bobby and I get married, now will it?"

"Married?" my daddy screeched. "Bronwyn, the man is serving life for murder, and you plan to marry him?"

"Kyle, he will not be spending his life in prison because I am working diligently to prove his innocence. And he won't be spending another minute in jail once he and I say *I do*. When we are married, people will understand. They'll know that surely Bronwyn Gail

Talmidge would not marry a man who had murdered his wife."

I couldn't breathe. My heart was on fire, and the top of my head felt like it was crawling with ants. I lay down on the landing and closed my eyes, willing my parents' conversation to go away, to rewind, to never have happened. But it wouldn't rewind, and the two of them just kept on talking—Daddy trying to reason with Mama and Mama insisting that she knew exactly what she was doing and that she didn't need to be reasoned with.

Finally I was able to find my breath and fill my lungs until they felt as if they would explode. My feeling was that I needed to save up as much air as I could, just in case I found myself unable to breathe again.

I wobbled to my feet, dropped my book on the stairs, and screamed as loudly as I could, "Stop it! Both of you stop talking right now!"

Then I ran down the stairs, not looking into the living room at my squabbling parents, and out the front door in my pajamas and made my way over to Miss Delphine's. I left the door wide open and let the screen slam with a bang behind me. By the time I'd jumped off the porch and streaked through the hedge between our house and Miss Delphine's, I was gasping for air.

"What it is, Briley?" Miss Delphine said when I pounded on the door and screamed, "Please, Miss Delphine, I need to come in. Right now."

"Darlin', you look like you've seen a ghost. Come on in here right this minute."

She grabbed her untied kimono shut and shuffled along on the backs of her bedroom slippers. Apparently, I'd caught her unfit for company, but that was of no concern to me at that moment. I needed Miss Delphine, needed her bad.

"Now tell me what's going on."

"Mama and Daddy," was all I could say before I busted out crying. I tried to talk through my blubbering, but all that would come out was gibberish.

"Just hold on right there a minute," Miss Delphine said when she pushed me down on the sofa and shuffled real fast down the hall in her half-on, half-off bedroom slippers.

While I waited, I heard Miss Delphine's opera coming from the kitchen, its wails mixed with my wails. We did not make a pretty duet, and in that tragic instance, I realized that opera still hadn't grown on me.

When Miss Delphine returned, she was toting a wet washrag. First she wiped my steaming face with it, and then she folded it up and held it on the back of my neck.

"Okay, when you can get ahold of yourself, you tell me what's going on and why you look so scared. Something awful must have happened to you, Sweetie," she said, laying her cool hand against my fiery cheek.

"Mama...," I squeaked and then commenced to bellowing again.

"Just take your time, Briley. We have all day."

Miss Delphine rubbed my back real gentle-like.

But every time I tried to tell her what I'd overhead Mama and Daddy talking about, I'd just bust out crying again.

"It's all right, Briley. It's all right, Darlin'." Then when I just wouldn't stop crying, she asked, "Would you like for me to go get your mama?"

"No!" I screamed. "I mean, no, ma'am," I said, 'cause if Bronwyn Gail Talmidge Beckwith had taught her daughter anything at all, it was to be polite. Too bad that woman didn't take her own advice. "I don't want to see my Mama. She's the cause of all this," I said, pounding my fist on my leg.

"Okay, Briley, you lie right down there on the sofa and calm down while I go cool off your washrag for you. I won't go get your mama, and you don't need to talk till you're good and ready."

I lay down like she told me to, my tears dripping on one of her fancy, fringed pillows. I wiped my eyes and then my runny nose on my pajama sleeve, while my crying slowed to a hic-hic.

When Miss Delphine came back, I figured I could talk, and I did want to tell her what had happened. Why, that's the reason I'd come over to her house in the first place. So I sat up, took the washrag from her, and wiped my face real good.

"My mama."

"What about your mama, Briley?"

"She's leaving, leaving my daddy. And me, too, I suppose."

"Briley, I'm so sorry. I know it won't help to say these things happen so often in families, but sometimes people just grow in different directions and it's hard to keep a marriage together. That's the reason I never married. Didn't think I'd be very successful at it," she said, smiling wistfully and wiping my hair away from my steaming face.

"But, Miss Delphine, it's not just that my mama is divorcing my daddy, she's divorcing my daddy so she can marry Dr. Joe Bobby."

"What?" Miss Delphine screeched and jumped up from the sofa. Then she sat down again real quick, saying, "I'm sorry, Briley, you just took me by surprise. I'll try real hard to keep an open mind about this."

An open mind? How could anybody keep an open mind about a woman leaving her husband for a man serving life in prison for murdering his wife? There was nothing reasonable or rational about it. It was just so crazy that I was sure when my Granny Evadelle found out, she'd say, "Well, Bronwyn has finally gone off her ga-zip."

"Thanks, Miss Delphine, that's awful thoughtful of you to try and keep an open mind, but I won't hold you to it in this instance."

When she was sure I was about as calmed down as I could be under the circumstances, she went into the kitchen and got me a Yoo-hoo. I heard her pop the top, and then she shuffled back into the living room and handed me the cold bottle. I held it up against my hot cheek, took a deep breath, and closed my eyes. It felt good to cool the heat that was festering in me.

I took a gulp of my Yoo-hoo and leaned back against Miss Delphine's soft, squishy, flowered sofa and thought about the situation I was in. I had finally succeeded in my quest for invisibility. And, it appeared, my family was going to become invisible too. What was I going to do? I was just fifteen years old, and fifteen year olds aren't supposed to figure out stuff like that.

I was still sitting there on Miss Delphine's sofa, pondering the situation, when the grandfather clock in Miss Delphine's parlor struck noon, and I heard Miss Delphine say, "Briley, Honey, you really need to let me fix you something to eat."

Twenty

There was just no dissuading Mama. Daddy, sweet and accommodating man that he was, just couldn't reason with her. And when Father Caleb down at the Holier-than-thou Episcopal Church couldn't reason with her either, the two of them had no choice but to call in the big guns.

I heard her coming a mile away. Granny Evadelle's big old green Cadillac came roaring down Magnolia Street and careened into our driveway on two wheels. She was out of the car before it could come to a halt. She flung her pocketbook over her shoulder and slammed the car door so hard, you'd have thought it was the car she was mad at. Then she came stomping up the sidewalk onto the porch, marching right on in the house without knocking, breezing right past me without even seeing me, which was no surprise to me at all, seeing as how I was invisible.

"Hey, Mother," my mama said, looking up from her computer research. She acted all bright and cheery, like her mother had just stopped by for tea or to invite her to go shopping for Sunday shoes.

"Don't you *hey, Mother* me, Bronwyn Gail Talmidge Beckwith," Granny Evadelle screeched and slammed her pocketbook down on an end table, sending Mama's Lladro angel flying across the room, knocking one of her wings clean off. The loss of an angel wing, though, seemed minor compared to Granny Evadelle's anger. "I am not here on a social visit, young lady. Have you completely lost your ever-lovin' mind?"

"Calm down now, Mother," my mama cooed.

"Don't you dare tell me to calm down. I will not calm down. What in the world has gotten into you to make you behave like a bloomin' idiot, Bronwyn? There was nothing in your raising that would cause you to act like a lunatic. And there's absolutely no mental illness on my side of the family. You surely must have gotten that lunacy from your father's side, God rest his soul."

"You're just being dramatic now, Mother," my mama clucked and smiled, tossing her unkempt hair and flashing a dimple.

"The very impudence!" my grandmother wailed. "If I could, I'd turn you over my knee and switch some sense into you."

But Granny Evadelle did not switch my mama, and nothing she said could make her change her mind. Mama just kept that I'm-not-all-there smile on her face, that smile that gave me the willies and caused the hair to stand up on my neck, and assured Granny Evadelle that she was following her destiny and that nothing anyone said or did could sway her from marrying her soulmate, Joe Bobby Tisdale.

That having been settled with all who had tried to knock some sense into her, Mama took her computer, her notebooks of research, and the clothes from her half of the closet and moved her center of operations downtown to Dr. Joe Bobby's house.

And while all this chaos swirled around me, no one asked what I wanted to do or where I wanted to go. It was just decided for me: I would continue to live with Daddy during the week at our house on Magnolia Street, while staying with Mama at Dr. Joe Bobby's place on weekends.

At first I just kind of wandered around in a confused state, but when all the dust settled and I could see the situation for what it really was, I missed my mama something dreadful when I wasn't with her. The house just felt like it had lost its Bronwyn aura, its electricity, and that loss of electricity just left me feeling limp and empty, with a hole in my heart. But, strange as this may sound, it turns out I missed her even when I was with her on weekends at Dr. Joe Bobby's house. That's 'cause she was so totally immersed in her research that she didn't even notice that I was around.

When suppertime would come, I'd say, "Mama, you hungry?" and she'd turn from the computer just long enough to smile and say, "Sure, Sugar, why don't you get some money out of my pocketbook and go get us a pizza."

I'd grab a twenty out of her wallet and ride my bike down to Pizza House—Bynum's version of Pizza Hut, since the real Pizza Hut wanted nothing to do with Bynum—and get us a half pepperoni, half veggie pizza, light sauce, extra cheese, just the way Mama liked it. When I'd get back, all ready to eat supper with my mama, she'd say she'd lost her appetite. Or she had more research to do.

So during the week I missed my mama, and on weekends I missed my mama while I ate pizza alone and watched her work away at her computer.

I'd say, "Mama, let's go to a movie," or "Mama, aren't we going to church this morning?" or "Mama, don't you want to watch TV?"

Her answer was always the same: "Sure, Sugar, just a few more minutes. I believe I'm about to make a break-through."

But each break-through just fizzled and never amounted to anything, except more piles of paper with her chicken scratching.

Mama remembered that she had left Daddy for Dr. Joe Bobby and filed for divorce, something I was hoping she'd forget to do until her mind returned and she came on back home to Daddy and me where she belonged. But that didn't happen. So while she was waiting for her divorce from Daddy to be finalized, she started planning her jailhouse wedding to Dr. Joe Bobby.

How she talked Dr. Joe Bobby into marrying her, I just can't imagine. But Bronwyn Gail Talmidge Beckwith can be awfully persuasive; when she wants something, she pretty much gets it. Like being a majorette. And homecoming queen. But this was a whole lot different than majoretting. Guess Dr. Joe Bobby figured he didn't have anything better to do and what'd he have to lose. And since Mama insisted on divorcing my daddy anyway, he may as well marry his best friend since forever. 'Cause she was certainly the only person who was standing by him while he sat in jail, accused of killing his wife.

Mama had envisioned a white gown and a cake and all, but she found out, much to her dismay, that formal weddings were not allowed in prison. All she'd be permitted was a justice of the peace asking Mama and Dr. Joe Bobby to say "I do," after which Dr. Joe Bobby would go directly back to his cell and Mama would have to go right home.

"Well, I knew we wouldn't be afforded a honeymoon," Mama said real snippy-like, "but I thought they'd at least let us have a little celebration with cake and punch in honor of our love."

But Mama would not settle for just a simple *I do.*

The legal system might be able to tell her what kind of wedding she could have, but no one could tell Bronwyn Beckwith how to dress to marry her one-and-only soulmate. So Mama went over to Savannah to Needham's Department Store where she got herself a white silk suit and an honest-to-god white bejeweled bridal veil. And to go with her suit and veil, she purchased some white four-inch peep-toe platform heels. When she got home from shopping, I was waiting on the front porch, my weekend visit having begun three hours earlier.

"Briley, I'm so glad you're here," she said, as if she hadn't expected me and hadn't noticed that she'd kept me waiting for three hours, locked out of the house. "Help me get my purchases out of the car, will you? Then I'll try on my weddin' ensemble for you. Won't that be fun?"

I didn't respond. She didn't notice.

"Come on upstairs with me," she cooed, and I reluctantly followed.

When we reached Mama's bedroom—the bedroom that used to be Dr. Joe Bobby and Miss Libby Beth's, the bedroom where Miss Libby Beth was found dead in her bed—Mama began shedding her shopping clothes, leaving them in a limp pile in the middle of the floor. When she got down to her bra and panties, I whimpered at the sight of what my mama had become. She had lost so much weight, that her once taut skin now hung in wrinkles across her middle and around her thighs. I could easily count her ribs, and her pelvis bones jutted out at her sides. Her once round boobs had shrunk till her bra looked practically empty, and her bikini panties were held up only by her sharp pelvis. She didn't seem to notice—her transformation or my horror.

"Briley, I just can't wait for you to see my weddin' outfit," Mama giggled, as she wrestled her purchases out of their wrappings.

She teetered back and forth in front of me in her platform heels, wedding suit, and veil, stopping at each turn to admire herself in the full-length mirror. She'd turn and smile and toss her hair and even wink, as if I weren't there to witness her strange show. She didn't even notice the bones and angles that had replaced her curves. She didn't realize that her legs looked like long, skinny Barbie legs stuck into those tall, clunky shoes, or that her new suit hung on her as if she were a coat hanger. She didn't see the purple circles beneath her eyes, her cracked lips, or her limp hair that was starved from lack of nutrition. I recognized then that my mama was fading away, sinking into some strange hole. I wanted so desperately to find a way to pull her back, to make her Mama again, to make her well again, to make her sane again.

The Saturday morning of the jailhouse nuptials arrived. Mama had been unsuccessful in getting Granny Evadelle to stand up for her when she married Dr. Joe Bobby. Granny Evadelle was still angry with her daughter for her foolish behavior, and she refused to budge until Bronwyn Gail Talmidge Beckwith came to her senses and admitted that she had acted like the lunatic Granny Evadelle proclaimed her to be.

"Bronwyn," her mother told her, "I will not be a party to this insanity. You go home to Kyle and Briley where you belong. Then I'll stand up for you."

But, of course, Mama ignored her and moved forward with her plans to become Mrs. Joe Bobby Tisdale.

And since Mama couldn't even convince Miss Eulalee, Dr. Joe Bobby's mother, to attend *that sham of a wedding*, which she called it, their only attendee would be me, and only because I really had no choice in the matter. What's worse, Mama even made me put on my one-and-only dress. Fortunately, I had new flats that didn't put quarter-size blisters on my heels.

The morning of the wedding brought a chilly breeze and a huge downpour. But Mama was not deterred. She actually took a shower, shaved her legs, and washed her lank hair. She dressed in all her wedding finery and covered it with her raincoat. Then she slipped plastic garbage bags over her shoes and secured them with rubber bands around her frail ankles. She rustled her way out to the car, and we set off for the wedding venue.

Dr. Joe Bobby was waiting for us, wearing his regular prison garb—khaki pants and a khaki-colored tee shirt. Mama had suggested a tux for the occasion, but the prison system nixed that idea. The happy groom looked anything but happy; his eyes were hollow, and his mouth was a grim slash. Mama didn't seem to notice as she shed her outerwear and took her place beside Dr. Joe Bobby in front of the Justice of the Peace.

The whole ordeal lasted no more than five minutes. It was so short, my mind didn't even have time to wander, the way it did during Sunday sermons. After the so-called ceremony, Dr. Joe Bobby was allowed a quick kiss with Mama before being shuttled right back to his cell. Mama heaved a huge sigh, but the smile, outlined perfectly in crimson, stayed in place. We drove back to Bynum in silence, Mama's painted-on smile never wavering.

Weekend after weekend I'd go stay with Mama, only to find her with each visit farther and farther down her tunnel, and me unable to drag her back.

Each Saturday morning she'd dress in her best outfits, which now hung like shapeless sacks on her gaunt frame, and slather make-up on her hollow cheeks and baggy eyes. Forcing a smile, she and I would drive the hour and a half to the penitentiary, so that she could spend the hour that she was allowed each week with her husband. She'd work to keep her fragile smile in place while she entertained Dr. Joe Bobby with all the trifling Bynum news and the latest on her research. Dr. Joe Bobby tried to appear appreciative, yet all the while he was unable to mask his misery. Was Dr. Joe Bobby regretting his marriage to my mama? That look of gloom said everything about his current situation was one great big regret.

I sat to one side and read, attempting to escape the melancholy that engulfed my mama and step-daddy's new marriage.

In between her brief prison visits, Mama filled more notebooks with indecipherable scribbles. She ate little and seemed to sleep none at all. She remained transfixed by her computer.

One weekend I fixed myself a bowl of Cheerios and accidentally knocked it off the counter, breaking the bowl and scattering cereal and splashing milk all over the kitchen floor. I stepped over my mess and headed for the garage for the mop, broom, and dustpan. When I opened the garage door, I gasped and jumped back. There I found boxes, hundreds of boxes, unopened and stacked floor to ceiling, front to back. I made my way into the chaos of cardboard to find out what it was and where it had all come from. Each box was labeled either QVC or HSN. There were boxes of vacuum cleaners, at least four by my count. I found several boxes of expensive cookware, three microwaves, a convection oven, two blenders, a Kitchenaid mixer, and three Cuisinarts. There were boxes of sheets and towels, as well as bedspreads and matching curtains—more than there were bedrooms to accommodate them. There were rugs and lamps and tables. Some smaller boxes held clothes, purses, shoes, jewelry, and perfume. I felt a chill of terror. Where had all this stuff come from? And why was it in Dr. Joe Bobby's garage?

I made my way back through the maze of boxes to the house, forgetting the mop and broom and the mess I had made in the kitchen. I ran to the living room and found Mama exactly where I'd left her, glued to her computer screen.

"Mama?" I said, tentatively, careful not to agitate her in her fragile state.

"What is it, Briley?" she asked, not looking my way.

"What's all that stuff in the garage?"

"Oh, that. I'm just preparing for Joe Bobby's return."

By obsessively shopping? By hoarding? Apparently research wasn't the only thing she had been doing on her computer. She must have been streaming QVC and HSN, as well, and shopping like a mad woman.

"What do all those boxes have to do with Dr. Joe Bobby's return?" I asked her, so confused.

"Briley, I'm going to have to cook and clean for him when he gets home, aren't I?"

"And all the clothes and jewelry?"

Then she looked at me real coyly and said, "Well, I do need to look all pretty for my husband, don't I?"

"But, Mama, how are you paying for all that stuff?"

"Briley, Joe Bobby is rich. He has lots of money, just lots and lots."

"But what happens, Mama, if you spend all of Dr. Joe Bobby's money?"

"No need to worry, Briley. When Joe Bobby gets out of prison, he can just make some more."

I felt my heart ache like someone had just punched it, and I found it real hard to breathe. I had tried to deny it for so long, but I finally had to accept the situation for what it was. It was official: my mama had finally gone batshit, lunatic, over-the-edge, end-of-the-road, down-the-tunnel, off her ga-zip crazy.

Twenty-one

"Miss Delphine."

Miss Delphine hadn't answered when I knocked on the door, but I knew she was home 'cause her big orange car-boat was in the garage. And Miss Delphine didn't leave home without her car-boat. So I just stuck my head in the door and called.

I could hear opera coming from the radio in the kitchen and a muffled voice coming from somewhere in the distance, so I crept on down the hall, calling, "Miss Delphine, you okay?"

"Yeah, I'm fine," she yelled. "I'm up here in the attic. Come on up."

I took the stairs up to the second floor and found the attic stairs unfolded and resting in the hall. I climbed the sagging, creaky steps and found Miss Delphine sitting on the attic floor, a green crocheted shawl draped around her shoulders, a brightly colored, appliqued skirt fanned out all around her. Her storm cloud of hair looked electrified, billowing out around her head, as if it were excited about something.

When my head appeared above the attic floor, Miss Delphine smiled at me and said, "Couldn't handle school today?"

"No, ma'am, I just can't concentrate with my mama going all crazy right in front of my eyes."

Rather than trying to reason with me or figure it out—Miss Delphine had stopped trying that long ago—she just said, "Come on over here and sit then. I have uncovered a treasure trove of long-forgotten memories."

Then she dived head-first into a huge steamer trunk and

rummaged around. Soon she emerged with an armload of memories. Dumping it all on the attic floor, she reached into the pile and pulled out something wrapped in crumpled, discolored tissue paper. Peeling away the frail wrapping, she uncovered a dainty little yellowed, lace baby dress.

"Look, Briley, it's my christening gown. And here's the little Charleston bonnet I wore with it. Have you ever seen one of these?" she asked, handing it to me.

"No, ma'am, I don't believe I have."

I fingered the sweet little bonnet, unable to imagine Miss Delphine's head ever being small enough to fit into it.

"It's made of linen hankies. Little girls wore them for their christenings, and when they grew up, they'd take the bonnet apart and carry one of the hankies in their weddings."

"That's neat," I said, turning the bonnet over and looking at the delicate lace, the tiny stitches.

"Yeah, but I guess I'll never be carrying a hanky down the aisle. But we won't let it go to waste. I'll give it to you when you have a little girl."

"I'd love that, Miss Delphine."

"Then I'll hold on to it for you. No need rushing things," she said, giggling.

I agreed that I had no plans to have children any time soon and got up to wander around her huge attic, filled with shelves of books and picture albums and clothes and furniture. There were old toys and games and even boxes of seashells.

I found a hat box full of fancy old hats that I figured had once belonged to Miss Delphine's mama. But I had a hard time imagining Mrs. Dudley wearing anything as fancy as flowered and sequined hats, since I'd only seen her in a grey house dress with an apron over it, except on Sundays when she didn't wear her apron.

"Did these hats belong to your mama?"

"Sure did. Hard to believe, isn't it?" she asked, like she'd read my mind. "I always thought my mama was born old. Then I found all these dresses and hats."

"They're real pretty. Where'd she wear this stuff? It doesn't look like Bynum wear."

"Sure doesn't, but my mama didn't always live in Bynum. She grew up in Savannah, and she went to cotillions and debutante balls.

She had planned to go to college and move up north and become a career woman."

"What happened?"

"My daddy happened," she said, in a pinched-lip sort of way.

"I don't know what that means, Miss Delphine."

"Well, Briley, my daddy sweet talked my mama and convinced her that she should be married to him, keeping house over in Bynum, rather than being an educated career woman up North. Apparently, he was quite the smooth talker when he was a young man."

I don't have much experience reading grown-ups' emotions, other than my mama and daddy, and sometimes I'm not real good at that. But something about the way Miss Delphine said that about her daddy made me think she was harboring a whole bunch of bitterness.

Then looking up at me with red-rimmed eyes, Miss Delphine said, "Briley, don't you ever let a boy sweet talk you into giving up your dreams to take care of him, 'cause it'll just leave you with a lifetime of resentment."

"Okay, Miss Delphine," I said, hoping that if the time ever came, I'd remember Miss Delphine's advice. Then I said, "Miss Delphine, is that why you moved up North, 'cause your mama wasn't able to?"

Then she peered off in the distance with a kind of wistful look on her face. "I never put that into words, Briley, but I believe that was part of the reason. My daddy did not want me to move away, said no daughter of his would live up there in that god-forsaken place. But Mama, she told me to follow my heart; otherwise, I'd never be happy. Guess she was trying to tell me that she'd never been happy, which made me real sad for her. And sad for me, since her only child hadn't been able to make her happy.

"My daddy was really angry that my mama put all those New York ideas into my head and encouraged me to go chase my dream. But she wouldn't back down, wouldn't obey him. She said it was too important. That put a wedge between my mama and daddy that I don't believe was ever fixed."

Shaking her head, Miss Delphine said, "Sorry, Briley, don't know what made me go on so. It's been ages since I've thought about my mama's shattered dreams and her encouraging me to follow mine. Just don't you let any old sweet-talking boy rob you of your dreams."

"Okay, Miss Delphine, I promise."

Getting back to my plundering, I lifted the lid of a cardboard box and found what looked like colored rocks—all blue and green and yellow and purple. I picked up the box—it was real heavy—and hauled it over to where Miss Delphine was sitting, still sifting through her treasures.

"Hey, Miss Delphine, what's this?" I lifted the lid so she could see what was inside.

"Oh, that's sea glass."

"Sea glass? Is that sort of like seashells?"

"No, not exactly. You see, seashells are made by nature, but sea glass is only cultivated by nature."

I didn't understand any more now than I did before I'd asked the question.

"What does that mean, Miss Delphine?"

"Briley, sea glass is not found in nature. It actually starts out as regular old glass bottles and jars that, somehow, end up in the ocean. They get all tossed around by the currents, and they break into smaller pieces. Then over the years, maybe even as many as fifty, those pieces of glass get all polished and the sharp edges get rounded out by salt-water currents and sand till they are as smooth as those pieces in that box."

"Where'd you get 'em?" I asked, while I rubbed a cool, smooth blue piece of sea glass over my cheek. It was hard to believe that it had once been a jagged, sharp broken piece of bottle at the bottom of the ocean, waiting patiently for years to become smooth enough to rub on my cheek.

"I collected sea glass all the time I was growing up. Big Mama, that's my mama's mama, had a summer home over on Tybee Island, and I used to go visit her every chance I'd get. She's the one who taught me how to find the very best, most colorful sea glass."

"And how'd she do that?" I asked her, hoping she'd offer to teach me too.

"You can find your best sea glass and shells too, where currents from opposite directions come together. They'll crash into each other, churning up all sorts of sea life, spewing it into piles out on the sand."

"That's neat, Miss Delphine. I sure would like to see that."

"Would you, Briley?"

"Yes'm, I most certainly would. I think this sea glass is about the prettiest stuff I've ever seen. And how it came about is most fascinating," I told her, still rubbing the smooth, blue pebble of glass against my cheek.

"I find, Briley, that the best time to hunt for sea glass is early in the morning, just as the sun comes up."

"Why's that?"

"If you wait till later, you run the risk of other collectors finding it first or high tide washing it all back out to sea."

"I can get up early, Miss Delphine."

"Well, then, Briley, we'll just have to take us a road trip out to Tybee, maybe pack us a lunch to spread on a quilt and eat on the beach, watching the waves and listening to the surf. You never know, we may just see a school of dolphins frolicking off shore."

"Miss Delphine, you make it sound like so much fun. I wish we could go right this minute!"

"Not this minute, Briley, but soon. I promise."

Twenty-two

Soon came in about a week.

Miss Delphine picked me up on a Saturday, over at Dr. Joe Bobby's house. I woke up well before daylight, so Miss Delphine and I could be out to Tybee—about an hour away—just when the sun was coming up.

When I came downstairs all dressed and ready to go, I found my mama already—or still—doing research. At first I thought I shouldn't leave her since I had so little time to spend with her, but I figured she probably wouldn't even realize I was gone. By that time she had lost track of time, even days, and always seemed surprised when I showed up on Friday afternoons. I assumed she'd be going to the penitentiary to see Dr. Joe Bobby—if she could remember that it was Saturday—but I certainly wouldn't mind missing a Saturday and going, instead, to Tybee Island with Miss Delphine to collect sea glass.

When Miss Delphine pulled up out front, I grabbed two pouches of Strawberry Pop-Tarts, two Yoo-hoos, and my jacket and headed for the door.

"Bye, Mama," I yelled. "See you later."

"Bye, Sugar. Have fun."

"Morning," Miss Delphine said when I jumped into her car-boat.

"Hey, there, want a Pop-Tart?"

"Think I'll pass, but I will have one of those Yoo-hoos you got there."

I unscrewed the tops and handed her one, as I took a swig and a bite of my Pop-Tart. We turned off Azalea street onto Main and saw Melvin Crone sitting under the street light in front of Mr. Jensen's drug store. The Savannah Times newspapers had been dumped on the sidewalk, waiting for Melvin to come along and bag them and toss them up on all the subscribers' porches. I waved as we passed, and Melvin just bobbed his head in greeting. We headed on out east of town in the direction of Savannah, and I remembered the time, not too long ago, Miss Delphine and I had taken that trip to Savannah to shop. We had so much fun. At least, I had so much fun. I was hoping that our trip to Tybee Island to hunt for sea glass was going to be fun too.

Heading toward the coast, directly into the sunrise, I could see the horizon begin to turn from black to dark purple. Soon it would fade to lavender, then pink, and finally gold, when the sun would start to peek over the edge of the earth. I used to see that happen when we'd visit my Daddy's mama in Charleston, and Daddy would take Mama and me out to Folly Beach early in the morning, just to see the sun come up. It was the most beautiful sight I'd ever seen. I figured I'd never again go to Folly Beach with my mama and daddy to watch the sun come up.

"You think we better hurry, Miss Delphine? We don't want anybody to get there before we do and get all the good sea glass."

"We'll be fine, Briley. There'll be plenty of sea glass for us."

But what I didn't tell her was that I wanted to hurry and get to the beach so that I could watch the sky turn from black to deep purple to pink and then to gold, and watch the sun peek over the edge of the earth—even if I couldn't see it with my mama and daddy.

By the time we reached Savannah, though, the sky had already turned to purple, and when we hit the road to Tybee, it had turned a beautiful gold. We would soon be staring directly into the morning sun. But that was okay. There would still be sea glass.

We drove the length of Tybee Island, heading for the south end, to a cove where Miss Delphine was certain there'd be plenty of colorful sea glass. The sleepy island was still asleep, for the most part, except for a few early-morning joggers and several old men in windbreakers and cotton trousers headed for the diner, the only establishment on Tybee Island open at that hour of the morning.

We found a parking spot with ease, since the orange car-boat was the only vehicle on the road at that hour.

"Here, Briley, grab these collecting bags and this old quilt. I'll get our picnic basket from the trunk of the car."

Once we'd gathered all our gear, we headed toward the beach.

There's something about the beach that always takes my breath away. It's not like I've never seen it before, but it always seems like such a surprise to me every time I see it: the beautiful stretch of smooth, white sand; the ocean reaching for as far as you can see, blue this morning but sometimes angry gray; the powerful waves, making deafening sounds as they crest and crash to the shore. As Miss Delphine spread our quilt on the sand, I just stared in wonder at how anything so perfect, so powerful could be so real.

"Beautiful, isn't it, Briley."

"Yes, ma'am, there's just nothing more perfect."

She stood and stared with me for a good long while before she said, "I guess we'd best head on to the cove before someone else beats us to the best sea glass."

As we trudged in the loose sand toward the cove, sea gulls soared overhead, sometimes swooping so low that Miss Delphine waved her arms and cried, "Shoo! We don't have anything for you. Go find your breakfast somewhere else."

Yet, they continued to follow us to the cove. When they finally realized that Miss Delphine was telling the truth and that we really didn't have anything for them, they soared off, I assumed to search elsewhere for their breakfast.

I thought we would find a huge mound of brightly colored sea glass, glistening in the morning sun, just waiting for us to scoop it up and take it home. Instead, we came upon a pile of shells, driftwood, seaweed, Styrofoam cups, a single flip-flop, a deflated pool toy, a plastic shovel, and several beer cans. I'm sure my disappointment showed.

"Come, Briley, help me pick up all this litter so that we can start sifting through the sand for our treasures."

We gathered all the cans and cups and other junk and carried them to a trash can at the edge of the sand. Then we returned, fell to our knees, and began sifting.

There were beautiful shells: whorled conch shells, shiny brown-spotted cowries, sand dollars, starfish, and just regular old scallop and clam shells. Some were bleached white, while others were vibrant shades of rose, green, and purple.

"Look, Miss Delphine! I've never seen so many shells. Can we have some of these too?"

"Of course, we can. Think how pretty they'll be, displayed in your room. Just put them right there in your bag."

As I gathered several still-hinged clam shells and gently placed them in the bottom of the bag, I spotted it: my first piece of sea glass. It was aqua blue, like the water of the Caribbean that I had seen in magazines. I reached down and picked it up. About two inches long and an inch wide, it was cool and smooth to the touch, polished to a frosty finish. I brushed off the sand and held it to my cheek, closed my eyes, and rubbed it round and round in circles.

"Look what you've found, Briley. It's gorgeous!" Miss Delphine cried.

I leaned forward and handed it to her.

"This is a winner. Perfection. Great find. Keep on looking. I'm sure there's a whole lot more."

We unearthed milky blue and deep jade, rich amber and amethyst. By the time we had sifted through the mound of treasures, we had filled our bags half-full, the sun was high in the sky, and our backs ached from our morning of stooping.

"What you say we head on back to our quilt for some lunch?" Miss Delphine said, rising and kneading her stiff, aching back.

I had no idea what time it was, but considering the sun was pretty high in the sky, I figured it was getting on toward noon. The mention of lunch made my stomach rumble.

We headed back to our quilt and Miss Delphine's cooler of food. She had packed chicken salad sandwiches, apples, dill pickles, and chocolate iced brownies.

Miss Delphine's chicken salad is the best in the world. I don't know what makes it better than anybody else's, and I just don't want to know. I want to believe that she puts some magic ingredient you can get only up in New York City. Her secret ingredient is probably something like Duke's mayonnaise, but, like I said, I'd just rather think it's magic.

Miss Delphine unwrapped our sandwiches and put them on paper plates. Then she doled out pickles and sliced apples.

"Want some water?"

"Sure," I said, reaching into the cooler for a frosty bottle.

We ate in silence and listened to the waves crashing on the shore.

The ocean was hypnotizing, and soon I felt myself getting droopy.

Miss Delphine shook me from my trance when she said, "How's your Power of Invisibility working out?"

"I think I've just about got it perfected, Miss Delphine."

"You like being invisible, Briley?"

I didn't answer her for a long time 'cause that's a really heavy question. It deserved a lot of thought before I said anything, and Miss Delphine knew it. So she just let me ponder.

Finally I told her, "You know, Miss Delphine, sometimes I like it, and sometimes I don't. When you're invisible, nobody can hurt you. Least, that's what I tell myself."

"I see," was all she said and took a bite of her sandwich.

"Sometimes being invisible can get mighty lonely, though. Sometimes I wish Whitney Burroughs would come back from New York and be my best friend. But I know that isn't going to happen, 'cause her daddy was transferred and Whitney already has new friends."

"Briley, Whitney isn't the only friend in the world. Have you tried befriending anyone else at Bynum Central High?"

"Miss Delphine, I've thought about that very thing, but that's harder than you might think."

"How's that, Briley?"

"Well, have you ever jumped double-dutch?"

"Do you mean jump rope?"

"Yes, ma'am, except it's jump rope with two big ropes."

"So…?"

"Well, when you jump double-dutch, you stand off to the side and shuffle your feet back and forth, waiting for that split second when you can jump into the middle of the ropes. If you go too soon or go too late, those ropes can sting your legs bad. They can even tangle up in your feet and fling you face down in the dust on the school playground. Yeah, making friends is kinda like double dutch. And, Miss Delphine, I just don't think I can run the risk of getting my legs burned or ending up face down in the dust."

"Briley, I understand that it can be hard. Why, can you imagine getting tossed into New York City all by yourself? Believe me, it wasn't easy. But it was something I wanted to do, had to do, so I put myself out there and made some really good friends. It was worth the risk."

But I knew I wouldn't try to make friends down at Bynum Central High. From the looks of things, everybody was already buddied up, and it didn't look like there was room for a fifth wheel. At least, I didn't want to run the risk of finding out. Just didn't think I could take falling face first in the dust. And I already had too many things that were stinging my legs.

Twenty-three

Saturdays would come, and Mama and I would drive to the penitentiary at Reidsville to visit Mama's husband, my step-daddy, Dr. Joe Bobby. If it wasn't embarrassing enough that Bronwyn Talmidge Beckwith, three-time State Champion Twirler, had left her husband and my daddy for a convicted murderer, I had to be a part of their Saturday visits, which were none too festive. The one saving grace was that I didn't run into anyone I knew out at Reidsville, except for Dr. Joe Bobby. And, thank goodness, I had my books and my iPad. As long as I had my nose in whatever I was reading, Mama and Dr. Joe Bobby pretty much ignored me and all but forgot I was there. That's not to say that Dr. Joe Bobby wasn't polite and welcoming. He's always been most kind to me—well, to everybody—but he had other pressing issues on his mind. Yet I was still convinced their ignoring me had something to do with my Power of Invisibility.

So Saturday after Saturday I'd make the long, boring trip with Mama, and Saturday after Saturday I'd sit in the corner of the visiting room, reading a book, while Mama and Dr. Joe Bobby had their sad, chaste, brief visits.

On one such sad, boring visit, I was still trying, unsuccessfully, to wade through *Fifty Shades of Grey* when I heard Mama say, "I didn't mean for it to turn out like this, Joe Bobby."

"I know you didn't, Bronwyn," Dr. Joe Bobby said.

"I'm so sorry."

I could hear the catch in my mama's throat, as she breathed a real heavy sigh.

"I know that, Bronwyn, but you couldn't help it."

"Joe Bobby, it was supposed to look like suicide."

When I heard my mama say that, my breath caught in my throat, and I just froze. I inched my iPad down so I could peek over the top. Mama looked at Dr. Joe Bobby all sweet and innocent-like. Dr. Joe Bobby just looked confused, with his face all scrunched up and questiony.

He finally squeaked out, "What do you mean, Bronwyn?"

"You know…Libby Beth. A suicide. I planned it to look like a suicide."

"You planned it?"

"Well, yeah…"

"Bronwyn, I don't understand what you mean by you planned it."

"Joe Bobby, I researched it on line and thought I had all the details worked out."

"Details? What details, Bronwyn? What research?"

"Suicide, silly. I read all about suicide, figured I could make it look like suicide. And I almost did."

"How, Bronwyn?" Dr. Joe Bobby croaked, his face an ashen color.

"Joe Bobby, I planned it for when you were going to be out of town on purpose. I figured that way they'd never suspect you, 'cause, as you know, they always suspect the husband. And then you had to go and leave your camping trip on that very night," Mama said real exasperated-like, as if Dr. Joe Bobby was to blame for things turning out the way they did. "I told Kyle I was going to bridge club, got all dressed up like I normally do. But, instead, I drove over to your and Libby Beth's house." Then she added real coyly, "My house now."

"Then what, Bronwyn?" Dr. Joe Bobby said, trying to keep his voice real level.

"Well, I'd put some plastic sheeting and garbage bags and gloves in the back of my car. So before I went in the house, I put the garbage bags on my feet and wrapped myself in the plastic sheeting. Then I slipped on the gloves. That way, I figured I wouldn't leave any prints or get any blood on my clothes." And then she whispered, "You know, from the potential splatter."

"I see."

Dr. Joe Bobby gritted his teeth, making the muscle in his jaw jump up and down. I could tell he was trying real hard to control himself.

Apparently, Mama didn't even notice 'cause she just kept on talking.

"Course, I didn't need a key, seeing as how I've had a key to your house since when you and Libby Beth moved in."

"That key was for emergencies, Bronwyn."

"Well, this was an emergency," Mama said, real testy. Regaining her composure, she continued, "Everything seemed to go just fine. Looked like suicide to me. Just guess I didn't consider the trajectory."

"The trajectory…" Dr. Joe Bobby croaked.

"And there's the thing about left hand, right hand. I could have sworn Libby Beth was left handed."

I watched the blood drain out of Dr. Joe Bobby's face and the muscle jump in his jaw. Mama just sat there smiling at him, like she'd done something to be real proud of.

"But why, Bronwyn?" he stammered.

"Why what?"

"Why did you read about suicide? Make it look like suicide? I don't understand, Bronwyn. Why did you feel the need to kill Libby Beth?"

I could tell by Dr. Joe Bobby's reaction that he finally realized he was dealing with a very unstable woman. What I don't understand is why he hadn't seen it long before. It was right there, slapping him in the face.

"For us, Joe Bobby," Mama said, reaching across the table for my step-daddy's hand.

He flinched and pulled away, like Mama had scrubbed her feet across a nylon rug and then shocked him with the static electricity.

"But, Bronwyn, why did you think I'd want you to do such a thing…for us?"

"Joe Bobby, you know that Libby Beth was just in the way. You and I were meant to be together all along. And we just couldn't be, as long as she was hanging around."

"You killed my wife, Bronwyn, and then let me go to prison for her murder."

"As I just said, Joe Bobby," Mama told him, all exasperated-like, "I didn't mean for it to happen that way. And if you hadn't gone and left that campsite, nobody would have even suspected you 'cause you'd have had an air-tight alibi. But, no, you had to go and screw things up."

The look of bewilderment on Dr. Joe Bobby's face matched my own confusion and astonishment.

"But you let me stay here in jail all this time, knowing I was innocent."

"But, Darlin', I've been working night and day to get you out," Mama cooed at him.

"And just how were you planning to get me out, Bronwyn?"

"Now, Joe Bobby," my mama snapped, "if I knew that, you wouldn't still be sitting here in prison, now would you?"

Dr. Joe Bobby was still looking like somebody had just slapped him right across the face when a prison guard stuck his head in the door and said, "Time's up, folks. Sorry, ma'am, but you're gonna have to leave now."

Mama stood, straightened her skirt, and leaned forward to kiss her husband good-bye. Dr. Joe Bobby didn't move a muscle, just stared at the floor. When he made no attempt to meet her halfway, Mama just kissed him on the forehead and said, "Cheer up now, Darlin', I'll have you out of here real soon. I just don't know how yet.

"Come along, Briley," Mama said over her shoulder, as she sashayed out the prison waiting room door, like confessing to murder was something she did just any old day of the week.

Seems Mama didn't have to figure out how to spring Dr. Joe Bobby out of prison, after all.

The sheriff's car was sitting in the driveway when we got back from Reidsville to Dr. Joe Bobby's house. As we pulled up to the garage, the driver side door of the cruiser opened, and out stepped Sheriff Peegram. A rather portly gentlemen, he hiked his trousers up under his protruding belly as best he could. His helper, whose name I didn't know but his face I recalled seeing in Aunt Sal's Donut Shoppe, stepped out and came around the front of the car. He rested his hand on the pistol at his side.

"Hey, Bronwyn," the sheriff said as he walked toward Mama. "Briley," he said, nodding toward me when he saw me get out of the car. But that's all he said in my direction.

"Hey, Burford, what you up to? Collecting money for the class reunion?"

"No, Bronwyn, me and Hal here," he said, pointing to his helper whose name I didn't know until then, "have come on official business."

"What official business?" my mama said, looking from Sheriff Peegram to Hal's hand on his gun.

"Can we go inside where we can talk?" Sheriff Peegram said, coaxing Mama toward the house.

"Sure, Burford, come on in. I'll fix us some tea," Mama said as I trailed behind.

As soon as we got inside, Sheriff Peegram turned to Mama and, with a heavy sadness in his eyes, said, "Bronwyn Gail Talmidge Tisdale, you are under arrest for the murder of Libby Beth Tisdale. You have the right to remain silent. Anything you say can and will be used against you in a court of law. You have the right to an attorney. If you cannot afford an attorney, one will be appointed for you."

Hal stood there in the hallway, rocking back on his heels, his hand still on his pistol, while Mama looked at Sheriff Peegram as he read her her rights.

"Bronwyn, do you understand what I just said to you?"

"Why, yes, I do, Burford," was all Mama said, quite matter of factly.

"Good, Bronwyn. Then you're just gonna have to come along with us down to the station."

"Burford," Mama sort of laughed, "that won't be at all necessary. I'll just stay right here till y'all need me. I promise I won't go anywhere. Why, I have no place to go."

"That's not possible, Bronwyn. We're gonna have to cuff you and take you in," the sheriff said, as Hal took his cue, released his gun, grabbed his cuffs, and, with a flourish, clamped them on Mama's wrists.

Then Sheriff Peegram turned to me and said, "Briley, you need to call your daddy to come get you."

"Mr. Peegram," I said, "my daddy is up in Charleston visiting my Aunt Clarice."

"You got any place you can go to? I don't want you staying here all by yourself."

"Yes, sir, I believe I can go over to Miss Delphine's house for the time being. I'm sure she won't mind."

"Good," said the sheriff, "we'll drive you on over just to make sure."

"But I got my bicycle. I can ride it over to her house."

"Briley, you just leave your bicycle here. You can get it later. We'll take you on over to Delphine's."

"Yes, sir," I said, not sure what was going to happen next and real scared to find out.

While Sheriff Peegram opened the front door of his official car for me to get in, Hal the helper opened the back door, put his hand on my mama's head, and sort of shoved her in the back seat.

"Scoot over," he said to her and got in the back seat beside her.

Along the way we didn't pass a soul we knew. I was glad. I didn't want anybody seeing me sitting in the front seat of the sheriff's car and my mama sitting in the back. When we got to Miss Delphine's house, Sheriff Peegram and I got out of the car and headed for the porch. I was too afraid to look back at my mama. I didn't want to see her sitting in the back seat of the sheriff's car, wire mesh holding her in.

"Afternoon, Delphine," Sheriff Peegram said and tipped his hat. "Can I speak to you for a minute? In private?"

"Sure, Burford," Miss Delphine said, eyeing him sort of suspicious-like and then peering out toward his car sitting in the driveway. Then she smiled at me and said, "Briley, why don't you go on in the kitchen and get you and me a Yoo-hoo. Burford, can I interest you in a Yoo-hoo?"

"No thanks, Delphine. I'm here on official business. Maybe some other time."

I guess while I was in the kitchen, Sheriff Peegram filled Miss Delphine in on the facts, but I couldn't hear what he was saying over that dang opera. But when I got back to the hall where Miss Delphine and Sheriff Peegram were standing and talking, she said, "Briley, I understand your daddy is up in Charleston."

"Yes, ma'am. He drove up there this weekend to see Aunt Clarice. He won't be back till tomorrow."

"Then I'm going to call him and let him know what's going on. In the meantime, you're just gonna be staying right here with me. Now, you run on in the parlor and drink your Yoo-hoo, and I'll be there in a minute."

While I was sitting on the parlor sofa, trying to drink my Yoo-hoo but not really having a taste for it at that time, I could hear Miss Delphine and the sheriff talking in hushed tones. I just couldn't make out what they were saying.

Finally I heard them moving toward the front door and Miss Delphine saying, "Now, Burford, I expect you to keep me posted on what's going on. Briley is in a fragile state, you know, and I need to be kept abreast, for her sake. You hear?"

"Yes'm, Delphine. I understand. I'll let you know what's what."

When she came into the parlor after seeing the sheriff out the door, she sat down beside me on the sofa and took me in her arms. There was just so much she could have said to me, but, instead, she chose not to say a single word. I'm glad that was her choice. I just needed for her to hold me real close and real quiet-like.

Words just wouldn't do.

Twenty-four

They'd just put Mama in the county jail when I woke up one night with a start. I saw a red glow at my window and thought, for sure, our house was on fire. I thought to myself, *Hasn't enough happened to my daddy and me without our house burning down?* I jumped up and ran to the window, ready to scream, "Daddy, wake up, the house is on fire!"

But instead of a house on fire, there was an ambulance sitting next door in Miss Delphine's driveway, its red lights spinning round and round. I ran across my bedroom, jumped into my tennis shoes on the run, and screamed, "Daddy, get up, something is wrong with Miss Delphine. Hurry, Daddy!"

I took the stairs three at a time, threw open the front door, clomped across the porch, and jumped to the ground, ignoring the steps. I sprinted across our yard and through the hedgerow to the ambulance and peered in. There was no Miss Delphine inside, so I headed toward her house. As I was running, I tripped on my shoelace and nearly fell flat on my face. While I stumbled and staggered to stay on my feet, Miss Delphine's front door opened, and a man in a dark blue uniform backed out of the house, pulling a stretcher after him. I ran up the steps to find Miss Delphine lying on the stretcher, an oxygen mask covering her face.

"Miss Delphine, it's me, Briley. What's the matter? What happened?"

"Miss," the uniformed guy said, "you're going to have to step aside so we can get the stretcher to the ambulance."

"But what's wrong with Miss Delphine?" I screamed.

"We can't say just yet, Miss. You're just going to have to move out of the way so we can take care of your friend."

I followed behind and watched the guy and his partner load Miss Delphine into the back of the ambulance. Once they had her in and situated, I started climbing in after her.

"Miss, you'll have to get out of the ambulance."

"No, I'm going with her."

"But only family can ride in the ambulance."

"She doesn't have family. No one. Not a single living soul. I'm as close to family as she's got. You can't stop me from going with her."

The EMT guy, who looked bigger and more menacing than he had before I started sassing him, took a deep breath, but before he could say anything else, I heard someone say, "Let her go, please."

I turned to see my daddy standing in the driveway, wearing just his pajamas and his bare feet. He smiled at me and shook his head.

Then he said, "You go on with Miss Delphine, Briley. I'll meet you at the hospital in a little while, just as soon as I can shower and put on my clothes."

I just shook my head at him, tears of fear now standing in my eyes.

Daddy and the ambulance guy exchanged a knowing look, and he said, "Okay, Miss, but you'll have to sit over there so we can work on your friend on the way to the hospital."

"Yes, sir."

I'd agree to anything, just as long as he'd let me ride along to the hospital with Miss Delphine.

I sat where the guy, whose name turned out to be Guy, told me to sit, close enough to reach Miss Delphine's hand. I picked it up, and it felt limp and bony and cold. It scared me so bad.

I whispered, "Miss Delphine, I'm here," and she gave my hand a real weak squeeze.

The guy who was Guy's helper got into the driver's seat and started the siren. Guy closed the back door to the ambulance, and we took off in the direction of the hospital. I looked out the back window at my daddy standing in Miss Delphine's yard. He stood right there, watching the ambulance drive away with me in it. I watched him till we turned left on Amaryllis Court and I lost sight of him. Then I turned my attention to Guy, who had stayed in back by Miss Delphine and went to work taking care of her.

He hooked all kinds of wires up to her and did all sorts of stuff to her, all the while saying real loud, "Stay with me, Miss Delphine. Hang in there. We're getting you to the hospital. You're doing great, Miss Delphine."

Bynum General is out west of Bynum about ten minutes from my house, but that was the longest ten-minute ride I've ever taken. I thought we'd never get Miss Delphine to that hospital. Guy's helper must have called ahead, though, because there were two people waiting at the emergency room entrance, a man and a woman, both wearing blue scrubs, waiting to help take care of Miss Delphine. Guy and the two hospital people took her on her stretcher out of the ambulance and whisked her into the emergency entrance.

I ran alongside, but when we got to the check-in desk, the woman in the scrubs who had been waiting for Miss Delphine said, "Honey, this is as far as you can go. You can sit over there in the waiting room, and someone will come get you when we've gotten your grandma stable."

"She's not my grandma. She's my best friend."

I must have looked and sounded terrified, because the woman put her hand on my shoulder, smiled, and said, "Don't worry. We'll take real good care of your best friend." Then she turned and followed the stretcher down the hall and through some swinging double doors.

I crossed the lobby to the waiting room, where I chose an orange, plastic molded chair. I liked it better than the green, but not by much. I was the only person in the waiting room at that hour, which happened to be 3:57 in the morning. Fluorescent lights buzzed and flickered overhead, and the intercom crackled with frantic words I could not understand. There was a TV with the sound turned off hooked way up high on the wall, and there was something on the screen about a desert in the Middle East. I couldn't tell what the reporter was saying because of the sound being turned off and because I couldn't read lips. Someone should have suggested closed captioning to the hospital if they weren't planning to provide any sound for the people who were waiting in fear in their waiting room.

But the program didn't look very interesting anyway, so I started thumbing through the magazines on the table beside my chair. What they say about outdated magazines in hospital waiting rooms is true. I found a Popular Mechanics, a Redbook, and Parenting, all dog-earned and tattered, all several years old. I thumbed through the Redbook to find many of the pages bearing holes, I'm guessing where coupons had once lived. I hadn't taken time to put on my glasses before rushing over to Miss Delphine's, so I couldn't read the tiny words too well. I squinted real hard but figured that old magazine wasn't really worth my squinting. So I put it back and wiped my hands on my pajamas, wondering how many sick people had thumbed through those same magazines in the past few years. I looked around for a bottle of Purell but couldn't find one.

There was a big red soft drink machine and a snack vending machine in the corner. I could have used a soda, but I hadn't brought any money with me.

I heard the air conditioning roar to life, and I instantly felt the chill. I pulled my knees up to my chest and buried my bare arms between my legs. I shivered—from cold and from fear.

"Honey, are you all right?" I looked up to see a gray-haired lady wearing a pink smock standing over me.

"Yes, ma'am. I'm just waiting for my friend. They took her back there on a stretcher," I said, pointing down the hall.

"You look cold, all folded up like that. Would you like for me to see if I can find you a blanket?"

"Yes, ma'am, that would be nice. I'm real cold. I shouldn't have come off without my jacket, but I just didn't have time to think."

"I understand. I'll be right back, Sugar."

As I sat and shivered, lights flickered, the air conditioner whirred, and the TV screen moved silently through the Middle East.

"Here you go, Honey. I heated it up for you."

She wrapped a wonderfully warm blanket around me and tucked it under my feet and legs.

"Thank you, that feels good."

"Would you like a soda while you wait?"

"Thank you, but I didn't bring any money."

"My treat," she said, moving toward the drink machine and fishing for change in her smock pocket. "What'll it be?" she asked, looking back over her shoulder.

I peered past her to the machine and scanned my choices.

"A Dr. Pepper, please. I think I'd like a Dr. Pepper."

"A Dr. Pepper it is," she said, as she fed the machine with coins and punched the button.

When she brought my drink to me, she asked, "Would you like a snack?"

"No, ma'am. A Dr. Pepper is fine. But thank you for asking. And thank you for the drink."

"My pleasure, Honey. I'll be right over at that desk if you need anything."

"Yes, ma'am," I said and took a sip of my soda, wishing that reporter would get out of that desert and into some place I wanted to see.

"Briley, are you okay?"

I looked up to see my daddy standing by me. I don't know why, but I just started crying at the sight of him. He crouched beside me and put his arms around me.

"It's okay, Honey. She'll be all right. They'll take real good care of her."

I put my head on my daddy's shoulder. He smelled so good, like tooth paste and after shave lotion. He had showered, shaved, and dressed for work before coming to the hospital. And it wasn't even five o'clock in the morning.

Looking up into his eyes, I said, "What next, Daddy?"

"I just don't know, Briley, but we'll take it as it comes. We're strong. Right?" he said and chucked me gently on my chin with his fist.

"I guess so, Daddy," and, holding out my Dr. Pepper, I asked him, "You want some? That lady over there bought it for me."

"Thanks, Briley," he said, taking it from me and having a sip.

"Here," he said, handing me a paper grocery bag, "I brought you a change of clothes and your jacket. And your tooth brush and comb. And your glasses. And I put your phone in there too."

"Thanks, I could use the jacket. It's cold in here, and my warm blanket is cooling off."

"Any word about Miss Delphine?"

"No, sir. Some lady promised someone would tell me as soon as they know something."

"In that case, we'll just sit here till time for you to go to school. I'll take you on my way to my office."

"Daddy, please don't make me go to school today," I begged. "Miss Delphine might wake up and need me."

Squinting his eyes and thinking about that for a second, Daddy said, "You're right, Briley. In this case I believe Miss Delphine is more important than school. You just stay right here today and look out for her." Then he patted me on the leg and said, "You want me to stay with you for a while?"

"Thanks, Daddy. I'd like that."

He sat in the chair next to me, and I leaned my head against his arm. I needed to feel him, just to make sure he was still there, and to smell his after shave lotion.

I dozed against my daddy until, at 8:00, he shook me gently and said, "Briley, I'm going to have to head on to the office. You sure you're going to be okay here by yourself?"

"Yes, sir, I'll be fine. I just want to be here when Miss Delphine wakes up."

"I understand." Then reaching into his wallet, he pulled out a twenty-dollar bill and said, "Here's some money for you to get something to eat. Please make sure you eat, you hear?"

"Yes, sir, I will."

Taking the bill from him, I dropped it into my paper bag of clothes.

"Now, you call me if you need me. In fact, you call me even if you don't need me. Okay?"

"Okay."

I knew that I could call my daddy whenever I wanted, that he'd stop whatever he was doing to talk to me; but I really needed to hear him say that he was there for me and wasn't going away and leaving me. He got up and kissed me on the top of my head and patted my back.

"You're a good girl, Briley. Sorry I don't tell you that enough. And I'm so sorry for what you've had to go through."

Giving my back one last pat, he smiled at me and headed out the emergency door. I turned and watched him walk across the parking lot, get into his car, and drive away. He turned as he passed by, saw me sitting in the window, and gave me a thumbs up.

"Miss?"

I looked up to see a man in scrubs standing over me.

"Yes?"

"Are you here with Delphine Dudley?"

"Yes, sir."

"I'm Dr. Balfour. I've been caring for Miss Dudley. We have

stabilized her and moved her to a private room. She is still quite groggy and won't be able to communicate with you just yet, but you may go to her room if you'd like. It would probably do her good to have you there when she wakes up."

"What's wrong with her, Dr. Balfour?"

"Well, Miss…"

"Briley. My name is Briley."

"Briley, because of HIPAA regulations, I am not at liberty to discuss Miss Dudley's diagnosis or condition with you. If she wishes to divulge this information when she awakens, then that will be fine. In the meantime, just be there for her."

"Yes, sir," I said, rose, picked up my paper bag of belongings, and followed Dr. Balfour.

When we reached the check-in desk in the lobby, Dr. Balfour said to the woman who had bought me the Dr. Pepper, "Edith, will you kindly direct Briley to room 402?"

"Of course, Dr. Balfour."

"Thank you, Edith," he said and disappeared through a set of stainless swinging doors.

"Sweetie, take that hallway right there to the elevators, which will be on your right, about halfway down. Go to floor number four. When you get off at four, turn right. Once you pass the nurses' station, turn left. Room 402 will be the last room on your right."

"Thank you, Miss Edith," I said, and headed for the elevator.

When I got to Room 402, I tiptoed in to find Miss Delphine lying in bed, looking peaceful and calm. Her hand no longer looked bony and waxy and frail, the way it had looked in the ambulance. I was so relieved. She looked just like her old self that drank Yoo-hoo, blew smoke circles, watched French movies, listened to opera, and liked it when I skipped school to keep her company.

Seeing as how she was sleeping and I couldn't do her any good while she slept, I took my grocery bag of clothes into the little bathroom attached to Miss Delphine's room so I could get dressed. 'Cause it was the middle of the morning by then and I still had on my pajamas.

I closed the bathroom door gently, but it still made a squeak. I figured somebody ought to tell the maintenance guy to bring his WD-40 up there and fix that squeak so it wouldn't annoy any sick people. I sat on the john and peered down into the bag that my daddy had brought me. Lying on top were my favorite, well-worn, needed-a-good-washing jeans.

Daddy was always saying, "Don't you think those jeans need a good washing?" and I'd tell him, "They'll let me know when they're ready, Daddy."

And Daddy always trusted my jeans' judgment.

He must have searched real hard to find my favorite jeans among all the clothes that I'd tossed on my bedroom floor.

Beneath my jeans was a tee shirt that daddy had bought me in an airport gift shop while he was on one of his business trips. On the front it said PI R ROUND. He had thought it was so funny when he'd seen it and had said when he gave it to me, "Just a little mathematical humor." He still thought it was funny and hadn't noticed that it was getting awfully snug on me. Perhaps he just didn't want to admit that I was growing up. Maybe he just wanted us to keep sharing our own little private math joke.

At the bottom of the bag he had put a bra and my pink and green striped thong. Daddies are not supposed to have to pack their daughters' underwear. I picked them up, still neatly folded, and felt the tears sting my eyes. I was lucky to have a daddy who would pack underwear for me. I bet most daddies didn't even know where their daughters kept their thongs.

I shed my pajamas and slipped on my thong and bra, which I was finally filling out, and pulled my tee shirt over my head. I stretched real hard to loosen it up a bit and then climbed into my comfy jeans.

Daddy had also packed a baggie with my deodorant, tooth brush, tooth paste, and a comb, along with my glasses and phone. Daddy hadn't missed a thing. I reached up under my tee shirt and rolled my deodorant around my pits and flapped my arms for it to dry. There's nothing I hate worse than deodorant sticking to my tee shirt. Then I brushed my teeth real good, 'cause you can never brush your braces too much. Those things are hard to clean. I ran a comb through my hair and dropped my pajamas and the rest of my stuff in my brown Piggly Wiggly bag and rolled it down real tight. I thought about cleaning my glasses but didn't really care how smudged they were, so I just stuck them on my face and squinted through them. Good enough. Then I tiptoed back into Miss Delphine's room and sat in the chair beside her bed and waited for her to wake up.

"Briley?"

I woke with a start. I hadn't intended to fall asleep.

"What are you doing here, Honey?"

"I came with you in the ambulance, Miss Delphine."

"You've been here all this time?"

"Yes, ma'am."

"Thank you so much," she said, reaching for my hand.

I was relieved to find that it felt just normal.

"What's wrong, Miss Delphine? Are you going to be okay?"

"Well, apparently, I had a mild heart attack. Guess that means there was a definite attack but that it resulted in no permanent damage. This time."

"Whew, that's a relief. So you're going to be okay?"

"Yes, Briley, I'll be okay, but they'll need for me to stay overnight, just to keep an eye on me for a little while."

"Yes, ma'am, I understand."

"Looks like I'm going to have to clean up my act, gir'friend," Miss Delphine said and chuckled.

"Yes, ma'am, I think you're right about that."

"Guess I'm going to have to give up my cigarettes."

"Yep, the cigarettes are going to have to go," I said, shaking my head in resignation.

"But I'm sure going to miss my smoke circles, Briley."

"Me, too, Miss Delphine, me too."

Twenty-five

Word spread real fast about what my mama had done. All of Bynum was struck dumb.

"Not Bronwyn Talmidge!"

"I thought she and Libby Beth were tight as ticks."

"You never know what a person will do for love."

"That girl had everything! So smart. And so pretty."

"Best nurse in all of Bynum."

"Why, she was even the State Twirling Champion—three years in a row, I believe."

Like being State Twirling Champion—three years in a row—would prevent somebody from committing murder.

"I seen her down at the Piggly Wiggly a good while back. I could tell some'pm wudn't quite right. Couldn't put my finger on it, but she just didn't seem all there. You know what I mean? Just some'pm was off…"

Then they'd cluck their tongues, shake their disbelieving heads, and say, "This is just gonna put Miss Evadelle in an early grave. Gonna kill her, for sure."

But the one that got me the most was, "Whatever is going to come of that poor child of hers?"

So I just invoked my Power of Invisibility, kept my eyes down, didn't make any sudden moves, and tried not to hear what was swirling all around me. I did have a diversion, though, as I was scheduled to shed my braces and transition from my thick glasses to contact lenses. Somehow, though, my mama's recent incarceration had thrown cold water all over my anticipation.

The most difficult part of that crazy time was returning to school. But after I'd watched my mama being taken away and making good and sure that Miss Delphine was going to be okay, Daddy said I just couldn't put my life on hold any longer and that I couldn't miss any more of my education.

"We all have hurdles, Briley—some higher than others—but we have no choice but to face them head-on."

I think he mixed up his metaphors and meant we had to leap over our hurdles, but I got the message. It wasn't a time to be picky, metaphorically speaking. But regardless of his pep talk, I dreaded facing Bynum Central High School.

The day of my return, I made myself a bologna sandwich, so that I wouldn't have to navigate the cafeteria line with all those inquiring minds and staring eyes. I dropped my sandwich in my backpack, strapped my pack on my back, and headed for my bike.

When I arrived at school, I pulled into the bike stand and made my way to the building. I hugged my chest tight and trained my eyes on my shoes and didn't make any sudden moves, hoping my Power of Invisibility would protect me. I made it through Algebra, English, and World History unscathed. None of my teachers called on me, and I was grateful they couldn't see me. When the noon bell rang for lunch, I sidestepped groups of fellow students clogging the hall, as I worked my way to the cafeteria. There I found an empty table in the far left corner.

I'd pulled out my sandwich and had begun eating it when I heard, "Is this seat taken?"

I looked up to see Kimmy Carson, one of the spirits, standing by my table, holding her lunch tray.

I glanced around the cafeteria to find plenty of empty seats. But Kimmy was choosing to sit at the table with me. But why? And how? I was invisible.

"No, it isn't taken," I told her and returned to my sandwich.

"Do you mind?" she asked, nodding at the table.

"Nah."

"Thanks."

She took the seat across from me.

Before she began eating, she bowed her head and closed her eyes. I assumed she was praying. When she finished, she took a deep breath, unfolded her napkin, placed it in her lap, and looked down at her shriveled fish sticks and niblets corn swimming in a greasy juice.

"That looks mighty tasty, don't you think?" she said, and we both laughed.

I just couldn't help myself. It felt good to laugh for the first time in I-don't-know-when and certainly for the very first time with one of the spirits.

"You were smart to bring a sandwich on fish stick day."

She took one bite and chewed for a long time before she swallowed real hard and looked up at me.

"I'm so sorry, Briley, just so, so sorry."

There were tears in her eyes.

"Thank you, Kimmy," was all I could say, 'cause I didn't want to cry at her kindness.

"If there's anything I can do…"

I just shook my head and, for some reason, knew she meant what she hadn't finished.

Just then Bethany Andrews, Sarah Williams, and Joanne Blair, all spirits, came up to the table and said, "Can we sit with y'all?"

Before Kimmy offered them a seat, she turned to me and whispered, "Is it okay?"

"Sure," I said and half-smiled at the girls.

They chatted about school for a while, and then Bethany said, "Briley, I didn't realize your eyes were so blue. They look so pretty with your new contacts."

I told her thanks but said I was having a hard time getting used to wearing them.

Sarah piped up and said, "You'll get used to them in no time. It just feels strange at first, sticking something in your eye."

Kimmy said that was right and assured me, too, that it wouldn't take long for me to get accustomed to them.

Joanne said, "I see you got your braces off too. Don't your teeth feel all little and slick? That felt really weird when I got mine off."

I laughed and ran my tongue over my teeth. She was right. They did feel little and slick.

"Hey, Briley," Kimmy said, "Gretchen is graduating this year, and there'll be a vacancy on the spirit squad. I think you'd be perfect. Why don't you try out? You can come over to my house this summer, and I'll help you with the routines. That way you'll have a head start on everybody else." She giggled and said, "That may not be fair, but we sure would like to have you on the squad."

All the others agreed, and then my eyes did fill with tears.

Wiping them with the back of my hand, I said, "Thanks, that's awful nice, but I won't be here next year. My dad has gotten a job in Florida. We're moving right after school lets out."

So they all told me they wished I weren't moving but were so jealous that I was going to get to live in Florida, where it's warm and the sun always shines.

Sarah said, "Yeah, I hear you can wear your bikini everywhere down in Florida, like to the grocery store and all." Then furrowing her brow and getting all serious, she said, "I guess you wouldn't wear your bikini to church, but really everywhere else." Then she just glowed and said, "I'd like that. I'd really like that."

When the bell rang for classes to start, we all stood and headed for the trash can to deposit the dregs of our lunches. Before stowing her tray, Kimmy picked up her cookie, oatmeal raisin, and broke it into two pieces. Handing me the larger piece, she said, "Here, eat this. That sandwich wasn't enough lunch to get you through the afternoon."

I'm not a big fan of the school cafeteria oatmeal cookies, but I gratefully accepted Kimmy's broken offering, as if it were some sort of communion wafer. I ate my share during Spanish class and decided that the cafeteria's *galletas de avena* was pretty good, after all, especially when it's shared with a friend.

A couple of days later, I was standing at my locker, fiddling with my lock before World History class. I'd had the same locker all year and still had trouble opening it. I remembered the combination, but, for some reason, it just didn't want to cooperate sometimes.

"Dang it!" I said and banged my fist on the door, hoping my anger would make it open.

"Need some help?"

I looked up to see Kurt leaning against the locker next to mine, his blonde hair dipping seductively over one eye.

"Just have a stubborn lock sometimes," I mumbled and felt my face flame.

"Tell me your number," he said, and winking at me, added, "promise I won't tell."

Growing hotter and hotter, I sputtered out my number while Kurt twirled the dial right, left, and right again. When he came to a stop, he slammed his palm on the locker door, and it popped right open.

Throwing his hands in the air, he said, "Easy peasy."

"Thanks," I said, the nervous perspiration dripping down my back.

"Hey, I hear you're moving to Florida."

"Yeah, my dad got a new job."

"Sorry to hear that," he said.

"Mmmmm, yeah…" I wasn't too good at teen small talk. I hadn't had much practice.

"What you say you and me go over to Benny's for a hot dog before you go?"

"Oh, well, um, Benny's…"

This really wasn't going very smoothly.

"No big deal. Just a hot dog."

"Okay, but I'm leaving Sunday."

"Then how about Friday? Say six o'clock?"

"I'll have to ask my dad, but I think it'll be all right."

"Great! I'll call you tonight," he said and backed down the hall to class.

As he was backing and winking at me, Mr. Shelton came out of his classroom, and Kurt backed right into him. He dropped all of his books and started apologizing to Mr. Shelton as he stooped and began gathering up scattered books, papers, and pencils. When he had retrieved all his belongings, he stood and glanced my way, his face as red as mine.

That's when I realized Kurt's secret. It was the same secret I had, the same secret I was almost certain every teenager had. Even the most confident teenager has that awkward, want-to-crawl-into-a-hole moment. There are times we all feel as if we don't belong, as if we don't fit in. It is at those times that we just wish we possessed the Power of Invisibility, so that others can't see our imperfections, our failures.

I raced home from school Friday and jumped into the shower, in preparation for my date with Kurt. All that was left to do was choose the perfect hotdog-eating outfit. I thought about my one and only dress but decided against it. I only wore it when my mama made me, and I figured my mama wasn't going to make me do anything ever again. As much as I hated my Bronwyn Orders, knowing I'd never hear them again made me real sad. So I got out a pair of jeans—a clean pair—and tried on every top from my dresser drawer and my closet. I finally settled on a blue flowered peasant blouse, which was real comfortable and looked like something teenagers would wear to Benny's for a hot dog.

Daddy wasn't quite sure what to say when I told him that Kurt had invited me on a date.

"Let me think about it, Briley, and I'll get back to you. Okay?"

"Okay, Daddy, but Kurt's calling me tonight. Can you get back to me by then?"

"Sure, sure…" he'd said, like a daddy whose little girl had grown up without his noticing and without his permission.

He went off to his bedroom to take off his suit and put on his jeans. And, I figured, to think about my date.

When he returned, he said, "Briley, I think you're too young to be dating." Before I could protest, he held up his hand. "But I know Kurt and his family, and I think he's a very fine boy. I trust that he'll treat you real respectfully. I also think you should be allowed to visit with your classmates before you leave Bynum. So tell Kurt that you may go, just as long as you go straight to Benny's and straight home. Deal?"

Smiling broadly, showing my slick, straight teeth, I said, "It's a deal, Daddy," and threw my arms around his waist and hugged him.

He patted my back and said, "Well, all right then…" and cleared his throat.

Kurt showed up at six on the dot. Daddy told me to wait in my bedroom, so that he could greet Kurt and have a word with him. I stayed upstairs out of sight, but instead of waiting in my bedroom, I stood at the top of the stairs, barely out of sight but clearly within ear shot.

"Hi, Mr. Beckwith," Kurt said in a semi-confident, meeting-dad-for-the-first-date sort of way.

"Hi, Kurt, come on in, and I'll call Briley." Leading Kurt into the living room, he said, "I understand you and Briley are going to Benny's tonight."

"Yes, sir, that's our plan."

"Well, you know that Briley is only fifteen, a little young for dating."

"Yes, sir, I understand."

"Good, Kurt. Now, I'm allowing you to take my daughter to Benny's on the condition that you go nowhere else and that you have her home by ten."

"Yes, sir, we won't go anywhere but Benny's. And I promise I'll bring her home by ten o'clock."

"Good, good, just so we're clear…" Daddy said and then called up the stairs, "Briley, Kurt's here."

And as I came down the stairs, I could hear daddy making small talk, asking Kurt if his daddy had been out to the lake fishing lately.

"Hi, Briley," Kurt said when I came into the living room. "You sure look nice. That's an awful pretty shirt."

I blushed, said, "Thanks," and told Daddy that I'd see him later.

Kurt led me to his car and even opened the door for me, like a real gentlemen. Then all the way to Benny's he made small talk, telling me he'd looked up the place where I was going to live in Florida, and that it seemed like a real nice place and he was sure I was going to love it.

I told him I didn't know too much about Florida but that Daddy had gone down to visit his new company and said it was real nice.

"And Sarah said you can wear your bikini just about anywhere you want, except maybe church. That sounds pretty convenient. You wouldn't ever have to worry about ever buying new clothes, just as long as you had a bathing suit."

Kurt just laughed and said, "You're funny, Briley."

Dating wasn't as hard as I'd suspected. Kurt was easy to talk to, and he was a real fine boy, just like Daddy had said. We got hot dogs and Cokes and were chatting about football—a subject that had never interested me but sounded right intriguing when Kurt talked about it—when we heard a big commotion outside.

Benny's front door burst open and all the Baptist kids came tumbling in, fresh from their BYF meeting down at the First-and-only-one-that-matters Southern Baptist Church. All the kids, which included most of the spirit squad, crowded around us, squeezed into the booth with us, and pulled up chairs to sit real close. By then they'd all heard that I was leaving, and each one of them wished me luck and told me they wished they were going to the land of sunshine with me, where you could wear bikinis just about anywhere, except church. I figured they'd been talking to Sarah.

"I'm sorry we didn't get to know you better, Briley," Angela Murchison said.

"Yeah, me too," I kind of mumbled.

She got real close and said, "We thought you didn't like us, for some reason."

That statement caught in my heart and explained a lot. My invisibility wasn't all their fault. I'd put up a shield; I had to accept a good deal of the blame.

"No, I just, I don't know…"

So she just smiled and put her arms around me and hugged me real hard, saying, "I bet you're just going to go down there to Florida and meet all kinds of new kids. You just march right in there and shown 'em what a good friend you are."

I said, "Thanks, Angela, I'll try."

"Briley, we gotta go," Kurt said, while I was soaking up all the fresh friendship to take to my new home. "It's almost ten o'clock, and I promised your daddy I'd get you home by ten."

So I said bye to everyone and got more hugs than I'd had in my entire life.

On the way home Kurt reached over and took my hand and said, "I'm so glad I got to know you, even if it was just for a little while. You're really cool, Briley."

"Thanks, Kurt, you're pretty cool yourself," I said, and we both laughed.

When he walked me to my door, he said, "I'm so sorry about your mom, Briley. But I hope you like your new home. I'm sure you'll make lots of new friends."

"Thanks, Kurt. That's what Angela said. I hope y'all are right."

Looking around and shuffling his feet, he said, "Briley, would you mind if I kissed you good-bye?"

I could feel myself blush, but I said, "I wouldn't mind at all. In fact, I think I'd like that."

So Kurt leaned in and kissed me gently on my lips. It was sweet and soft, and in that moment I knew that I would remember Kurt and love him forever for giving me my very first kiss.

After he kissed me, he smiled and said, "You know, Briley, you're real pretty. Don't hide anymore. You go down to Icafui, Florida, and you show all those people just how pretty you are. Okay?"

"Okay," I said but didn't blush this time. No one had ever told me I was pretty but Miss Delphine—and Mama, of course—and I thought she'd said it just because she's sweet and thought I needed to hear it. But when Kurt told me I was pretty, I actually believed him. And I actually felt pretty.

"Bye, Briley," he said, as he backed down the sidewalk, careful not to collide with anyone or anything.

He didn't promise to text and neither did I, but that was okay. We both knew I'd have new friends to share texts.

When I went into the house, I found Daddy waiting for me in the living room.

Before he could say a word, I said, "Yes, Daddy, he's a fine boy, a very fine boy."

Daddy just smiled. "Yeah, I had a feeling."

Wanting to live in the evening a bit longer, I said, "Daddy, I'm a little tired. I think I'll go on upstairs. See you in the morning. We've got packing to do and a long journey ahead of us."

Twenty-six

The next day Daddy woke me early, calling, "Up and at 'em. We've got packing to do."

Daddy had brought home boxes, and it would be my job to pack up all the things in my closet so they'd be ready when the movers came the following morning.

After folding all my clothes that were on hangers and putting them in boxes, I pulled my vanity stool over to the closet, so that I could reach all the dusty stuff on the high shelf, things I hadn't seen or used in years. I pulled down my old roller skates and a mini baton that Mama had given me one Christmas when I was a little girl. I'd never learned how to twirl the thing, though Mama had tried so hard to teach me. I found a yellow sand pail and a red shovel that Daddy had gotten me on one of our beach trips to Folly Beach, up in South Carolina. He had helped me make, like, a hundred sand castles. That was a really fun trip. And there was my Madame Alexander box with the mint-condition Cinderella doll inside. Granny Evadelle had given her to me, her only granddaughter, because her only child, Bronwyn, had so loved Madame Alexander dolls. I had thought Cinderella was so beautiful, the most beautiful doll I had ever seen, but was afraid to play with her, for fear of messing her up. So from time to time I'd take her down and look at her, still in her box, and then would put her back on her shelf where she would stay perfect—just like Granny Evadelle's daughter.

I took the box from the shelf and sat on the floor. I lifted the lid and folded back the pink tissue paper. I picked up Cinderella for the first time and held her to me, as I wrapped my arms around her and kissed her golden hair. I would donate the rest of the toys on the high closet shelf to Goodwill. But I would save Cinderella for my little girl. I would stand her on my daughter's dresser, where she could hold her and dress her and brush her hair. Cinderella would no longer be perfect, but she would be real, just like me, just like my little girl.

As I was placing Cinderella back in her box, I noticed something beneath the tissue. Lifting the pink paper, I saw the unopened pack of Pall Mall filters that I had bought from Mr. Jensen the day I dyed my hair shocking pink. At the time, I thought I needed to learn to blow smoke circles. I was so glad I'd changed my mind.

I dropped the Pall Mall filters in my overflowing trash can and put all the toys, except for Cinderella, in a box and marked it *Goodwill.* I taped the boxes of clothes shut and marked them *Briley's Room,* so that the movers would know where to put them when they arrived at my Daddy's and my new house in Icafui, Florida.

Cinderella would ride to Icafui with Daddy and me.

I picked up the box of sea glass that Miss Delphine and I had collected on Tybee Island. I ran my fingers through the colorful pieces. They felt so cool, and all the jagged edges had worn down over time until they were smooth and beautiful. I sort of felt like sea glass. My whole self had been shattered, broken into little jagged pieces, but I knew that over time my jagged edges would be smoothed down and polished and that I'd be beautiful. Maybe not Bronwyn beautiful, but Briley beautiful.

"Daddy, I'll be back in a little bit. I'm gonna go say bye to a friend."

"Okay, Briley," Daddy called, sticking his head out the kitchen door where he was boxing up stuff. "Don't you be gone too long, you hear? We have to get all these dishes wrapped and packed before the movers come."

"Okay, Daddy, I'll be back to help you soon."

I left the house, letting the screen door slam after me, and hopped off the front porch. My bike was lying on its side by the walkway, its kickstand still and forever broken.

Heaving it from the ground, I climbed on and cruised out into the street. Except for an old stray tabby cat slinking along, Magnolia

Street was deserted, as it usually was. I picked up speed till I got to Main, where I careened around the corner and headed in the direction of Azalea Drive. Between Al's Shoe Repair Shoppe and Miss Sheila's Beauty Parlor, I took a sharp right onto Azalea. At the second house on the left, I bounced into the driveway and came to a stop at the enormous live oak that canopied the front yard.

I ducked under the drapes of Spanish moss that hung from the oak's branches, careful not to let it drag in my hair. One of the first lessons every Georgia kid learns is never put Spanish moss on your head. It'll eat you up with chiggers. But, despite the warning, every Georgia kid has to make a wig out of Spanish moss just once. 'Cause just once is all it takes.

I dropped my bike on the sandy ground, 'cause grass just won't grow beneath the big old branches of a live oak, and ducked under the Spanish moss once again. I shook my head real good, just to make sure no chiggers were hitching a ride in my hair.

I took the steps two at a time up to the porch of a house I had dearly loved all my life and had spent weekends in for a brief time. I loved the big, wide porch; I loved the great, tall, two-story columns that held up the roof; most of all, I loved the red, wooden swing that hung on long chains and provided me hours of entertainment as my parents visited with their best friends when they had lived in the house together.

Knowing this was probably the last chance I'd get to sit in the old, red swing, I crossed the porch and eased myself down. The chains had rusted since I'd first sat in the swing, and they creaked and screeched as I settled in. When I'd first sat in the swing, my baby legs didn't even reach the edge of the seat. Mama would have to give me a push to get me going. Now my feet touched the ground, and I could give myself a push. I swayed back and forth for a few minutes, giving myself a good-bye swing. Then I dragged my foot across the worn porch, my shoe clicking across each warped board, slowing myself to a stop. I got up and walked over to bang on the double screen doors. I rapped three sharp times, and soon I heard someone coming to greet me.

"Hey, Briley."

"Hey, Dr. Joe Bobby. I just wanted to come say *bye* before Daddy and I head out."

"I'm glad you did. Want to come on in? I just made a pitcher of lemonade."

"No, sir. I can't stay long. Daddy is waiting for me to help him pack dishes before the movers come to pick them up."

"You excited about going?"

"Hmmm, I don't know if you'd call it excited," I told him, looking down at my tennis shoes and nudging the welcome mat with my toe.

I'd already decided what I was feeling was halfway between happy and scared, the way Dr. Joe Bobby's swing used to make me feel when I was a little kid. Someone would give me a shove, get me started real good, and then I'd take over. I'd pump and pump till I had the swing going as high as I could get it, and my heart would be in my throat. Then I'd leap from the swing at its highest point and sail through the air, happy and scared at the same time, till I landed with a thud that made my feet sting and my knees buckle. Yep, Daddy's and my move to Icafui, Florida, was sort of making my feet sting and my knees buckle.

"I think you'd call it a cross between happy and scared, Dr. Joe Bobby."

"I guess I can understand that, Briley," he said, smiling and shaking his head.

"I'm sorry, Dr. Joe Bobby."

"Me too, Briley."

"You know, if you hadn't told on my mama, I would have. At least, I hope I would have. Tattling on your mama for being a murderer would be a hard thing to do, but it would be the right thing to do, especially if an innocent man was taking the blame for it. I just hope I'd have done the right thing."

"I'm sure you would have, Briley. You're a really good person. But I'm just glad you didn't have to tattle on your mama."

"Me too."

"By the way, Briley, how did you know that your mama was responsible for Libby Beth's death?"

"Well, Dr. Joe Bobby, people think that since I always have my nose in a book, I can't hear what is going on. I may not be able to see when I'm reading, but reading does not render me deaf. I've heard lots of stuff that I probably shouldn't have been hearing—like mama confessing to you that she was the one who shot Miss Libby Beth."

"I'm sorry you had to hear that, Briley."

"Yeah, I was sorry I had to hear it too. But, more than that, I was sorry it was true."

"Me too…"

"Hey, Dr. Joe Bobby, will you do me a big favor?"

"What's that Briley?"

"Will you look in on Miss Delphine from time to time? I reckon she's gonna be mighty lonesome when Daddy and I leave."

"Sure, Briley, I suppose I could do that."

"Maybe y'all could have an appletini."

Since Miss Delphine had given up her Pall Mall filters, she had taken a liking to appletinis. "I have to have at least one vice, don't I?" she'd said and laughed real hard.

Dr. Joe Bobby smiled and said, "I could probably handle an appletini."

"Good, I'm sure that'll delight her no end."

"I'll give that some thought," he told me, smiling at me again.

"And maybe you could hang around and watch one of her French movies with her. And don't worry if you don't speak French. They've got the English words at the bottom of the screen. And if you're like me and can't follow the words and pictures at the same time, Miss Delphine will be more than happy to translate for you."

"That might be a good thing to do, Briley."

"And you might want to bone up on your opera before you go."

"That's good to know."

"Dr. Joe Bobby?"

"Yeah?"

"You still my step-daddy?"

"Reckon I am, long as I'm married to your mama."

"You gonna stay married to my mama?"

"Probably not, Briley, probably not."

"I understand, Dr. Joe Bobby. Don't blame you one bit."

"But, you know, you and I will always have a connection."

"You got that right."

"'Cause I was the very first person to see that pretty face coming into this world," he said, reaching over and cupping my chin with his hand.

I blushed and pulled away, still not real comfortable with compliments, and said, "Yes, sir, you sure were."

But I had a real hard question to ask him, and I wasn't sure I could get it out, but I had to try. I needed to know the answer. Fact is, it was one of the main reasons I'd come to Dr. Joe Bobby's house in the first place.

"Dr. Joe Bobby, why'd you marry my mama?"

He took a real deep sigh and looked down at his hands. They were knotted together, resting on his thighs. Finally, he looked me in the eye and said, "Briley, that's something I've been asking myself, and this is the best I can come up with. Your mama and I have loved each other since we were babies. We did everything together. We laughed at the same foolishness, finished each other's sentences. Why, I guess you'd say we were like an old married couple even when we were young'uns."

"Yeah, everybody says y'all were best friends forever," I said.

"That we were. And when we got to high school, we even talked about dating. But we decided that might hurt our friendship, and neither one of us wanted that."

"Makes sense."

"But then I went to jail, and your mama was the only person who didn't give up on me. Only person who believed in me."

"Now we know why," I said, and Dr. Joe Bobby agreed with a sad nod and a shrug of his shoulders.

"Briley, even my own mama thought I'd killed Libby Beth. She said if Hey Boy Turner couldn't even prove my innocence, then I must be guilty. But Bronwyn was always there, always believed in me. I guess that's all the excuse I have, Briley."

"I think I understand, Dr. Joe Bobby. Bronwyn Gail Talmidge can be awful persuasive. Why, there were times she almost persuaded me I could be a majorette."

Dr. Joe Bobby chuckled a little and said, "Yeah, she's right persuasive, but that doesn't excuse what happened. I just hope you'll forgive me, 'cause I'm awful sorry for the pain I've caused your family."

"Sure, Dr. Joe Bobby, I forgive you."

"Thanks, Briley. That means a lot to me."

I felt a cry lump rising in my throat, so before it could develop into a full-blown cry, I said, "Well, Dr. Joe Bobby, I'd best be getting on back home. Those plates aren't going to wrap and pack themselves."

"Okay, Briley, you keep in touch, you hear?"

"Yes, sir, I will."

I knew I probably wouldn't keep in touch. I figured Dr. Joe Bobby knew it too.

I sauntered down the steps, taking them a lot slower going down than I had going up.

I ducked under the draping Spanish moss, and Dr. Joe Bobby called out, "Careful you don't get any chiggers in your hair."

I grabbed my bike, ducked again, and said, "Thanks, Dr. Joe Bobby, I'll be careful."

But I gave my head a good shake, just to be on the safe side.

Then I hopped on my bike and rode out of Dr. Joe Bobby's yard and headed for home to help Daddy pack some dishes.

Twenty-seven

"You ready, Sport?"

Daddy had taken to calling me Sport, something he'd never done before, but I reckon he figured with this new phase of our life starting, we probably needed new names for each other. I'd let him call me Sport if he wanted, but I decided I'd just stick with Daddy, if it was all the same to him.

"Sure, just let me go say bye to Miss Delphine."

"Okay, Sport." It sounded like he was really getting into this new-name thing.

I raced across Miss Delphine's lush June lawn, feeling it squish under my feet, and bounded up the steps to her front porch. I pounded on her screen door and called, "Hey, Miss Delphine, it's me, Briley."

I heard her shuffling from the back of her house in her bedroom slippers until she appeared in the square patch of early morning light streaming through the screen. She was wearing her red kimono, the same kimono she'd been wearing that morning she coaxed me from the bus stop and convinced me that skipping school was a good idea. I'll never regret my decision to believe her.

"Hey, Briley, guess you've come to say the old good-bye."

"Yes, ma'am, I guess I have."

"Come on in and have one last Yoo-hoo for the road," she said, holding the screen door open for me.

I could hear her ever-present opera seeping from the radio in her kitchen. Though I'd never acquired the taste and it certainly did not ooze from my soul, I was glad Miss Delphine would have her opera to keep her company after I was gone.

"No, ma'am, I can't stay. Daddy's waiting for me in the car," I said, turning and pointing toward Daddy, sitting patiently behind the wheel of his silver Hyundai. He smiled and waved when he saw me looking.

"I'll miss you, Miss Delphine."

"Yeah, same here, Briley. You've made my life here in Bynum real yellow, and for that I thank you. But I fear you'll be taking my yellow with you."

"Miss Delphine, Bynum's not so bad."

Miss Delphine just smiled a wistful smile of resignation. That smile made me sad for her. Even I know Bynum isn't New York City. Why, it isn't even Savannah.

"Hold on, I have something for you," she said and retreated into the darkness of her house. While I waited, I swatted at the swarm of no-see-ums that had taken up residence around my head. When she returned, she was carrying a neon-pink scarf scattered with brightly colored hibiscus. "Here, take this with you and think of me when you wear it." Then she wrapped it round and round my neck.

"It's beautiful, Miss Delphine. Thank you. I think it'll fit right in down there in Florida."

"Since you've given up your shocking-pink hair, you need a shocking-pink scarf to compensate," she said and stroked my cheek lovingly.

"I agree," I said, fingering my new scarf.

"And I got this for you at an exotic shop up in New York," she said, handing me a small package.

We both laughed real hard. Turns out the exotic oil she used to make her house smell so good was nothing but a lavender Glade Plug-in she'd bought down at the Piggly Wiggly.

"Plug this into your new bedroom wall and think of me."

"I'll do just that, Miss Delphine." Then I asked her, "You going to be okay, Miss Delphine?"

"Yeah, Briley, I'm going to be just fine. The doctors have given me a clean bill of health. And as long as I stay away from the smoke circles, I'll live to be an old, cranky lady."

"Miss Delphine, I can't imagine you ever being an old, cranky lady," I said and believed it.

"I'll try not to be cranky, Briley." Then smiling a real sad smile, she said, "I'm so sorry about your mama, Briley."

I felt the tears gathering.

"Thank you, Miss Delphine. I'm sorry too, but I guess there's just nothing we can do about it but accept it and move on."

"Good attitude," Miss Delphine said, knowing full well that a girl will never move beyond her mama murdering her second husband's first wife. That's a mouthful for a daughter to say and a really hard thing to wrap her head around.

"Bye now, Miss Delphine." I stepped forward to give her a hug.

She held me real tight and patted my back, and I could feel her thin body shiver a little, like she was holding back tears. I let go before I could start crying—about my mama and about leaving Miss Delphine—and headed back down the stairs. I just couldn't look back. It's really hard to walk away from the best friend you've ever had, knowing you'll never find another quite like her. Looking back would be unbearable.

"Fasten your seatbelt, Sport. We've got a long ride ahead of us."

As I fastened my seatbelt, Daddy backed away from the only real home I'd ever known. 'Course, I'd lived in Dr. Joe Bobby's house uptown for a while, but it just never felt like home to me. I took a big, long look, knowing it was probably the last time I'd ever lay eyes on that house. So much had happened while I was living there—a lot of stuff I'd just rather forget, so I figured I wasn't going to miss it all that much.

I didn't know the people who had bought our house. I do know that they had just moved to town from somewhere up North and that they were smitten—their word, not mine—with our tree-lined street and the antebellum style of our house. I really didn't care what they liked; I just hoped they'd be nice and that they'd look in on Miss Delphine from time to time. Maybe they'd even be opera lovers.

We cruised down Maple Avenue past Granny Evadelle's house, home of the shrine to Bronwyn Gail Talmidge, three-time Georgia Twirling Champ. Granny Evadelle told Mama she was going to send her to an early grave when she up and divorced Daddy and married an incarcerated, convicted murderer. She didn't quite go to her grave then, but when it came to light that Mama was actually the murderer of Dr. Joe Bobby's wife and not Dr. Joe Bobby himself, that just finished Granny Evadelle off. And who could blame her? It's not every day your daughter murders somebody.

We took a sharp right at Main Street and nearly ran over Peevis Spurlock who was riding his ten-speed right down the middle of the street. Daddy said Peevis was loose a few screws. I believe Daddy was right about that. When we passed the Rexall Drug Store, we saw Mr. Jensen flipping over his red OPEN sign. He smiled through the pharmacy window and threw up his hand in greeting—or maybe good-bye. I waved back and smiled on the inside at the memory of me buying pink hair dye and Pall Mall filter cigarettes from Mr. Jensen. That was a long time ago. I don't believe Mr. Jensen ever tattled on me about the Pall Malls filters. I always liked Mr. Jensen.

We passed the Holier-than-thou Episcopal Church, where Mama and Daddy had been married, where I'd been baptized, and where Mama and Dr. Joe Bobby had been baptized on the very same sultry July day all those years ago. I wondered if Daddy and I would find us a new church in Icafui or if Daddy was fed up with organized religion and would just try to wing it when it came to the saving of my mortal soul.

We whizzed out the west side of Bynum, past the county jail where Mama had been held briefly before they sent her away. Once she confessed to that open-and-shut case, she was whisked off to the State Penitentiary in Reidsville, where they threw away the key, because that's just what you get for premeditation.

After Mama was sent over to Reidsville, Daddy would take me to visit her on Saturdays. I really didn't want to go, didn't want to see my mama locked up that way, but I didn't have a choice. Visiting day at Reidsville meant family came to visit. Daddy and I were pretty silent on our rides to the penitentiary, me staring out the window at a landscape that looked lots more drab and deserted now that my mama was locked up, Daddy clutching the steering wheel and clenching his teeth. Once we arrived, Daddy would park in the lot reserved for visitors. Then he'd sit in the car for the hour I was allowed with my mama, an hour that seemed like a forever.

While I was waiting for the guards to herd the prisoners into the visiting room, I'd stand in line up against a drab green cinderblock wall with all the other kids coming to see their mamas, most of them lots younger than me. The little girls would be all dressed up in what looked like their Easter outfits, their skirts all starched and sticking out real prissy. They'd have on little lacy socks and patent leather shoes, and their hair would be combed real neat and put up in ponytails or braids. And the little boys would be just as fixed up as the little girls—wearing their shiny shoes, with their hair all wet and slicked over with comb tracks, like their meemaws had spit on their heads just before they got out of the car.

The last Saturday I saw my mama, she came rushing into the visiting room with a yellow writing pad under her arm. After she hugged and kissed me, she said, "Briley, have you checked into majorette tryouts yet?" Before I could answer, she sat down at the gray, metal table and motioned for me to sit too. Then she slammed the pad of paper on the table, spun it around so that I could see, and poked furiously at it with her finger. She had bitten her nails so short, that there was dried blood all around the ends. And her once soft, smooth hands were dry and cracked and sounded like taffeta rustling when she rubbed them together.

"What are you poking at, Mama?" I said, as she continued to pound her finger on the pad of paper.

"There, there, don't you see it?"

"See what, Mama?"

"The break-through. I told you I'd find it. Look right there," she cried with relief. "I found it, Darlin'. It has been such a struggle, but it has all paid off."

"What do you mean, Mama?"

"The evidence, Briley," she said, real exasperated with me. "It's the evidence I've been looking for, the proof that Joe Bobby is innocent. And he'll be free, just as soon as I can present my findings to the authorities."

I looked at Mama's evidence, her proof that Joe Bobby was innocent. It could have been Arabic or Sanskrit, neither of which my mama wrote nor spoke. It was hen-scratch, gibberish.

And she didn't even realize that Dr. Joe Bobby was already a free man.

I hated seeing my mama in her condition, but thinking about not seeing her for a very long time—because Icafui, Florida, down in the Everglades, is a pretty far piece from Reidsville, Georgia—brought a lump to my throat and a recollection to my mind: one day Mama was doing her research, and I needed her attention real bad. I can't remember just why I needed her attention. Maybe I just needed her to notice me, yet she had lost sight of everything but her efforts to get Dr. Joe Bobby released from prison. But I needed my mama, needed her bad. She was good as gone, though. Real gone. And I got mad. Awfully mad.

So I just screamed at her, "What good is having a mama anyway? You've never taught me a thing. Everything I've ever learned, I've taught myself!"

Now, riding down the highway, headed for Icafui, Florida, I thought about screaming that my mama had never taught me a thing. And I remembered that look of sadness that came across her face when I'd said it. But I knew that really wasn't true. It was just my anger talking.

First off, my mama carried me inside her belly for a good part of a year, and that can't be an easy thing to do. I have no first-hand knowledge, but I've heard lots of pregnant ladies complaining. Why, just the week before, I'd heard Sarah Conners down at the Rexall, talking about her morning sickness and heartburn and swollen ankles and varicose veins. And that's just what I heard in passing. I didn't stick around to hear about all of the other horrors of her pregnancy. Surely, Mama went through all those things with me, but I never heard her complain one bit about what I put her through.

She'd just say, "Briley, I was so happy when I found out you were a little girl. That's all I ever wanted—a sweet little girl to love to bits. You were a joy, Briley, a perfect joy."

Thinking about that made my heart hurt and sing at the same time. And I realized, for the very first time, that I hadn't done anything at all to stop being her joy, to make her stop loving me to bits. She'd changed. Not me. It's still hard for a girl to accept that her mama got sick—not crazy—and just couldn't help herself. It wasn't much to hang onto, but it was something, a start.

And, yes, before her sickness she taught me things—lots of things. Why, she taught me how to use a spoon and how to pee in the toilet, instead of in my pants. She taught me how to look before crossing the street and pump a swing and ride a bicycle. She taught me how to hold a pencil to draw and write my name, and she bought me coloring books and crayons down at Mr. Jensen's Rexall drug store and taught me how to color. And I certainly wouldn't have been able to read at the age of three if my mama hadn't taken me to the library every Wednesday and waited patiently while I picked out the six books I was allowed to borrow for the week. Then she'd read those six books to me as many times as I asked her to read them—

until I was able to read those six books to her. Yeah, my mama taught me lots, and that's just skimming the surface.

So I'll forgive her sickness 'cause she taught me about forgiveness too.

She'd say, "Briley, you don't love people just when they're doing what you want them to do. You love them all the time and forgive them when they need forgiving, 'cause people just aren't perfect."

And that was something, coming from my perfect mama.

So I'll love her and work real hard on the forgiving part.

"You thirsty, Sport?" Daddy asked and shook me out of my daydreams.

We were about two hours outside Bynum, and the drive was rendering me a bit thirsty.

"Yes, sir, I think I could use me a Yoo-hoo. How about you?"

"I was thinking the same thing. What you say we stop at the next truck stop we see?"

"I'll keep my eyes peeled," I told him.

When we were just a couple miles from the Georgia-Florida State line, a Stuckey's loomed in the distance. Thinking about Stuckey's made my taste buds begin salivating for one of those sweet and salty peanut logs.

"How about that Stuckey's up there?"

"I think that'll work, Sport."

"Think we can get us a peanut log too, Daddy?"

"Why, sure. You can't stop at Stuckey's without getting yourself a peanut log, now can you, Sport?"

I figured by now it was official. My new name was Sport.

Daddy swerved into the Stuckey's parking lot and pulled up to the gas pump and said, "You need to pee?"

"Yes, sir."

"Then you run on inside and find yourself a restroom, and I'll be on in when I finish filling up."

I sauntered across the parking lot, the steam already rising from the asphalt in the morning sun. It was a sultry south Georgia morning, but I was told that Georgia summers would feel brisk compared to where I was going.

"Them Florida summers down there in the Everglades are killers, Briley," Leon Biddles told me one morning while he and I were sitting on the courthouse steps playing with his pitbull, Hobo, and watching passersby. "Humidity so thick you can see it hanging in the air. Mosquitos big as your hand. And, what's more, they got pythons fat as a fire hose down there. I seen videos of 'em just hopping down the side of the road."

Sure made me anxious about moving to Icafui. But I figured stifling humidity and palm-sized mosquitos were far better than the sadness I was leaving behind, though I wasn't so sure about the pythons.

When I came out of the restroom that stunk like BO and poop and pine air freshener, I found Daddy already at the check-out counter with two bottles of Yoo-hoo and a giant-size Stuckey's peanut log. While he was rummaging around in his billfold for his credit card to pay for our purchases, I noticed a cardboard display of fingernail polish on the counter, next to the register.

"Daddy, you s'pose I could get me a bottle of fingernail polish?"

"Sure thing, Sport. Just put it over here so I can pay for it with the rest of our stuff."

Perusing the display, I said, "Which color do you like best, Daddy?" hoping he'd pick the Emerald, which was green with gold flecks.

He pulled his glasses down on the bridge of his nose and squinted at the display. He lifted a few bottles out of their cardboard cutouts, one at a time, and replaced each of them before settling on Amethyst, a deep purple with silver glitter. It wasn't Emerald, but it was right pretty.

"This one. I think I like this one, Sport."

"Yeah, me too, Daddy. That's the one I would have picked," I said, and something about my Daddy picking out a bottle of fingernail polish for me made my heart feel so good.

Back in the car I unscrewed the tops on our Yoo-hoos and nestled them in the drink holders in the console.

"You want some peanut log, Daddy?"

"Nah, not right now. Maybe later."

"Me neither. It'll make a good treat down the road, though," I said, and tucked it in the outside pocket of my pink flowered backpack.

I kicked off my sandals and propped by feet on the dashboard. Then I clamped my fingernail polish bottle between my knees and unscrewed the cap. Daddy fiddled with the radio, trying to find some good traveling music.

When he landed on an opera station, I said, "Nah, I've had my fill of opera. Miss Delphine said it would grow on me, even ooze out of my soul, but it just never did."

"All right, then, we'll just keep on searching till we find something to our liking."

He punched the scan button until it hit upon Carrie Underwood singing "Jesus Take the Wheel."

"I think that's a pretty good traveling song, don't you, Sport?" Daddy said and tapped his thumb on the steering wheel in time to the music.

"That I do, Daddy."

We both hummed along with Carrie a while until I said, "Daddy, did you mind giving up your insurance business?"

"Not a bit, Sport, not a bit. I think owning my own business took too much time away from my family. I needed to pay more attention to you and your mama. I believe I'm going to like working for somebody else, let them have all the responsibility of business ownership. I'm especially going to like spending more time with my girl." Then he looked over at me, smiled, and patted me on my leg.

We went on back to humming along with Carrie, as I painted the fingernails on my left hand Amethyst. Then I held them up to the sunlight to watch the glitter sparkle.

"Real pretty, don't you think?" I said to Daddy and stuck my hand out for him to see.

"Yeah, real nice, Sport. Makes you look mighty grown-up," he said, with a sad, pinched smile.

Then I went back to painting my other hand.

After a few miles of silence, Daddy asked, "How does it feel to have your braces off?"

I reckoned he was just trying to fill up the empty space between us. Daddy and I had a lot of empty space to fill up.

"Feels great," I told him, smiling real big at him and running my tongue over my straight teeth.

They looked prettier and straighter than I ever dreamed they could be, and they felt so slick and smooth on my tongue. I was glad Dr. Pepperdine had let me get my braces off before I headed for Florida. It's hard enough being the new kid in school when the reason you're there in the first place is because your mama killed her second husband's first wife and you and your daddy just had to move away. A mouth full of braces would have just added insult to injury.

"And thanks for the contacts too, Daddy," I said, batting my eyes at him. "Sometimes they make my eyes feel real scratchy, but it's worth it to be rid of those big, old clunky glasses."

"I understand," he said, grabbing the side of his glasses and wagging it up and down at me. "Maybe I'll just get me some contacts too."

Once I got my contacts and shed my braces, I decided that I just didn't need neon pink hair anymore. It had served its purpose—proving my Power of Invisibility—but I had moved beyond that. So Daddy gave me money to go down to Miss Sheila's Beauty Parlor to have my hair fixed. She stripped out the pink dye and colored my hair back to its natural brown. Then she cut my homemade asymmetrical hairdo into a swingy, layered style that actually made my fine, thin hair look thick and bouncy.

When I finished painting my nails, I pulled out my iPad, careful not to smudge the polish. I booted up and clicked on my Kindle app.

Scrolling through my library, I said, "Daddy, did Mama ever tell you about the time she and I were to Barnes and Noble and I asked her to buy me a copy of *Fifty Shades of Grey*?"

Daddy laughed out loud and said, "No, I haven't heard that story. What did your mama say?"

"Of course, she said that it was inappropriate for a girl my age and that I most certainly could not have it."

"And we both know that your mama knows what's inappropriate," he said, and we laughed to keep from crying.

"But look here, Daddy," I said, clicking on *Fifty Shades of Grey* and turning the screen to where he could see.

Daddy laughed real hard and said, "Sport, I just don't know what to do with the likes of you."

"Yeah, Daddy, that's what Granny Evadelle always said. By the way, I bought this book with an Amazon gift card that Granny Evadelle gave me."

And that made my daddy laugh till he was wheezing and banging his fist on the steering wheel. When he finally composed himself and wiped his eyes on the back of his hand, he said, "Well, what did you think of it? The book, that is?"

"I don't know, Daddy. The writing was so bad, I just couldn't get all the way to the sex part."

And that made Daddy laugh even more.

While he was still in a good mood, I said, "Daddy, I have a confession to make."

"What's that, Sport?"

"Every morning, before the sun comes up, I've been going out to Yamasee Lake."

"Yeah, I know."

Surprised, I said, "How'd you know?"

"I saw Jess Tillman uptown one day and he told me that he saw you ride your bike by his house every morning, before sunrise. I figured the only place you could be going was out to the lake."

"Did you mind that I was sneaking out of the house early in the morning?"

"Nah, I figured you needed to go. Otherwise you wouldn't have."

"Yes, sir, I did."

"I'm sure you felt the need to get away from your mama's troubles."

"Yeah, she was acting awful loony."

"Briley, she's your mom. I don't want you calling her loony. She's a very sick woman. She can't help it."

I thought that was awful kind of my daddy to say that about my mama. I still thought she was loony, but I would never again say that to my daddy.

Then he told me, "I used to stand in our bedroom window and watch you leave the house early in the morning. I'd see you ride your bike out of the driveway, and then you'd get lost to me behind Elsbeth Reynolds' grove of magnolias. But you'd reappear on the other side, and I'd watch you go all the way down to the lake road and take a right. Then I'd watch till you became a little dot and disappeared from my sight."

It touched me that my daddy cared enough to stop trying to help my mama long enough to watch me ride out of sight on my bicycle. But it also surprised me that he could see me, seeing as how I'd been exercising my Power of Invisibility.

"Daddy, the lake is real pretty early in the morning. It's perfectly quiet, except for the cicadas. And the fog just nestles all around the water, like a layer of cotton candy."

"Sounds beautiful. And peaceful."

"Yeah, it is. And you know what else? I was my most invisible when I was out at the lake."

"Really? You mean nobody could see you?"

"Yes, sir, that's right."

"Did you like being invisible?"

"I did, 'cause sometimes I needed to be invisible. That way stuff couldn't touch me, couldn't hurt me."

"I understand. I'm just so sorry for the stuff that did hurt you, Briley. And I'm sorry I didn't do a better job of protecting you."

"I know. But you just couldn't help it. You sort of had your hands real full."

"I'll try real hard this time to keep things from hurting you."

"Thank you, Daddy."

We drove on in silence for a while, till I said, "I'm sorry you didn't go out to the lake with me."

"Me too. I think I'd have liked that."

"You think we could find us a lake in Florida?"

"I'm sure we can."

"Will we go to our lake early in the morning?"

"We'll go to our lake any time we want."

"But, Daddy, I don't think I'm going to be invisible anymore. I want to be a visible girl in my new life down in Icafui, Florida."

"I think that's a good idea, Sport."

"Daddy, do you think, maybe, we could get us a dog too? I bet a dog would like to go to our lake with us."

I figured while I was asking for stuff, I'd just throw a dog in and see what he'd say.

"I think a dog would be a great idea, Sport. I like dogs, don't you?" he said, looking over at me and smiling.

"I sure do, Daddy. One time I asked Mama if I could have a dog, and she told me if I could find one that would brush its own teeth and wipe its own butt, she'd think about it."

Daddy busted out laughing and said, "Yep, that sounds just like your mama."

Then he just shook his head back and forth, thinking about my mama, the lady he loved until she went loony. My word, not his.

"I used to have a dog when I was a boy. I named her Muffett."

"Why'd you name it Muffett?"

"When I was little, my mama, your Granny, used to read a poem to me about Little Miss Muffett. I thought Muffett sounded like it would make a good dog's name, so I said, 'Mama, if I ever get me a dog, I'm just gonna name it Muffett.'"

"And you did."

"And I did."

"What kind of dog was Muffett?"

"Oh, she was just a shaggy little mutt. Don't know what kind of mixed-up breed she was."

"But I bet she was cute."

"Yeah, she was a good dog. I really loved her, but do you know who that little dog loved most?"

"No, who?"

"My mama. I'd go off to school, and those two would stay at home together. She was real good company for my mama, and they got to be mighty good buddies. No matter where my mama was, Muffett was right by her side. And every time mama would sit down, that little dog would nestle down right beside her."

"What happened to your dog, Daddy?"

"Well, Sport, when I was off at college, she got sick and had to be put down. Just about broke my mama's heart."

"That's so sad."

"Yeah, Honey, it's sad, but most folks outlive their dogs. You sure you're up for that?"

"I believe I am, Daddy. I'm not looking to bring any more sadness into our lives, but I think a dog would bring you and me a whole bunch of joy. Don't you think?"

"I agree. So it's settled. We're gonna get us a good old dog."

That having been settled to my advantage, and without a promise that the dog would brush its own teeth and wipe its own butt, I picked up my Kindle and said, "Want me to read you some *Fifty Shades of Grey*?"

And Daddy laughed again real hard.

I loved making my daddy laugh. It made me want to laugh too. I was hoping my daddy and I were going to do a lot of laughing in our new life in Icafui, Florida, where my new name would be Sport, the humidity is so thick you can see it hanging in the air, and the mosquitos are as big as your hand. And where there are pythons the size of fire hoses, hopping down the side of the road.

And where I didn't want to be invisible.

ABOUT THE AUTHOR

Padgett Gerler was born on the coast of South Carolina but grew up in the Shenandoah Valley of Virginia. In the 1980's she relocated to Raleigh, North Carolina, to attend North Carolina State University. Upon graduating with a BA in accounting, she passed the CPA exam and began her career as a certified public accountant, first in public accounting and then as a CFO in corporate accounting. In 2010 she left accounting to pursue a career in writing. Prior to *Invisible Girl,* Padgett published her novels, *Getting the Important Things Right, Lessons I Learned from Nick Nack, The Gifts of Pelican Isle,* and *What Does Love Sound Like? Lessons I Learned from Nick Nack* was awarded the indieBRAG Medallion, as well as honorable mention in the 2014 Writer's Digest Self-Published Book Awards competition. *The Gifts of Pelican Isle* was an Award-Winning Finalist in the 2018 Best Book Awards sponsored by American Book Fest. She also authored the short story "I Know This Happened 'Cause Somebody Seen It," which was published in the anthology *Self-Rising Flowers.* She is the first-place recipient of the Southwest Manuscripters Short Story Award for her short story "The Art of Dying." Padgett and her husband, Ed, reside on pastoral and inspirational Winchester Lake in Raleigh, North Carolina.

ADVANCE PRAISE FOR INVISIBLE GIRL

Invisible Girl by Padgett Gerler is as much a novel about a young girl's journey to find her authentic self as it is a love letter to small town Southern life complete with double first names, grand Fourth of July parades, ham biscuits from the kind but gossipy Baptist ladies, and prevalent Spanish moss sure to give you chiggers as soon as you touch it. Serve yourself up some sweet iced tea with lots of ice and get ready for a witty and gritty ride that will make you feel indelibly connected to these memorable characters.

Alice Osborn, author of
Heroes Without Capes

Characteristic of Gerler's writing, both the confines and the compassion of the South come through in Invisible Girl, where the mystery is just as much about finding out who you are as whodunnit.

Cristel Orrand, author of
Khayal

Once again, award-winning author Padgett Gerler has delivered a story that tugs at the very depths of personal emotion…Mrs. Gerler included some real-life, well-timed humor that added to the enjoyment.

Harry James Krebs, author of
The Benjamin Tucker Series

This is a heartfelt, hopeful story that portrays a child's drive to overcome the insanity and desperation befallen her family. The tight writing and the suspense about the actual crime and its aftermath will keep readers engaged to the end.

Jorge Cortese, author of
The Sound of a Broken Chain

Padgett Gerler is a fine storyteller, deftly blending southern charm with contemporary wit, humor, and gravity. She takes us on a compelling journey through the eyes of teen Briley Beckwith, astute but uncertain, trying to find her way through the typical travails of adolescence…and much more.

Hugh Willard, author of
Degotoga

Padgett Gerler shares this story through gifted dialogue and detail. She brings Briley's voice to life as she takes the reader through an unforgettable year.

Kathryn Watson Quigg, author of
To Any Soldier: A Novel of Vietnam Letters

You will see the Spanish moss, taste the Yoo-hoo, and laugh at the witty expressions, but serious undertones seep through the simplicity of this tiny southern town. Fans of Fannie Flagg's *Fried Green Tomatoes* will not be disappointed.

Leslie Tall Manning, author of
I am Elephant, I am Butterfly

Padgett shares a fascinating story. I'm not a girl…however, it's easy to identify with the heroine, as well as her friends and family. I enthusiastically recommend this novel!

Mike Boyd, editor of
Marooned on Margo

Gerler's beautifully crafted descriptions place you right in the middle of the action…and will have you reliving the book's unfolding events long after you put the book down.

Tracie Barton-Barrett, author of
Buried Deep In Our Hearts

72414409R00131

Made in the USA
Columbia, SC
30 August 2019